NOBLE HOLIDAYS

FOUR SWEET VICTORIAN CHRISTMAS ROMANCE NOVELLAS

ANTHEA LAWSON

FIDDLEHEAD PRESS

NOBLE HOLIDAYS includes

A Countess for Christmas
A Duke for Midwinter
A Prince for Yuletide
A Nobleman's Noel

Cover by Kim Killion

Editing by Red Circle Ink, Copy Editing by Arran at Editing720

QUALITY CONTROL: If you encounter any typos or formatting problems, please contact anthea@anthealawson.com so they may be corrected.

For more historical romance, visit the author at www.anthealawson.com ~ Sign up for notice of new releases plus get a bonus story! - http://www.tinyletter.com/AntheaLawson

ISBN: 978-1-68013-057-7

CONTENTS

A COUNTESS FOR CHRISTMAS

November 6, 1814
  Tarrick Hall, Suffolk

DEAR MISS CECILIA FAIRFAX,

Do not be unduly alarmed, but I am writing on behalf of your brother, Marcus. He is well, but suffered a hunting accident that has left his eyesight temporarily damaged, and I have agreed to help him navigate his correspondence.

His first wish was to write to you, and assure you he is (mostly) unharmed. Although he believes your first impulse will be to rush to his side, he would urge most strongly that you remain at home, tending to your father. In addition, Marcus asks that you make no mention of his current infirmity, so as not to lay an additional burden upon the viscount so soon after the loss of your mother.

As the accident occurred here at my estate, I am taking every measure to provide for your brother and ensure he is receiving the best of medical care. The doctor is confident Marcus will regain his eyesight within the month.

Marcus would like to assure you he plans to return as usual to Wilt-

shire for the Christmas season. He sends his love and reminds you that you are "a willow in the wind."

Yours, etc.

Liam Cahill Barrett, 5th Earl of Tarrick

CECILIA FAIRFAX SANK BACK into the tapestry-upholstered chair, the letter trembling slightly in her hand. A hunting accident? Oh, Marcus!

The fire burning in the parlor grate did little to ward off the chill creeping through her. She supposed she should be grateful her twin brother hadn't blown his foot off, or shot the Earl of Tarrick in the shoulder, but still—the timing was wretched.

Forcing her breathing to calm, Cecilia sat forward and re-read the letter, searching for clues to Marcus's true condition. The "mostly" was clearly the earl's addition, as her brother was known to always put things in the rosiest light possible.

"Mostly" unharmed. It was small comfort.

She had known, the previous week, that something had happened to Marcus, through that curious bond they shared as twins. On Tuesday afternoon, while sitting with Father, her eyes had suddenly stung and burned, and her heart thumped like an enormous drum, tuned so tightly the next beat might make it burst. She had gasped aloud, and Father had asked what was the matter.

She'd made a vague reply, and the episode passed, but anxiety for Marcus had lodged like an iron splinter in her chest.

And now she knew.

The splinter still ached and pricked, however. She *did* want to rush to his side—but he was right. Father was fragile, and there was no reasonable excuse she could make for leaving Wiltshire.

You are a willow in the wind. How she wished it were so, but ever since Mother's death—a slow, consuming illness that had claimed her life in early January—Cecilia had felt brittle. A sharp wind could snap her in half.

If she let it.

Cecilia refolded the letter into crisp lines. She was strong enough to carry on, despite her idiotic twin rendering himself blind. Despite Father's recurring cough that left him weak and irritable. Despite the approaching holiday season—drat Marcus for reminding her.

Last Christmas, Mother had been ill, and the holiday had passed with none of the spirit and gaiety that usually filled Wilton House. This year, she fully expected Christmas to be excruciating, especially as Father had decreed it was time to put off their mourning.

"Your mother would not have wanted to see us so dreary, all in black." He had patted her cheek. "The color makes you look terribly pale, my dear. No, we shall make an end of mourning and celebrate Christmas in her honor—with life and light and color, as befits her favorite season."

How could Cecilia deny him? For well over a year the house had been swathed in sadness. And so, she was determined to make the holidays everything her father wanted—despite the absence of the viscountess, who had filled their lives with warmth.

Ignoring the chasm of grief inside her, as she ignored it every day, Cecilia went to her writing desk to compose a reply.

November 12
Wilton House, Wiltshire

DEAR LORD TARRICK,

Thank you for your letter. I am not pleased with my brother for his continual exploits, but most relieved to hear the injury is not permanent.

3

In our family, tales of his near-fatalities are notorious. Please keep him away from any sharp corners and stairs – secure him to the bed if necessary, or perhaps a leash might be in order.

As soon as he is recovered enough to travel, inform him his presence at home is greatly desired. Do keep me informed as to his wellbeing.

And thank you, sir, for tending to him. I commend your willingness to host what must be a demanding houseguest. Remind him that he is a stone in the sea.

We are in your debt.

Very sincerely yours,

Cecilia Fairfax

"A STONE IN THE SEA?" Liam Barrett glanced over the top of the page to where his reluctant guest, Marcus, lay on the bed, a bandage over his eyes.

The guest suite where Marcus was installed was dim, on the doctor's orders. Floor-to-ceiling green drapes were drawn across the tall windows, and coals glowed redly on the hearth, lending heat but no light to the room. Liam had drawn a chair up directly beside the bed and lit the lamp on the bedside table. The warm yellow glow fell over the page, illuminating the firm curves of Cecilia Fairfax's writing.

Marcus smiled, though the expression was closer to a grimace. "No matter what trouble I'm in, I'll get washed back to shore eventually."

Liam scanned the letter again. There was a sharp humor to Cecilia Fairfax's words. He wasn't entirely certain if he liked the woman for it.

"Your sister is all kindness. A leash?"

"No doubt Cecy pictures me leaping about blindly without a care in the world." Marcus let out a low breath. "Despite what she says, I am not constantly risking my life."

"Only occasionally?" Liam lifted a brow. "Although we were but acquaintances at Oxford, I heard stories of your escapades."

Marcus flushed, his fair coloring showing his reaction clearly. No doubt he was glad of the linen laid across his face, so he would not to have to meet Liam's eyes.

"I was young then, as you know," Marcus said. "My mother insisted I enter school early, though perhaps I should have waited."

He was still young, to Liam's mind. Although Liam was two years his elder, it felt as though a decade gaped between them. Perhaps that was due to the burdens of the Earldom falling early on Liam's shoulders, while Marcus was a carefree younger son. Or perhaps because of the cheerful way the young man strode into whatever life offered, while Liam knew himself to be far more dour in nature.

"You may regale me with stories of your exploits later," Liam said, curiously interested to hear them; perhaps because he himself had led a rather staid life as a student. "Doctor Smith will be here shortly, and after his visit you may dictate more assurances to your sister."

November 18
Tarrick Hall, Suffolk

Dear Miss Fairfax,

I am writing again at your brother's direction, to say that a leash will not be necessary. I have personally provided a cane for his perambulations about the house, and the stairs are well-guarded by attack lions. Rest assured no more accidents will befall Marcus while he is under my roof.

His recovery is proceeding apace, and the doctor is encouraged that he will be able to travel in two week's time.

Yours, etc.

Liam Barrett, Earl of Tarrick

CECILIA COULDN'T HELP SMILING at the earl's letter, despite her ongoing concern for Marcus. Attack lions, indeed. The Earl of Tarrick was reputed to be a rather grim fellow, but his letter somewhat belied that reputation.

She absently stared at the mottled November sky through the parlor windows, trying to recall what she knew of the earl. There was some history of family tragedy, and the unfortunate fact of his Irish blood. Not only had his mother been Irish, but, horrifyingly, Catholic as well, according to the gossips. He did not spend much time about in Society.

The winter light shone weakly into the parlor, making the wallpaper seem more gray than peach. She held the letter up to the mullioned windows and studied the vigorous, looping handwriting. It was impossible to tell anything about the writer, other than he crossed his T's with a line a trifle too broad.

"Mistress?" Martha, one of the maids, stepped into the parlor. "Begging your pardon, but Mrs. Bess would like to speak with you concerning the draperies."

"Of course." Cecilia swallowed a sigh. "I must reply to a letter, but inform her I will be down shortly."

"Yes, mistress." Martha bobbed a quick curtsey and was gone as quickly as she had come.

She was one of the village girls, hired less than a year ago, and so full of darting energy that she made Cecilia feel a bit tattered around the edges.

Fingers chilled, she rose and pulled her shawl more tightly about her shoulders. The dark brown wool was unbecoming, but it was the warmest she had. This time of year, she was always cold

—but a cup of tea would revive her, certainly. Enough to meet with Bess.

Dear Bess. She had been the housekeeper for as long as Cecilia could recall, and even then she had been old.

Mother's illness had taxed all of them. Father most of all, but Bess had suffered as well. Recently, she had taken to wandering in her attention, sometimes leaving crucial things undone. It was past time to provide her a proper retirement, but somehow Cecilia had been unable to bring herself to break the news to Bess that she was relieved of her longtime position as housekeeper to the Fairfaxes.

Soon, though. Once the household was out of mourning, and the holidays endured—*celebrated*, she amended—there would be time enough to restructure the running of Wilton House.

"ANOTHER LETTER FROM WILTSHIRE, MY LORD." The butler bowed before Liam's desk, then handed him the correspondence. The envelope, addressed in Cecilia Fairfax's neatly swirling script, was smooth beneath Liam's fingers.

"Thank you, Hobbs. Please alert the cook to send luncheon up to Mr. Fairfax's room." Liam rose, glad enough to leave the estate business untended for a short while.

It was foolish, how such a small thing as a letter could become the brightest thing in his day. A letter that was not even written to him.

He did not like to think how empty his house would feel, once Marcus departed. It was not that Liam was lonely, exactly. But solitude was a heavy weight, and he had become accustomed, over the last handful of weeks, to having that weight lightened.

Marcus Fairfax was an unfailingly cheerful fellow, with an amazing number of stories. He had a witty way of spinning them out, the fire crackling cheerfully in his room, the warmth of brandy settling in Liam's stomach while the warmth of words settled in his mind. Marcus's tales of his times at Oxford were amusing, yet Liam found himself enjoying the stories of Marcus's childhood even more.

Perhaps it was because his own youth had been empty of siblings, and a mother, and the type of family home that Wilton House sounded to be. It was like peeping into a baker's shop and seeing the warm loaves, golden on the racks, when all one had ever eaten was stale, hard bread. Even though Liam had never tasted that life, he liked to hear that it existed outside the pages of treacley books written for children.

Though Marcus's claims that Wilton was haunted did strain credulity a bit—especially the stories where he and his sister had played hide-and-seek with the ghost of a young girl.

"She almost always won," Marcus told him. "The ghost, I mean."

"One would think."

"You don't believe me, but she exists. Or existed. She died from influenza in 1783, at the age of nine—it's in the family bible. Elizabeth Fairfax. Would have been my and Cecy's great-great aunt."

"How do you know it's her?" Despite his skepticism, Liam found himself interested.

"The clothing, mostly. She's not dressed as a serving girl—her skirts are wide and very old-fashioned. Besides, the Fairfaxes have lived at Wilton House for over two-hundred years. So even if she's not Lizzy, she's an ancestor."

Liam shook his head and, letter in hand, ascended the broad staircase. What a fanciful fellow his guest was.

He paused a moment to set his palm atop one of the carved marble lions standing guard at the top of the stairs. The stone was cool against his hand. So far, the statues had done their job, and Marcus had not tumbled down the stairs. Of course, the maids were happy to assist and accompany the cheerful young gentleman about the house whenever he tired of the confines of his rooms.

"Another letter," Liam said, striding into the suite where Marcus was currently housed.

The rooms were done up in deep green—a soothing color, if only Marcus had been able to see it.

"Cecilia is nothing if not punctual," Marcus said, glancing up from his seat by the fire. The linen bandage across his eyes gave him the look of a jaunty oracle. "Come, read it to me."

Liam joined him, settling into the second armchair pulled before the hearth. When he opened the letter, he smelled the distant memory of flowers.

November 24
Wilton House, Wiltshire

Dear Lord Tarrick,

I am relieved to hear of the lions guarding your stairs. Perhaps you could send one home with Marcus, as he could use such a pet to keep him out of harm's way – although I hesitate to think what such a beast would do for his reception in Society, once he returns to London.

Now, Marcus, I must tell you it has not yet snowed here, so you may give up any thoughts of pelting me with snowballs the moment you walk in the door, as is your wont. Besides, with your recent injury, I would be forced to aim for your chest and not your head, so it is just as well the season remains cold and clear.

In all seriousness, will you need any extra provision made for your care when you arrive? I am not entirely certain I trust the reports that your eyesight will be completely cured—and if such is the case, I implore you to strain Lord Tarrick's hospitality a bit longer, and do not undertake to travel until you are truly ready to do so.

Your loving sister, Cecilia

MARCUS LEANED BACK, his face turned toward the fire.

"Will I be fit for travel, do you think?" For a moment his smile slipped, revealing the worry beneath.

"Doctor Smith is planning to remove the bandages tomorrow, is he not?" Liam asked.

"Well." Marcus leaned his chin on his fist. "I confess, I've peeked a time or two. I'm afraid my sight will not be miraculously restored overnight."

"Can you see anything at all?"

Guilt rose up like briars in Liam's throat. If he had blinded Marcus Fairfax, he owed the man a debt he could never repay.

As if sensing the direction of his thoughts, Marcus shook his head. "See here, Tarrick, guns misfire. It was my great misfortune to be behind the barrel of one at the time—but that is a risk a gentleman takes when shooting."

"It was my gun," Liam said. "I bear the responsibility."

"To answer your question—I can make out shapes. I can see the brightness of the fire, and lighter patches in the room that might be the windows. It is an improvement, certainly."

Liam crossed his arms. An improvement—but not a recovery.

"Your family has suffered some hardships recently, correct?" he asked.

"I do not remain here simply for your scintillating company," Marcus said. "My mother has been dead nearly a year, and I am not certain Father is finding it worthwhile enough to stay on this mortal plane without her."

"He must have loved her very much." Liam couldn't imagine.

Marcus let out a sigh edged with sorrow. "She was the sun the entire household revolved around. They are struggling enough, without me casting another dark cloud upon their existence."

"Your sister seems well enough." Liam waved the letter, again catching the faint scent of flowers.

"Cecy puts on an admirable front." Marcus frowned. "A pity about the snow. She needs something to make her smile, especially now."

"Now?" Liam leaned forward.

"She is caring for Father, readying the house for the holidays, and carrying the secret of my injury. Too many burdens."

"You called her a willow in the wind." Liam could imagine her —a slender, pale thing like her brother, bowed down by the weight of her obligations.

Marcus nodded slowly. "I only hope she doesn't break."

DECEMBER 1
Tarrick Hall, Suffolk

DEAR CECY,

You will notice that Lord Tarrick is still serving as my secretary. I believe he missed his true calling in life—it's a pity he was born into the gentry. (Miss Fairfax, I cannot let such a slight upon the characters of secretaries pass. I assure you that, even were I not the Earl of Tarrick, I would make a poor secretary. Indeed, if you can decipher my writing, I commend you.)

Do not be alarmed, but the doctor has ordered me to wait another week until I travel. He fears the jouncing of a coach may disrupt the progress of my returning sight. And it is returning, have no fears on that account.

You have not written much of Father. Is everything well? Will our esteemed elder brother be joining us for the holidays, or will we be lucky enough to avoid his family this go-round?

Expect me to arrive by 20 December. The earl has kindly offered his coach to transport me to Wiltshire, so you see I'll be traveling in great comfort.

Until then I remain,
Your loving brother, Marcus

(P.S. I MUST ADD *that your brother's eyesight is slow to return. He is reluctant to speak of it and add to your burdens, but I do believe you'd be happier forewarned. T)*

CECILIA SMILED as she read the angular, dark writing. The earl's letters were not difficult to decipher—although she noticed his penmanship had declined slightly from the first, more formal missive he'd sent on her brother's behalf.

She tapped the letter thoughtfully against her lips. Was the Earl of Tarrick as dark and angular as his handwriting?

Oh, foolishness. She needed to be readying rooms for Marcus, and discussing meals with the cook, and making sure Mrs. Bess had not ordered the servants to hang all the washing outside to freeze, forgetting it was winter.

There was, too, the work to be done in preparation for her brother's visit. Edward and his fretful wife, Honoria, and their clamorous set of boys would be descending imminently (like a flock of harpies, Marcus was fond of saying). Cecilia did not, quite, agree. Honoria was not as strident as a harpy, though she did find fault with almost everything around her. And everyone. Poor Edward.

Still, receiving the earl's—or rather, Marcus's—letters, provided a welcome respite. A few stolen minutes where she could retire to the parlor, sink into the overstuffed wingback, and be *elsewhere* for a brief time.

Always too brief, however. Letting out a low breath, Cecilia went to her desk to compose a reply to the earl. She certainly had no time to spin fancies about a man she was likely never to meet.

A pang went through her as she pulled out a fresh sheet of

paper. She would not receive another letter from Tarrick Hall, as Marcus would be departing there within the week. She was glad the earl had warned her that her brother's recovery was not as complete as he would have her believe. He seemed quite the gentleman, the Earl of Tarrick. Swallowing back something that tasted suspiciously of disappointment, Cecilia dipped her pen and began to write.

DECEMBER 8
Wilton House

DEAR LORD TARRICK,

I am not certain this letter will reach you before my brother's departure, so I shall not include exhortations for safe travel (which no doubt he will ignore in any case).

Again, thank you for caring for him whilst he recovered from his injuries, and for your frequent letters. And the guard lions, of course. Please give them a pat of gratitude from me – provided they do not bite your fingers off.

Perhaps some day we will have the good fortune to meet in London.

My brother and I are deeply in your debt.

Most gratefully,

Cecilia Fairfax

"THERE YOU ARE," Liam said, slipping the letter back into its envelope and nodding to Marcus, seated across from him. The cozy fire burning on the hearth belied the chill in Liam's bones. "Homeward bound at last. No doubt you'll be happy to shake the dust of Tarrick Hall from your feet."

How long would it be until another guest graced the set of rooms? Years? Liam crossed his arms, banishing the thought.

"You've been an excellent host." Marcus squinted happily at him. "In fact, I have a splendid idea."

"If it involves remaining here another few weeks, I can't say I agree. Your vision is improving daily, and you are wanted home for Christmas. Is your sister-in-law truly that dreadful, that you'd wish to remain here?" Liam glanced at the half-packed trunks lined up by the door of Marcus's room.

Marcus waved his hand in dismissal. "Cecy and I manage to prop one another up during Horrible Honoria's visits. No, I think you ought to come with me to Wiltshire for Christmas!" He grinned. "I'll be able to repay your hospitality, and you'll have a marvelous time."

"You expect me to believe that, after regaling me with tales of your sour relatives?" Liam tamped down the sudden surge of interest that ran warmly through his veins. "I am quite content here at Tarrick Hall, though I thank you for your offer."

He tried not to think of the empty hallways, the lack of greenery and holiday cheer. Did he not, every Christmas Eve, sit beside the fire and drink a fine glass of port? Did he not go for a long ramble about his estate, savoring his property, despite the winter's cold?

"Quite content?" Marcus let out a snort. "Let me guess. You give the servants a Christmas holiday and send them off, then sit alone beside the hearth in your study, eating cold ham. Perhaps indulging in a brandy or two."

"It is not a bad life." Liam lifted one shoulder in what was meant to be a shrug. "I'm happy enough."

He did not examine too closely the itch that had lodged beneath his ribs at the thought of going to Wiltshire with Marcus Fairfax. And meeting Miss Cecilia Fairfax.

"If you're happy here, then you're easily pleased, and my sister-in-law will prove no obstacle to your greater joy." Marcus reached forward and took him by the shoulder. "Do come, Tarrick. Or are you afraid of the ghost?"

"I take no alarm at the figments of a boy's overactive imagination."

"Lizzy's real," Marcus said, letting go of Liam's shoulder. "It would serve you right to meet her in the upper hallway. You must come to Wilton House, just for that comeuppance. Besides, I know Cecilia would like to meet you."

Liam had not read him that crossed-out line in Miss Fairfax's letter—the one about possibly meeting some day, that had made him stumble briefly in his narrative—but clearly her brother knew her well.

"I hardly think your sister would welcome the unexpected burden of my arrival."

"How often has she said we are in your debt?" Marcus raised a blond eyebrow. "She will be glad to repay it, I assure you. Besides, I am still not recovered enough to read, or count out my bills correctly. What if the coachman takes a wrong turn? What if the innkeeper decides to take advantage of my infirmity? I need you, sir, to see me safely home."

"That's a patent lie."

"I wager it won't take you long to pack." Marcus leaned back, smiling. "You'll be ready to leave before I am."

"I'm not coming with you, Mr. Fairfax."

CECILIA SAT AT HER DESK, resolutely keeping herself from rereading the earl's—Marcus's—letters. Instead, she busied herself with making lists of all the tasks still looming, before the holidays at last came to a close. The maid, Martha, hurried into her sitting room—a welcome distraction.

"Mistress," Martha said, "the Earl of Tarrick's coach is coming up the drive."

"Indeed?" Cecilia rose from her desk and went to the window.

As the maid had said, a large black coach was approaching, the side emblazoned with the earl's coat of arms. Thank goodness. Having Marcus home would lift some of the weight pressing down upon her. And he had arrived just in time—Christmas was only a handful of days away.

Giving her hair a quick smooth, Cecilia hurried down the stairs. No need to change from her worn gray muslin. It was just Marcus, after all.

She arrived in the entryway as the butler opened the door.

Marcus strode in. "Cecy?" he called.

"Here," she said.

As soon as she spoke, he turned toward her, a wide smile on his face, and opened his arms.

She embraced him, then drew back, grasping his shoulders.

"You still can't see," she said.

"Why of course I—"

"Don't deny it." She gave him a little shake. Drat her brother, pretending he was well.

His smile faded. "I can see—but details are blurry. You blended with the shadows."

At least the earl had forewarned her. She sent a prayer of thanks to the man, wherever he might be.

"There's one more thing," her brother said. "I brought a guest for Christmas."

"What?" Sudden apprehension jolted through her, and her fingers tightened on his shoulders. "Who is with you?"

She knew the answer, however. Who else could it be?

"The Earl of Tarrick," her brother said. "You don't mind, do you?"

"I..."

"He's just outside. I'll go fetch him."

Her throat was dry, her nerves suddenly fluttering. A pox on her impulsive, generous brother. As if the holidays were not complicated enough.

Whirling, she rang for the maid, counting the seconds until the girl hurried up.

"Martha, we need another set of rooms made up immediately. Marcus has brought the Earl of Tarrick to stay for the holidays."

The maid's eyes went wide. "Of course, Mistress. The gold rooms?"

"Those will do very well. Make haste."

Martha bobbed a curtsy and hurried off.

Moments later, Marcus reappeared in the doorway, followed by his guest. The Earl of Tarrick was tall and solidly built. As she had imagined, he was dark and angular, with steely gray eyes set in a forbiddingly remote face. Judging from his expression, he rarely smiled.

He removed his hat, revealing hair as black as a raven's wing.

Marcus stepped forward. "Tarrick, allow me to present my sister, Miss Cecilia Fairfax. Cecy, this is Liam Barrett, the Earl of Tarrick."

"Miss Fairfax, the pleasure is mine." The earl made her a stiffly correct bow.

Judging by his appearance, she would have expected his voice to be rough and growly, but the earl's tone was surprisingly smooth—like a cup of warm chocolate.

Cecilia dipped a curtsey, wishing she were not wearing her drabbest gown. Would the earl mistake her for a shadow, as her brother had? No. Indeed, his gaze rested on her a trifle too long, and she felt heat rush into her cheeks. What dreadful stories had Marcus told about her?

"Lord Tarrick," she said. "Please, come into the parlor. Your rooms will be ready as soon as possible, given that I had no notice of your arrival."

She shot her brother a narrow-eyed glare. Surely Marcus could not see her expression, but he grinned back at her anyhow.

"My apologies for the unexpected visit," the earl said. "Your brother insisted."

Cecilia ushered them into the parlor, where a fire was burning merrily, thank heavens.

"Marcus is too persuasive for his own good," she said, wishing the earl had resisted. Well, half-wishing. "Make yourselves comfortable. I must see to the maids."

"Cecy, sit with us." Marcus made a grab for her hand, and missed. "Let Mrs. Bess arrange things."

"I cannot. Please excuse me." She nodded at the earl. "Marcus, offer our guest some brandy. It's on the sideboard."

"I'll pour," the earl said, an unexpected dry humor in his tone.

Cecilia shot him a glance, but his eyes were as cool as ever. Heart pounding in her chest, she hurried out of the room. Heavens, she had so much to arrange.

LIAM WATCHED Miss Fairfax leave the parlor, her step firm, her chin high. She was, as he'd suspected, as fair as her brother, with the same long, slim nose and smoky blue eyes. There, the similarities ended. Her brother was more sturdily built, while she was—yes, willowy was the word. Where Marcus was full of open humor about the world, his sister seemed much more contained, her expression guarded.

He glanced about the room, which seemed cheery and warm. No black draperies hung at the windows to signal the family's ongoing grief, yet Miss Fairfax had been wearing a markedly dreary gown.

"Is your family still in mourning?" Liam asked.

"No," Marcus said. "Father has declared we'll celebrate the holidays without that pall. Mother loved this season. I forgot to warn you—there will be singing. And a yule log, and greenery, and the best pudding you've ever tasted."

"It sounds splendid." And like no Christmas he'd ever known.

"Brandy?" Marcus gestured in the general direction of the sideboard. "When Cecy commands, we must obey."

Liam found the crystal decanter and poured them two glasses. He made a point of handing Marcus his brandy, not releasing it until he was certain his host had a firm grip.

"How will you keep your father from noticing your blindness?" Liam asked. He took a swallow of brandy, a bright fire warming the inside of his mouth.

"Father is…" Marcus threw back a swig of his own drink. "The last time I visited home, he was so overtaken by his own infirmity he would not notice anyone else's."

"What's the nature of his illness?"

"A broken heart, mostly, with gout and rheumatism complicating matters." A rare, pensive look crossed Marcus's face. "He's old, you know. Cecy and I were rather a surprise, coming a good fifteen years after Edward was born."

At least they had been loved—that much was clear. Liam drank his brandy and stared out the window. Bare branches etched a sky pearling into evening.

"Your brother and his family arrive soon?"

"Tomorrow or the next day. At which point, you and I shall go riding, and make many expeditions to gather boughs in the forest."

"Are evergreens that difficult to find in this part of Wiltshire?"

Marcus made a face. "No. The difficulty lies within the walls. Come, I'll introduce you to Father, and we'll see about settling you into your rooms."

Liam set his half-empty glass of brandy aside, and followed Marcus. Not for the first time, he wondered if coming here had been a mistake. Well, and he could always leave again. He'd delivered Marcus safely home, and met the pale, lovely Cecilia Fairfax. His escape was parked in the stables, should family interactions prove too difficult for his taste.

And what of Miss Fairfax? an errant voice inside him whispered. Has she any refuge at all? A coach to bear her away? The excuse of rambling about in the woods?

The uncomfortable answer was, no. There had been a shadow behind her eyes, a trapped look like that of a hare pursued by the shivering howls of wolves.

He suspected Cecilia Fairfax was running nearly as fast as she could, inside, where no one would ever see.

"Begging your pardon, Mistress, but Martha said as how there was nest in the chimney of the gold bedroom. Well, there was, and now the carpets are sooty. And there's, er, a pair of swallows loose in the room."

"The laundry soap is wet through, completely ruined—how shall we wash all the linens in time for your elder brother's arrival tomorrow?"

"Mistress, cook says the partridges are all burnt on one side. So sorry—would half a bird each do for dinner?"

"Mrs. Bess has set herself to polishing the silver, and there's no forks fit to dine with. Please come!"

"Milady, the best bottle of claret has gone missing. Perhaps you might check your father's study?"

Cecilia paused inside the study, her fingers tight around the neck of the half-full claret bottle. Instead of opening the door and returning to the hallway, she leaned against it, resting her forehead against the slab of oak. If only she could keep all her troubles from reaching her, held at bay by the solid wooden door.

Dinner was going to be dreadful; all the mishaps of the afternoon compounded by the presence of the Earl of Tarrick. If it were only family, they could smile through their difficulties, but having a stranger in their midst made everything more difficult.

She could hear Martha calling for her. Taking a deep breath, Cecilia opened the door and stepped into the hallway. They would have to make the best of it, as ever.

As she had feared, dinner was a strained affair. The earl, seated on Father's right, watched everything with his cool gray eyes and said very little. Father had nipped too much of the claret and alternately pontificated at length about the joys of family and lapsed into long silences.

Marcus was his usual cheerful self, though he was using his utensils in an odd manner. Both knife and fork were engaged in poking and chasing bits of food around the china, and each successful mouthful was lifted carefully to his lips, with a few near-misses. Luckily, Father was too far gone to notice when a stray piece of turnip tumbled off Marcus's fork to lie forlornly on the white tablecloth.

"You have a charming home, sir," the earl said to Cecilia's father.

"Twas all my wife's doing. She had the touch, you know. Domesticity. Children about the knee." He peered from beneath his bushy white brows and scanned the table. "I say, where is Edward and his brood?"

"They arrive tomorrow," Cecilia said, doing her utmost to keep her voice even, though her heart pounded at the thought.

There was so very much to do.

LIAM SLEPT WELL ENOUGH, though it had been years since he'd slumbered on a mattress other than his own. The maid had come in that morning to rake up the coals, and a fresh fire burned merrily on the hearth. Before leaving the room, she informed him that breakfast would be laid out shortly in the morning room.

He rose to dress, for the first time regretting the lack of a valet. Not that he was incapable of donning his own clothing, but he was well aware he did not possess any elegant flair. He did not know the most fashionable ways of tying his cravat, he did not have anyone to pull his coat just so across his shoulders or keep his boots polished to a high shine.

Vanity. Liam shook his head, but still spent an extra moment in front of the mirror, tidying his sleep-rumpled hair. He leaned forward, trying to see his face as a stranger might.

His eyes were unremarkable. His jaw too wide, his cheeks too hollowed. His hair might hold a certain appeal—years ago a young lady had told him it was like black silk—but other than that, he had very little to recommend him.

With a sigh, he straightened and tugged his cravat back into place. Truly, he would be better off finding some excuse to leave. This moping about in front of mirrors was inexcusable.

The Fairfaxes kept country hours, for which he was thankful, being an early riser. The smell of eggs and bacon wafted down the hall, and he increased his strides. A true English breakfast would be a pleasurable change from his usual bowl of oatmeal. Of course, his servants would cook him bacon and eggs if he asked, but it was simpler to have a bowl of porridge each morning. Less trouble for everyone.

A strange noise reached his ears, and he paused. He did not think the household boasted any pets, yet a quiet mewling issued from a nearby passageway.

For a scant second, his skin prickled. Was it the fabled ghost of Wilton House?

Certainly not. It was the sound of a living creature in distress. Liam turned the corner and paused outside a small paneled door —a closet of some kind. By the sound of it, the creature had been prisoned within.

He turned the knob and gently opened the door a few inches.

Light slanted into the small room, revealing shelves stacked high with linens.

"Here, now," he said softly. "Come out, kitten."

No sign of the creature. Liam pulled the door wide, then jumped back in surprise as the *ghost*—no, no, it was only Miss Fairfax—whirled to face him. He caught a glimpse of tear-wet cheeks and disheveled blonde hair before she turned her face from the light.

"Go away." Her voice wavered unsteadily.

"I beg your pardon," he said.

Gentlemanly courtesy demanded he shut the door and depart, never to mention the fact that he had found Cecilia Fairfax weeping inconsolably in the upstairs linen closet.

She sniffed, her hands balled in a pillowcase that had no doubt been muffling her sobs, and something within Liam gave way.

Instead of withdrawing, he stepped into the closet and shut the door behind him. The air smelled of lavender, and he heard Cecilia's skirts rustle in the dimness.

"Whatever are you—"

"Come here." He opened his arms.

She could not see him, he was certain of it, yet she stepped forward, just enough that he could touch her shoulders. She let out a shivering sob, and he folded her against him, murmuring hushing syllables from some long-forgotten time.

Her hands fastened on his coat and she clung there, crying, while he held her. In the close darkness they were not mere acquaintances, not earl and miss. No, they were elements of the world, meeting as inexorably as shadow and light. Greif and comfort. Loss, and love.

A strange, perfect contentment settled over Liam. He would stand there for centuries letting Cecilia Fairfax drench his shoulder with her tears, if that was what she required of him.

At last, the storm of weeping abated. Cecilia's sobs turned to sniffles.

"Oh dear," she said, stepping back. "I must beg your pardon, Lord Tarrick. This is most—irregular."

Liam reluctantly let her go, the cloth of her sleeve wisping against his fingers. He supposed she was correct. Proper young ladies did not inhabit linen closets, weeping into the arms of unexpected guests. Still, he could not be sorry for the circumstance.

"Are you sufficiently recovered, Miss Fairfax?"

She drew in a breath, yet did not speak. Liam felt the gossamer touch of her fingertips across his cheek, so light he might have imagined it. But he had not. He held very still, the scent of linens and lavender suffusing his senses.

"Yes," she finally said. "Thank you."

He wished there was light enough for him to see her, so that he might take her hand and press a warm kiss across the back of it.

There was no good way to bid her farewell. He reached behind him, the knob cool beneath his fingers, and opened the door just wide enough to slip out into the hallway. She did not follow, and Liam gently closed the door behind him, wishing for something he could not name.

CECILIA SCRUBBED her face with the pillowcase, then inhaled, trying to catch a last hint of the earl's spicy scent. She'd been beyond shocked when he'd come into her hiding place, and for a panicked moment had thought he was going to press his advances upon her.

But no—he had offered his warm, broad shoulder for her to weep upon, without hesitation. Without questions.

And then he had left, and a treacherously large part of her wished he had not.

She cracked open the closet door. The hallway was empty—everyone no doubt gone down to breakfast. She could not face the earl across the table. Nor her brother, who though he might not see her red-rimmed eyes and tearstained face, would be able to hear the remnants of weeping in her voice.

Besides, there was too much to do, and her stomach tangled in knots again just thinking of it.

Clutching the crumpled pillowcase, Cecilia stole back to her room and the towering list of tasks awaiting her. She would have Martha bring her up some tea and toast, and spend the morning planning Christmas dinner, including provisions for the staff. And then Boxing Day, with father's usual gifts to the servants...

Three hours later, the butler interrupted her.

"Miss Fairfax, the Widow Pomfrey has come to call," he said.

Cecilia loosened her grip on her teacup. For a stark moment she thought Edward and his family had arrived, too early. But she welcomed the stout widow's company, enough to take a respite from her work.

"My dear girl," Widow Pomfrey said when Cecilia entered the parlor. "You look a bit pale. Come, tell me—how fares your family?"

She held out her hands. Cecilia took them and let the widow draw her over by the fire. Widow Pomfrey was the physical opposite of the late Lady Fairfax—small and plump, with merry dark eyes and a hardy constitution. Yet the two women had shared a warmth of spirit that had made them fast friends.

"Marcus is home now for Christmas," Cecilia said. "He is... well. Edward is expected later today."

"And your father?"

The widow's tone revealed nothing but kind interest, but Cecilia suspected the woman nurtured a fondness for Lord Fairfax. After Mother's death, Widow Pomfrey had been a frequent visitor, providing help and advice to Cecilia, and bringing the family her famous pies. Indeed, the widow's pies were one of the few things that could tempt Father into eating, those first dreadful months.

"Father is regaining his strength, and his cheer." It was only a small lie.

"I am most pleased to hear it." The widow smiled, her eyes crinkling almost closed in the roundness of her face.

On impulse, Cecilia squeezed her hands. "Come spend Christmas Eve with us."

"Oh, well, I..."

Was that a blush on Widow Pomfrey's cheeks? She had no children to spend the holiday with, no family nearby. Indeed, the more Cecilia contemplated the idea, the more it satisfied her. Marcus was not the only one who could invite guests, after all.

"Please, do come," Cecilia said. "It will save me from having to explain to Father why we must have inferior pies. We need you."

"In that case, I shall come. And bring mince, and apple. It will be lovely to see your entire family again."

"We also have another guest." Cecilia withdrew her hands from the widow's soft grasp. "The Earl of Tarrick is visiting. He's a friend of Marcus."

"Do tell." The widow's eyebrows rose, nearly to the edge of her lace cap. "Is he handsome?"

Now Cecilia feared it was her turn to blush—though perhaps the widow would attribute the flush on her cheeks to the warmth of the fire, instead of the thought of the earl's arms around her.

"I suppose he is," Cecilia said. "Though I haven't given the matter much thought."

My, she was becoming an accomplished liar. The instant Liam Barrett had stepped into the front entry, she had been struck by his appearance. And a bit intimidated—though his gray eyes and lack of smiles seemed less remote to her, now that she had sobbed upon his shoulder.

Perhaps he was not aloof, so much as shy? She blinked at the thought. Not everyone was as outgoing as Marcus. The earl's reserve was understandable. And beneath that cool exterior was a surprisingly kindhearted man.

"Have you any brighter gowns?" Widow Pomfrey asked, glancing at the dark blue wool Cecilia wore. It was clear the widow had inclinations toward matchmaking.

"I've only just met the earl," Cecilia said.

It was true—although it was *also* true she'd been corresponding with him for well over a month. Not that the widow needed more fuel for her fire.

"Something to bring out the color in your cheeks." Widow Pomfrey tilted her head.

Cecilia had a red gown—a beautiful satin one, edged in white. It had been made up, along with dozens of others, for the Season she was supposed to have had in London. Before Mother fell ill, and their plans for Cecilia's grand coming-out fell into ruin.

Swallowing past the sudden tears crowding her throat, she nodded. "I do have a red gown."

"Then you must wear it. You are a lovely young lady, Cecilia, and if the earl does not see as much, he must be a blind man."

Not as blind as Marcus, she hoped. Was her brother's eyesight ever going to fully recover? What would Father do, once he knew?

The widow must have seen the worry in her eyes, for she gave Cecilia another smile, and rose to her feet.

"I've kept you long enough, my dear. Do tender my regards to your father. And your brothers, of course."

Cecilia showed her to the door, then stood on the step as the Widow Pomfrey departed. The winter chill seeped into her bones. The sky was low, clouds promising snow. She only hoped it would bide another few days—until Edward and his family arrived, until the greenery had been collected from the woods. Tomorrow she must send Marcus out to gather boughs and holly.

As the afternoon wore on, Cecilia found it difficult to concentrate. Every noise had her jumping up to scan the drive for Edward's coach. She had checked and double-checked that his rooms were ready, that the fires were lit, the water for washing

ANTHEA LAWSON

brought up—although none of it would be to Honoria's satisfaction.

Evening descended early, and still they had not arrived.

At dinner—another quiet affair—the butler approached the head of the table.

"I beg your pardon, my lord," he said to Cecilia's father, "but this message was just delivered by one of the village boys."

Fear darted through Cecilia. She had not wanted Edward to come, but she hoped no ill had befallen him or his family. Across the table, Marcus tensed. He set his fork down, the tines clinking against his plate.

"Read it, Father," he urged.

Their father unfolded the paper and read the note aloud.

DEAREST FATHER,

I regret to inform you that my family will be unable to spend Christmas at Wilton House. The boys have fallen ill—nothing too dire, the doctor assures us, just an upset of the digestion that seems to be striking many in the neighborhood. Still we thought it best we not travel during this time.

"THANK GOODNESS," Marcus said under his breath. "Can you imagine having the urchins here, spewing their dinner about?"

"Marcus!" Cecilia sent him a quelling glance.

IN ADDITION, we wanted to share the joyous news that Honoria is in a delicate condition—which, however, adds to the inadvisability of travel.

Our thoughts are with you and my siblings, and know that my family will be celebrating Christmas with you in spirit, if not in person.

Your respectful son,
Edward

CECILIA SWAYED BACK against her chair, relief deflating the tension that had filled her almost to bursting all day.

Edward and his family were not coming! She would not have to bear Honoria's sharp words when nothing met her impossibly high expectations, or run about after two wild and rambunctious boys, since Honoria refused to bring the nanny along yet pled a headache whenever her offspring needed tending. Best of all, Cecilia would not have to watch Edward silently endure his wife's scathing remarks, a trapped look tightening his features that she could do nothing to ease.

She closed her eyes in a silent prayer of thanks.

When she opened them again, she found the earl watching her from across the table. There was a sympathetic spark in his gray eyes, as if he could read her thoughts. She smiled at him, and for a moment thought he would smile in return.

Then Marcus knocked over his wineglass while groping for it, and the moment was broken, lost amidst the commotion of tidying up.

LIAM LAID an armful of holly into the back of the wagon, ignoring the sharp pricks of the leaves. Despite his hat, his ears were tingling with cold. The sun remained hidden behind swirls of cloud, only occasionally peeping out to send a shaft of light through the bare winter woods.

"Well done," Marcus said, unloading his own burden of boughs. "That's more than enough to decorate all of Wiltshire in greenery. And look what I found."

He pointed to a balled mass of foliage growing on one of the branches.

"Your eyesight must be improving, to discover such a treasure," Liam said. "Er, what is it?"

Marcus clapped him on the back. "It's mistletoe, my good man! Full of berries to steal a kiss with."

"Ah." Liam knew of the tradition, of course, but to his recollection had never seen the plant, let alone put it to use.

"Is that your only response?" Marcus grinned. "My vision is clear enough to see how you and my sister nearly smile at one another, before you both recall yourselves."

Liam coughed—not an entirely feigned response. "I do beg your pardon."

"I won't forgive you."

"You won't?" Liam looked closely at Marcus. "Please understand, I have no designs upon your sister."

It was a small lie, but really, he couldn't confess to the man the growing warmth of feeling he had for Cecilia. No, it was not the done thing for a houseguest to suddenly fall in love with his host's sister.

His fingers closed hard around a sprig of holly, the thorned bite of it recalling him to his senses. In love? What an impossible notion.

Marcus had stopped smiling. "I see. That's a pity. Come, then— one more pile of boughs and we can return to the house."

They completed their task in silence, Liam turning over their conversation in his head like a handful of polished stones. Had Marcus been encouraging him, or simply trying to determine the lay of Liam's affections? Or had Marcus been warning him off in some oblique manner that he was too thick-skulled to fathom? How *did* the gentry go about these things?

Lord, he was thrice a fool. If he had any sense at all, he'd order his coach made ready and ride back to Tarrick Hall that very evening.

But somehow he could not bear the notion of jostling away in his empty, cold vehicle; away from the warmth of Wilton House, away from the holiday he had, curiously, come to anticipate. Away from a particular set of stormy blue eyes that hid a vulnerability he understood all too well.

Their return to the house was greeted with merry cries and the bustle of the servants bearing the greenery away. They would deck the hall later with swags of sweet-smelling boughs, and no doubt hang the kissing-ball of mistletoe someplace amusingly prominent. Perhaps at the center of the wide opening leading to the parlor.

"Come in," Cecilia said, her smile seeming to warm further as she turned it on him. "There's mulled cider. You must be chilled."

He was, but it was nothing a simple cup of cider could cure. No, it was the bleakness of the rest of his life, a windswept plain spread out before him, that chilled him to the bone. He should never have come to Wiltshire. A man dying of frostbite does not want any excruciating thawing. Far better to freeze solid without interruptions along the way.

Still, he let her lead him to the cozy parlor, took the cider and lifted it to his lips. Cecilia Fairfax should not suffer for this grim mood that had fallen upon him.

As soon as he had drained his cup, he made her a stiff bow. "I must attend to some estate business in my rooms. I beg that you will excuse me until dinner."

"Oh." The sparkle in her eyes dimmed, and he was sorry to be the cause. "Don't let us keep you."

Marcus made a disagreeable noise from his slouched position on the settee, but said nothing. Feeling unaccountably weary, Liam headed for the shelter of a door he could close behind him.

Four hours later, he emerged, a bit warmer in body, if not spirit, to find the hallway sifted in gray evening shadows. The maids had not yet lit the sconces on the wall.

As he closed his door, movement caught the corner of his eye.

A slight figure in skirts stood at the end of the hall. He turned, prepared to give the errant maid a congenial nod, but no one was there.

Odd.

Liam blinked. He might have mistaken a hanging drapery for a maid, in the dim light—except that there were no draperies in the vicinity. Ignoring the chill at the back of his neck, he strode down the hall.

At the head of the stairs, he met a flushed maid carrying a candle. She bobbed him a quick curtsey and proceeded past him to light the sconces.

"Lord Tarrick?" It was Cecilia's voice. "Is that you? I was just coming to fetch you for supper."

"It is," Liam said, descending to where his hostess waited at the foot of the stairs, her slender hand resting on the carved newel-post. "My apologies for keeping you waiting."

He offered his arm, as a gentleman should. At least he knew *some* of the proper protocols.

"Not at all." She slipped her hand through his elbow, and together they proceeded toward the dining room.

As they passed the parlor, Cecilia let out a sharp cry and stumbled against him.

"Miss Fairfax!" He immediately caught her by the shoulders. "Are you well?"

She shook her head and glanced about, a suspicious tilt to her brows. Clearly not finding what she was looking for in the warmly-lit hall, she gave him a half-distracted smile.

"My apologies, my lord. I thought… well. No matter. Clearly I am clumsier than I'd imagined."

"I don't find you clumsy in the least." He ought to release her, now that she had regained her balance, but his hands seemed incapable of lifting from her shoulders.

A faint flush colored her cheeks as she lifted her head and met his gaze. Then her eyes slid to a point somewhat above his head, and her flush deepened.

What was… Ah yes. If he was not mistaken, they stood directly below the ball of mistletoe.

He gave her a heartbeat's chance to pull away. Instead Cecilia swayed imperceptibly closer to him. Her lips, when they were not pressed into an anxious line, were full. And eminently kissable.

Locking away all rational thought, Liam leaned forward. Their gazes met, with a shiver that sped down his spine. Then, deliberately, she closed her eyes and tipped her face up to his.

Heart jolting like a runaway coach, he lowered his head and brushed his mouth over hers. Soft, warm—and then warmth sparked to vivid flame. He pressed his lips more firmly to hers, and she sighed, her mouth opening slightly beneath his. His tongue, most traitorous and ungentlemanly, took advantage, dipping in to taste her sweetness. Fire spiraled through him, and a curious sensation of rightness. Cecilia Fairfax belonged in his arms, her slender fingers curling through his hair, her body pressed close, her mouth pliable and delicious beneath his.

But they stood in the center of Wilton House, and a kiss that he'd meant to be a gentle caress had blazed all out of proportion. Liam forced his head to lift, away from the warmth of her lips; forced himself to step back and release her, though his blood clamored for more. *Sweep her into your arms, carry her up the stairs,* a wild, reckless part of him demanded.

She stared at him, her eyes bright, her cheeks becomingly rosy. Then, slowly, she smiled.

"Happy Christmas, Lord Tarrick," she said, no trace of disdain in her voice.

"Likewise, Cecy—Miss Fairfax. Though we are a bit early, are we not? Christmas is two days hence."

She glanced up. "There is no rule about when the mistletoe may be used. Though now you must pick a berry and give it to me."

He reached up and plucked one of the small white berries. It was hard and smooth, like wax. She held out her cupped hand and he dropped it in.

"What will you do with it?" he asked.

Her smile took on a mischievous edge as she slipped the berry in her pocket. "Come along, sir. Supper awaits."

He finished escorting her to the dining room, and they spoke no more of the kiss—the splendid, secret kiss now indelibly engraved in his memory. He would sleep, and wake, and sleep again with the remembered feeling of his lips on hers. For years, no doubt. Years upon years. He could not decide if that was a wonderful thing, or a terrible one.

Either way, he would never regret that kiss.

CHRISTMAS EVE CAME INEXORABLY—AND it *was* evening, despite Cecilia's best efforts to hold the day at bay. She had spent the hours in a whirlwind, making sure all was in readiness for the holiday. Cakes were baked, the Yule log ready to light in the parlor's hearth, and all her gifts wrapped.

The Widow Pomfrey had arrived, pies in hand, as promised. She was keeping Father company before dinner, while Cecilia dressed.

Cecilia sat before the glass in her room, brushing her hair. Martha had helped her don the red satin gown, and the fabric glowed richly in the light. Too richly, perhaps. Her skin looked pale in contrast, her eyes wide and weary. She was not certain she was worthy of such a pretty gown.

Although the earl had kissed her, pretty or not.

Ah, that kiss. She had lain awake far too long the previous night, rekindling the moment behind her closed eyes. The serious look he had given her, the warmth of his lips upon hers, the solid strength as his arms had closed about her, the stunning softness of his raven-black hair between her fingers.

She had not meant to end up beneath the mistletoe with the earl. Perhaps she had dreamed of it, but she never would have maneuvered him so blatantly. No—that had been the ghost's doing. Sneaky little thing, to push Cecilia so violently at just the opportune moment. It was unlike Lizzy, to make such an overt showing.

Not that the ghost of the girl had been visible, but still. Cecilia could hardly explain such a thing to their guest, and so had passed it off as clumsiness.

"Mistress?" Martha said, interrupting her thoughts. "Cook says all is in readiness. Shall I call the family to dinner?"

"Yes—in ten minutes."

Cecilia caught her hair up and coiled it into a bun. Watching her, Martha *tsked*.

"Now, mistress, let me fix your hair. It won't take but a moment."

Without waiting for assent, the maid set the curling iron in the fire, then pulled a few strands of pale hair free from Cecilia's bun. Deftly, she curled them, the soft ringlets falling about Cecilia's face.

"That's better," Martha said. "Though you need something more. Those ruby-studded combs."

"I couldn't." Cecilia's response was automatic.

The combs had belonged to Mother, and though Cecilia had inherited all her jewelry, she had not touched it since her mother's death.

"Now, mistress, your dear mother would have wanted you to look well. Especially tonight."

Martha winked at her, and Cecilia flushed. Did all the servants know of her growing affection for Lord Tarrick?

"Oh, very well. But be quick about it."

She waved at the jewelry box on the dressing table, where the mistletoe berry was concealed like a small, precious pearl. Smiling, Martha plucked the combs out and deftly inserted them into Cecilia's coiffure. The gems winked and shone, set off by her pale hair.

"Lovely," the maid said. "I'll go fetch the family now."

After she left, Cecilia spent a moment admiring her reflection. She did look well—in a waifish sort of way. Enough to please the earl, or so she hoped.

She rose and collected the last gift to bring down to the parlor —a book wrapped in brown paper and sealed with red wax, for Lord Tarrick. After hours of consideration, she had settled on her beloved copy of *Lyrical Ballads* by Wordsworth and Coleridge. The poems had often comforted her, and she wanted to give him something of personal value, that showed the esteem in which she held him.

Something that would thank him for that most splendid kiss.

DINNER WAS A JOLLY AFFAIR—IN no small part because Cecilia could not help the little bubbles of joy that cascaded through her whenever she met the earl's gaze. Oh, it was foolish of her, but she could not help but indulge in her feelings.

He would leave soon enough, she knew it. But he was here now, and it was Christmas time, and so she let her smiles come freely. The Widow Pomfrey added to the air of merriment as well, with her unfailing good humor and witty stories of life in the village. And, of course, her delicious pies.

After dinner they repaired to the parlor, where the Yule log crackled merrily. Cecilia was careful to give the mistletoe a wide berth, though she could feel the earl's gaze upon her as she entered the room.

She went to the pianoforte and began to play the family's favorite carol; *God Rest Ye Merry Gentlemen*. Marcus took up the melody first, his baritone clear and strong. The widow joined him in a wobbly alto, quickly shored up by Father's tenor.

Cecilia sang softly, but it was difficult for her to keep her place in the music and sing out at the same time.

A shadow fell over the page, and she glanced up to see Lord Tarrick standing at her shoulder. Quietly, he began to sing as well, reading the words off the sheet music. His voice was low and deep, a bit husky as if from disuse, but tuneful enough.

When the carol ended, she turned and smiled at him.

"I didn't know you sang."

"I don't." His gray eyes were serious. "Until now."

Their gazes held, until Marcus cleared his throat.

"Here we Come a Wassailing!" he cried.

Despite the merry noise of caroling issuing from the parlor, no actual wassailers arrived at Wilton House. No doubt they thought the estate still in mourning. After the family and their guests had drunk their fill of the spiced wine, Cecilia directed the rest to be shared out among the servants.

At last, late into the evening, the small party wound to a close.

"My heavens," Widow Pomfrey exclaimed, glancing at the pocketwatch pinned to her gown, "Look at the hour! I must be returning home."

"Oh, do stay," Cecilia said. "I had an extra room made ready, just in case."

It took very little coaxing to persuade the widow to stay, and soon enough they were all making for their beds. Cecilia lingered a moment in the parlor, to make sure the Yule log was well banked.

Satisfied, she stepped into the hall, only to catch light and movement near the kitchen. Likely it was only a servant nipping the last of the wine, but Cecilia turned her steps in that direction. The kitchen was empty, the door gaping wide, admitting the frigid night air.

She paused at the threshold, rubbing the gooseflesh from her arms.

"Hello?" she called. "Is anyone outside?"

At the corner of the house she caught sight of a white-capped figure carrying a lantern. Heedless of the cold, Cecilia hurried out.

"Mrs. Bess!" she cried, when she was near enough to recognize the figure. "Whatever are you doing?"

The old woman had descended the steps leading to the cellar and was fumbling with her keys. At Cecilia's voice, she looked up.

"We must have plum cordial for tomorrow."

"Certainly," Cecilia said, "but we can fetch it in the morning."

"No, no." Mrs. Bess's voice was anxious and thin. "It's a Wilton House tradition. Plum cordial for Christmas."

Clearly the old housekeeper's mind would not rest until she was holding a bottle of cordial. Cecilia descended the steps as Mrs. Bess unlocked the cellar door. She took the lantern from the housekeeper's chilled fingers.

"Stay here," Cecilia said. "I'll find the cordial."

She hurried into the musty confines of the cellar, once again wishing they had an interior access. But Wilton House was oddly built, and no-one had seen fit to make the cellar convenient to reach.

In the lamplight, the rows of glass jars and bottles glinted like foreign treasure; amber and verdigris and old rubies. Cecilia located the plum cordial at the far end of the cellar. The glass was cool beneath her fingers as she carried it to where Mrs. Bess waited by the door.

"Here we are." Cecilia handed the old housekeeper the cordial. "Now, back to our warm beds." Her words left a white plume in the air.

"Oh." Mrs. Bess squinted at the bottle. "Plum cordial. But oughtn't we to have two? For the guests?"

Reining in her impatience, Cecilia turned and proceeded back to the shelf. She set down the lantern and was just reaching for another bottle of cordial when the cellar door slammed shut.

"Mrs. Bess?" She whirled and hurried to the now-closed door. "Hello?"

She tried the latch. It was locked, and dismay crept through her, even colder than the chill night air. Had Mrs. Bess forgotten that she was in the cellar? It was entirely too plausible.

"Mrs. Bess? Let me out!" she called, pounding on the door. The wood absorbed her fistfalls, turning them to soft thumps.

Cecilia pivoted and grabbed a jar of pickles, beating it against the door until she feared the glass would shatter. There was no reply. Mrs. Bess did not return.

Still, Cecilia called and pounded until her throat was sore and her hands ached. Swallowing back her fear, she slumped against the cold stone wall. There was nothing for it—she would have to wait until morning, and hope that someone would venture out to the cellar. Although the kitchen was completely well-stocked with everything they would possibly need on the morrow. Her chances of being discovered were not good—unless Mrs. Bess recalled their night-time trip.

Shivering, Cecilia glanced about the cellar. Potatoes were lumped in one corner in their rough burlap sacks. Uncaring of the mess, she dumped them out and wrapped the coarse material around her. She was still cold beyond belief, but she would survive the night. She would—and in the morrow she would win free of the cellar. Somehow.

Clinging to that thought, Cecilia closed her eyes and sank into frost-laden, fitful sleep.

LIAM WOKE, cold beneath his blankets despite the coals still glowing on the hearth. He pulled the covers up about his chin, but sleep was gone. After a solid half-hour of chasing after it, he gave up and rose, donning his clothing. A quick glance between the curtains showed the edge of dawn shading the horizon. Christmas Day was here—and he had nothing to give Cecilia.

Or perhaps he had everything to give. But would she accept?

He sat on the edge of the unmade bed, turning his signet ring back and forth between his fingers. The gold was warm, the sapphire bezel gleaming in the dim light. Hope and fear alternated, strobing across his soul until he was dizzy.

What was he even contemplating?

He could not ask Cecilia Fairfax to marry him. They scarcely knew one another. No, he would depart on the morrow. If they continued to correspond, or if Marcus invited him for another visit, *then* he might muster up the courage. But he could not do it now. It was the outside of foolishness, especially since she had no reason to tell him yes. Why would she?

Far better to wait.

Mind made up, the clamor of emotions beneath his skin stilled. Liam slid the signet ring back on his finger.

A quiet knock sounded at his door, and the dark-haired maid slipped into the room. She drew up short at the sight of him. Her eyes darted to the rumpled covers, then back to him, and she bobbed a quick curtsey.

"Good morning, milord." She hesitated a moment, then went to the hearth and began building up the fire.

Prompted by some impulse, Liam asked, "Is everything well?"

"Oh!" The maid glanced up at him. "Truthfully, milord? Miss Cecilia has disappeared."

"What?" He rose abruptly. "Disappeared, how?"

"No one knows. Her bed wasn't slept in, and she's nowhere to be found."

Ah, that explained the furtive glance at his bed—as if the servants had thought their errant mistress would perhaps be found there. He cleared his throat.

"Is the family awake?"

"Yes, they're in the parlor. They're organizing search parties, if you want to ride out."

Cecilia Fairfax missing. An impossible hole opened in the fabric of his world. How could he come back to court her if she was *gone*?

Leaving the maid, he strode into the hallway. He could not believe Cecilia had simply disappeared. Not here, in the serene heart of Wiltshire, surrounded by family and friends.

A flicker of movement at the head of the stairs made him glance up, and Liam stumbled to a halt. A girl stood there, garbed in an odd, old-fashioned dress.

But that was not what sent a shiver prickling over his skin. It was that he could see right through her to the paneled walls, her figure transparent as mist.

"Lizzy?" he whispered, his mouth dry as paper.

She nodded and beckoned urgently, then glided down the staircase. Liam stood frozen for a heartbeat, then sprang forward. He did not think the ghost meant him harm. Did she know what had befallen Cecilia?

At the foot of the stairs, he glanced wildly about, then spotted Lizzy's pale form hovering near the front door.

"Outside?" he asked.

In answer, the ghost passed through the solid mahogany door and was gone. Liam hurried to follow. He undid the lock and threw open the door, just as Marcus emerged from the parlor.

"Tarrick," Marcus said, "what the devil are you doing?"

"Lizzy went outside," Liam replied, a bit incoherently.

There wasn't time to explain. He bolted down the front steps, Marcus close behind. A tattered bit of mist rounded the corner of the house, and Liam pursued. He halted outside the mounded rows of the kitchen garden. There was no sign of the ghost.

"Where are you?" he cried, his voice cracking on the last syllable. Cecilia could not be lost to him. He would not allow it.

"Are you out of your head?" Marcus asked, drawing up beside him.

"Hush." Liam slashed his hand downward.

A muffled thumping issued from the far corner of the house. Liam hastened toward the sound, pausing at the head of a rough stone staircase running down the outside wall.

"The cellar!" Marcus said.

The two of them sprinted down the stairs to the door at the bottom. Liam grasped the handle, but the door was locked. At the sound of the rattling latch, the thumping ceased.

"Help!" It was Cecilia's voice, issuing from behind the cellar door.

"Cecy?" her brother called. "Can you hear me?"

"Marcus—I'm here." Her reply was faint, but present.

"Thank God."

Liam agreed—but Cecilia was still locked in the cellar. "Who has the keys?" he demanded.

Marcus frowned. "Mrs. Bess. I'll go find her." He ran up the steps, pausing at the top. "You stay here."

As if Liam would budge from the spot.

"Miss Fairfax," he called through the door, "Cecilia. Are you unharmed?"

"Mostly, though I'm a bit chilled." Her voice was weaker than he liked.

"Your brother has gone to find the keys. We'll have you out of there in a thrice."

"Liam?" There was a desperate ring to her words. "Please keep talking to me."

"What should I say?"

"Anything. I just—I need to hear the sound of someone's voice. Your voice."

He drew in a deep breath and then, before he could persuade himself otherwise, said the words.

"Miss Fairfax, will you marry me?"

Silence, underscored by the heavy beating of his heart.

"Excuse me? Are you jesting?"

"Never. I know the situation is hardly..." Damnation. What was he thinking, asking Cecilia to marry him through the thick expanse of a wooden door. He was a coward of the first order. "That is to say—here comes your brother."

Liam stepped back as Marcus bounded down the stairs, a ring of keys in his hand. Behind him came Lord Fairfax, the Widow Pomfrey, and a cluster of servants, white-haired Mrs. Bess among them.

"Which key is it, Cecy?" Marcus rattled the ring in frustration.

"The smaller iron one," she called back.

Marcus fitted it into the lock and, after another excruciating second, it turned. He threw open the door to reveal the wan and trembling form of his sister, coarse burlap sacks wrapped around her shoulders and upper body.

Without a word, Liam stepped into the dank interior and swept Cecilia up into his arms. She made no protest, only blinked and turned her face to his chest when they emerged into the light.

"Brandy," he said, ascending the stairs with her. "And blankets —in the parlor. Is there a closer entrance into the house?"

"Here," her father said, holding open a door that led into the kitchen.

Liam bore his precious burden to the parlor and sank down before the fire, still holding Cecilia. Shivers ran through her, and bedamned if he was going to let her go.

Unless, of course, she wanted him to. Terrible though the prospect might be.

"Here," Marcus said, holding out a glass of brandy.

Cecilia lifted her head, her eyes the color of a bruise, and took a tiny sip.

"More," Liam said. "You must get warm."

She took a larger drink, then coughed and shuddered as the brandy went down.

"Blankets, milord." The dark-haired maid hastened to the hearth, her arms full of woven wool.

As if the sight of the maid was a catalyst, Cecilia sat up and gently slid from Liam's arms. She pulled off the burlap sacking, leaving streaks of grime on her red dress and a smudge on her cheek. Before she could start shivering again, the maid draped a blanket about her shoulders, and another across her lap.

"Thank you," Cecilia said, glancing about the room. "Thank you all. I'm so glad you found me."

"How the devil did you get locked in the cellar?" Marcus said.

"Poor Mrs. Bess is wandering in her wits. She didn't mean to lock me in, but I fear she forgot my presence." Cecilia shook her head. "I didn't want to relieve her of her duties."

"And look at the cost to you, poor dear," the Widow Pomfrey said.

"She must be retired," Cecilia's father said, in a tone that brooked no argument. "Immediately."

Cecilia bit her lip. "Yes, but I have no one to take her place."

"As to that…" The widow glanced at Lord Fairfax, a faint blush suffusing her round cheeks. "Please let me assist you. I know a woman from the village who might suit admirably."

"Excellent," Cecilia said, meeting the widow's gaze.

Liam had the impression some small, secret communication known only to women passed between them, for the widow smiled and Cecilia nodded again.

"Lord Tarrick," Cecilia said, turning to him. "I believe you asked me a question."

He stiffened, the blood catching in his veins.

"I did."

"Would you do me the favor of asking it again?"

"Here?" He glanced about the parlor, from Marcus sitting on the carpet beside his sister, to Lord Fairfax and Widow Pomfrey, to the dark-haired maid.

"Yes." Cecilia's voice was clear and firm.

Very well. His chest tightened, but he was hers to command. Liam shifted onto his knees and faced her. Taking her hands in his —her fingers still too cold for his liking—he swallowed once, for courage.

"Miss Cecilia Fairfax. Would you do me the very great honor of becoming my wife?"

The room stilled. Even the flames in the hearth seemed to pause. Liam could scarcely breathe.

Cecilia tipped her head.

Liam wanted to close his eyes, wanted to leap to his feet and rush back to the isolated safety of Tarrick Hall, never to come out again. Instead he forced himself to wait, the signet ring heavy on his finger.

At last, Cecilia smiled, and it was like the sun coming out from behind the clouds in a blaze of promise. His heart gave a tremendous thump, then settled into a new, stronger rhythm, borne by a sense of hope beyond anything he had ever felt.

"Yes, Liam. I will marry you." She leaned forward and kissed him, gently, on the lips.

The world spun from that point of contact, the moon revolved, the planets danced, all because Cecilia Fairfax had consented to be his bride. Something inside Liam mended— something he had not even known was broken, until recent months.

Marcus let out a whoop and clapped him on the back, the maid cheered, and Lord Fairfax smiled broadly.

"I beg your forgiveness, sir," Liam said, glancing up to her father. "I ought to have asked you first, but—"

"I understand," Cecilia's father said. "Sometimes the heart precedes the head in such matters. You have my blessing."

Liam slipped the gold signet of the Earls of Tarrick from his finger and handed it to Cecilia. The sapphire shone in her cupped hand.

"This is all I have to give you," he said. "My name, my title. My heart. Everything I am and everything I have is yours, Cecilia Fairfax."

"It is more than enough, Liam." Tears shone in her eyes, brighter than the sapphire in his ring. "More than I had ever hoped for."

"Happy Christmas, my countess," he said.

Something half-seen at the edge of his vision made him glance to the doorway. The transparent figure of Lizzy stood there, smiling. As he watched, she faded away, leaving only mortal joy to fill the parlor.

Which was, indeed, enough.

A DUKE FOR MIDWINTER

PART ONE

The coach jolted, a rough sway to one side that made Selene Banning's lap robe slide off, taking her book with it. The lamp on her side of the coach guttered and went out, the wick foundering in its own oil. Selene scooped her book off the floor, then tucked it away. It was growing too dim inside the coach to read, and the story had not been able to distract her from the predicament she feared she'd placed herself in.

Her fingers, despite the fur-lined gloves she wore, were clumsy from the cold. The spatter of sleet against the windows made her shiver. She ought to have waited to depart for London, but when she, her companion Hetty, and the driver and footman had set out, the storm they were now fighting had been merely a dark smudge on the horizon.

"Are we nearly to the next town?" Hetty shot an anxious glance out the window of the coach. Nothing could be seen but their wavering reflections, backed by blowing gusts of icy rain.

"No doubt we are." Selene endeavored to keep her voice assured, though she had not been attending to their whereabouts. All she knew was that they had ridden through Downham Market some time ago, and that Cambridge still lay some distance ahead.

She stole a quick glance at the silver watch pinned to her bodice. Half-four, and growing darker outside by the moment. Foreboding pinched her breath.

"You must stay warm." Hetty retrieved the lap robe and tucked it about Selene's knees. "Wouldn't do to arrive in London for the holidays with a chill."

"I might say the same." Selene gave her companion a look, and Hetty tightened her shawl about her shoulders.

Her companion was a decade older than Selene, but acted as if she were more than twice her mistress's age, bustling and clucking like a mother hen. Of course, she was used to fretting over two charges, not one, which meant that on this journey the brunt of Hetty's attention fell upon Selene. Her younger sister, Eliana, was already in London, by special request of the queen.

Golden-haired, lovely Eliana, who would certainly make a stunning match. She was as different from Selene as the sun from the moon. Compared to Eliana, Selene's thick brown hair was reduced to a mousey brown, her strong nose seemed overlarge, her eyes too melancholy. But truly, she could not be bitter. Eliana was too open-hearted and sweet to resent—though sometimes, in the deep of night, Selene lay awake and wished that her own features were not quite so unremarkable.

While she was wishing, she supposed she ought to be less firm in her opinions. Her unwillingness to compromise had lost her her first, and most likely *only*, offer of marriage. In the three years since, there had been no more suitors for her hand.

But she was who she was, and her future became more clear with every passing year. Eliana was the one who would wed a handsome lord, while Selene would retire to the country, tend to her horses, and adore her nieces and nephews as she carried on into spinsterhood.

If she managed to make it to London in one piece. Trying not to let her worry show on her face, she peered out the window again. The stretch of road was empty, with no habitations in sight.

She should have gone to Town with the family, not stayed behind to help with her favorite mare's foaling. She should have heeded the stable master's worries about the weather instead of overriding him with glib reassurances. She should have curbed her impatience, which had blinded her to the dark storm on the horizon.

Better to spend a cold and lonely Christmas at Banning Hall, despite the bleakness that had come over her in the past months. But oh, she had so wanted to be in London with her family.

The coach shuddered again and she heard the horses whinny in fright. She wrestled the window down and was rewarded with a faceful of wind-driven sleet. Shading her eyes with her gloved hand, which did little to mitigate the icy blast, she squinted. She could barely make out the hunched figure of the driver.

"Benjamin!" she shouted. "Is everything well? Any sign of a town?"

Her words were whipped from her lips, but the driver heard.

"Nothing, Mistress" he called back.

Mouth set, Selene closed the window. There must be a village soon, or at least a farmhouse where they might take shelter

The coach slewed violently and Hetty let out a shriek. Selene watched in horror as they tipped over. Her book banged against the ceiling and she braced herself, catching Hetty's arm as her companion tumbled past.

A sickening crunch, the high whinny of a horse, and the curtains caught fire from the flame of the remaining lamp. Hastily, Selene beat the fire out with her muff. The stench of scorched rabbit fur filled the air.

"Are you all right?" she asked Hetty.

Despite Selene's aid, her companion had crashed into the corner. Hetty lifted her head and winced.

"I think my arm might be broken," she said.

"Stay still." Selene clambered across the seats, unwinding her woolen muffler. "We must bind it until a doctor can examine you."

Fear rose up, but she shoved it away. They might be capsized in the midst of a worsening blizzard, Hetty injured, and far from any help, but she would not let it overwhelm her.

First, she must tend to Hetty, and then somehow exit the coach and assist Benjamin and John with the horses. Hopefully they had leaped clear when the coach tipped, and had been spared injury. She strained, listening for their voices over the terrified neighs of the horses, but heard nothing.

Hetty bit her lip as Selene bound her arm to her body, but bravely bore up. Gently, Selene helped settle her companion on the seat—the bench of which now served as part of the floor. The pallor in Hetty's face was worrisome.

One matter at a time.

"I must help with the horses," Selene said. Thank heavens the panicked whinnies had ceased—but if the horses were still in harness, they could easily injure themselves. At least she could now hear Benjamin and John calling to one another. Neither of them sounded hurt, and she sent up a prayer of thanks for that small mercy.

"Mistress?" It was Benjamin, knocking on the underside of the coach. "Are you unharmed?"

"Yes," she called back. "But Hetty is not. I'm climbing out now."

"Very good," he said.

"Please," Hetty said, "be careful." Her voice caught on the last word.

Selene nodded briskly at her companion, then studied the coach door, now located just above her head. She could probably wrestle it open, but levering herself up and out would be another matter entirely. And Hetty would not be able to help her.

Blast.

She scanned the tipped interior—the fallen lap robes, the scorched muff. Ah, the basket of provisions. Would it be sturdy enough to take her weight? She must try.

"Tuck yourself into the corner as much as you may," Selene

said to her maid. "And mind your head—I'm afraid I might need to kick rather ungracefully."

Hetty nodded, wedging herself against the corner, where the ceiling was now a wall.

Selene considered a moment, then dragged the lidded basket under the door. Beneath the toes of her boots, the coach window was laid over flattened grasses mixed with mud and snow. The dimness she had remarked upon earlier was growing—the storm hastening nightfall.

"Mind your head," she told Hetty, satisfied the basket was properly positioned.

She would have to be swift, and pray that the basket would not break under her feet. Step up, fling open the door, grip the sides of the coach and pull herself out.

"Good luck," Hetty said.

With a brisk nod, Selene launched herself into motion. The basket creaked ominously beneath her weight, but held. Bless the sturdy wicker construction.

It was easy enough to reach the door handle, but took considerably more strength than she had bargained for to push the door up. There was a bad moment when the wind bore down against it —but then, in the maddeningly capricious way of weather, it reversed direction and ripped the door from her hands. It banged open against the side of the coach with a loud thwack.

She heard voices, but all her concentration was on levering herself from the coach. A quick lunge up, and she managed to hook her elbows over the door frame.

The icy wind hit her in the face as her head and shoulders emerged, snowflakes stinging her cheeks. She drew in a quick breath and swung her legs, hoping that Hetty had the sense to duck away from her kicks.

One boot found purchase on the back of the cushioned bench, and she rose a bit more, trying to wiggle herself onto the body of the coach.

ANTHEA LAWSON

Her foot slipped, and she began sliding back down. *No, oh drat it...*

A dark figure appeared out of the storm. The coach rocked as he quickly clambered up. Before she lost her grasp entirely and tumbled back down into the interior, strong arms caught her about the waist and lifted her free.

He steadied her, blocking the worst of the wind with his body as she got her feet under her. The surface of the coach was too slippery for her to stand confidently, so she ended up in a half crouch and eyed the ground below.

"I'll lower you down," he said in a resonant, cultured voice. "Take hold of my arms."

She peered at him. From the first she had known it was not Benjamin—the rotund driver had neither the grace nor the agility to climb upon a toppled coach. Nor was it the footman, John, for he was a thin fellow who spoke with a rustic accent.

The man kneeling beside her was clearly a gentleman, judging by his assured manner and the fine cut of his coat. Snowflakes caught in his dark hair, and his blue eyes regarded her steadily.

"My companion, Miss Miller, is still within," she said. "Her arm is injured."

"Ah." He shot a glance down into the shadowy interior. "If I lift her, do you think you could help her emerge?"

"Of course."

A brief smile flitted across his lips before he lowered himself into the doorway.

"Look out below," he called.

Hetty made a muffled sound of assent, and their mysterious rescuer slipped into the coach. He landed with a soft thud, and Selene was glad he hadn't crushed the basket or stumbled over it and hurt himself.

A few moments later, Hetty partially emerged. Selene knelt forward.

"Wrap your arm about my waist," she said. "Yes, there you go."

Though she hadn't the strength to pluck her maid free, as the gentleman had done for her, Selene managed to crawl backward along the paneled coach's sides, pulling Hetty with her. It was difficult, since her maid's injured arm clearly pained her, but after a brief struggle, and a helpful boost from below, Hetty was free.

"Oh, nicely done," Selene said.

She cast a quick glance to the front of the coach. Despite the driving snow, she was able to see that Benjamin and John had managed to untangle the horses. Both animals seemed unharmed, thank heavens.

A moment later the gentleman levered himself out of the door, then hunkered beside them where they perched on the coach. The ground seemed rather farther away than she would have liked.

"I'll go first," he said to Selene. "Lower your companion to me."

She nodded her agreement, and he all but bounded down from the overturned coach. The man seemed positively invigorated by their adventure. And, if she were entirely honest, Selene was of a somewhat similar mind. Hetty's arm aside, and the fact that they had tipped their coach heavens knew where in the middle of a wretched snow storm, it was certainly a departure from the humdrum of the everyday.

She and Hetty carefully scooted to the edge of the coach, mindful of the wheels. Below, the gentleman awaited, arms outstretched.

"I'll keep hold of your waist as long as I can," Selene told her companion. "Ready?"

Hetty gave her a grim nod, and in moments had slid down without mishap into the gentleman's arms. He carefully helped her stand on the snow-covered grasses, then looked up at Selene.

"Miss?" He lifted his arms.

She gathered her skirts about her, dangled her legs over the edge, and let herself slip off the coach. He caught her deftly, and even through her thick woolen gown and cloak, his body was shockingly warm and solid.

"Banning," she said, a curious catch in her throat. "Miss Selene Banning."

"A pleasure, despite the rather unconventional manner of our meeting," he said, his voice vibrating against her. "I am..."

He paused a moment, his dark blue eyes catching hers, and her heart made an odd little flip in her chest. She stood still within the shelter of his embrace, snowflakes melting against her cheeks and tangling in her lashes. It was rather improper, but she did not step away.

"Yes?" she prompted. "You are?"

"Jared Kendrick, Baron Collingwood, at your service." With that, he stepped back and made her a bow. "Where are you bound in such a storm, Miss Banning?"

"London." Without his warmth around her, the wind was suddenly icy. "I am going to join my family for the holidays. Or rather, I was."

She'd never heard of Baron Collingwood—but then, England was littered with minor nobility. There was no denying Jared Kendrick was a gentleman, at any rate.

She turned to survey the tipped coach. Hetty huddled by its side, her injured arm cradled close, and John and Benjamin held the horses, who stamped impatiently.

"Are you both uninjured?" she asked to them. "Can we right the coach?"

"Afraid not," Benjamin said. "That is, we're well enough—a few bruises here and there—but the axle's cracked. I wouldn't trust it in this weather. We'll have to come back and make repairs once the snow clears."

"For now, I'm afraid the storm is only going to get worse," Sir Kendrick said. "Luckily, there's an inn not far down the road. I passed it perhaps half an hour ago."

"I'm much relived to hear it," Selene said. "Are you on foot?" She glanced through the thickening whiteness. He was right, the storm was growing more severe.

"Ah, no." He gave a short laugh. "My horse, Admiral, is a patient beast. He waits yonder."

He pointed, and she could just make out a dark shape tethered to a bush at the side of the road.

"I'm sorry to leave the coach," Hetty said regretfully.

"As am I," Selene said. "But it can't be helped."

At least their luggage was accessible, lashed on the roof and now touching the ground. She would be able to bring her valise, packed with a few necessities.

"I don't suppose you have extra saddles and bridles?" the baron asked, glancing at the coach horses.

"I'm afraid not." Without tack, the horses would not make effective mounts, which meant the driver and footman would have to lead them to the inn.

"Can you ride astride?" Sir Kendrick asked.

"Yes." It wouldn't be comfortable, with her skirts bunched up. But she had borrowed her brother William's trousers often enough to ride about the countryside. As long as she kept her hair tucked beneath a hat and wore a bulky coat, she hadn't feared shocking the neighbors too badly.

"Then you must mount Admiral," Sir Kendrick said. "You can steady your companion in front of the saddle. I'll lead my horse, and your men can take the carriage horses."

It was a sensible suggestion. She beckoned to John, who handed his horse to Benjamin and fought his way against the wind to fetch her and Hetty's valises. Soon enough they were ready to embark.

Sir Kendrick retrieved Admiral from the side of the road. The horse was a tall black gelding, but did not seem overly skittish, standing quietly as the baron assisted Selene up. She set one booted foot in his cupped hands, and managed to gain the saddle, though her skirts twisted dreadfully. She pulled them down as best she could, grateful for her warm woolen leggings. At least her cloak concealed the worst of her awkwardly displayed limbs.

There was no use in blushing at the impropriety—not while the snow swirled about them in earnest. She hoped the road remained visible. It would be a dreadful fate to freeze to death stumbling in circles around some farmer's pastures.

But she refused to dwell on such morbid fancies. They would reach the inn and wait out the storm in warmth and comfort. She clung firmly to the thought.

It took both Sir Kendrick and John to boost Hetty onto the horse in front of Selene. Though her companion did not cry out, Hetty's face was very pale by the time she was properly settled in front of Selene.

"I've got you," Selene said, holding her about the waist.

Since the baron would be leading his horse, Selene would not need to guide Admiral, and could direct her attention to steadying her companion and keeping them both safely mounted.

"All secure?" Sir Kendrick asked.

"Well enough," she replied, taking a firmer grip on Hetty as Admiral launched into motion.

They made a sorry parade: a baron afoot, a woman riding astride with her injured companion, and two coach horses trailing unhappily behind two men not best suited for a long trudge through a winter storm.

Selene wrapped her muffler around her face and rather grimly held on to Hetty. She could feel her companion shivering as the icy wind blasted about them. After the first ten minutes, the world was nothing but white and cold and discomfort. She focused on the dim figure of Sir Kendrick who, head bowed against the storm, led them forward.

The road disappeared under swirling snow, but he kept them upon it—she was not quite sure how. When at last a building loomed up, windows bright against the encroaching night, she could scarce believe it. They would not die in the snowstorm after all! She let out a relieved breath, which quickly turned to icy crystals and was swept away by a frigid gust.

The baron led them directly to the stables, where two lads appeared to take the horses. Admiral stood calmly as the baron helped Hetty dismount. Although their breath plumed in the stable air, it felt wonderful to be out of the biting wind. Selene began to believe she might actually be warm again, at some point in the future.

When it was her turn to dismount, she could barely move her legs. They felt frozen to the horse's sides. With effort, she slung her left leg over the pommel and, skirts all akimbo, slid down once more into Sir Kendrick's arms.

He steadied her, his grasp warm and solid, and gave her a slight smile. It was remarkably comforting to be in his embrace. She gave in to the impulse to lean against him. Surely it was not too untoward after the ordeal they'd just been through.

"Thank you, so very much," she said, looking up into his face. "Without your help this evening…"

She shivered, and his arms tightened about her.

"I am glad to be of service, Miss Banning. Now, let's get all of you inside."

She took a breath and stepped away, setting back the hood of her cloak. The ice on the sides was beginning to melt, the wet wool clammy against her face.

"Come," she said, slipping her arm about Hetty. "I hope there is a doctor in the village."

Sir Kendrick led the way into the courtyard. The air stole Selene's breath, and snowflakes whirled about her face. Fortunately, it was only a few paces to the inn door. She squinted up at the sign as they went in, faintly making out the shape of a red hound.

"Oh, heavens! Come in, come in." A tall, plump woman bustled up to greet them, calling for her husband to bring hot toddies.

Soon enough, Selene and Hetty were installed in the inn's best suite, ensconced in armchairs before the fire and sipping heated cinnamon-laced brandy. There had been some confusion about rooms for the gentlemen, but Sir Kendrick had insisted that the ladies go and warm up as soon as possible. He'd given his word to make sure her men were well situated.

As it happened, there was indeed a village doctor. The innkeeper had sent for him to tend to Hetty's arm, and in the meantime, the brandy seemed to be helping. Selene watched her companion over the rim of her own cup, glad to see the lines of pain and cold ease from Hetty's face.

Selene suspected her own expression was relaxing, as well. She was not accustomed to such strong spirits, but the spiced alcohol warmed her all the way down to her toes. It was a wonderful sensation, despite the dampness of her gown, which the crackling fire was already drying.

"We are so fortunate Sir Kendrick rescued us," Hetty said. "Without his help, I fear we would have perished this night."

"Certainly not." Selene kept her tone bracing, though that very thought had crossed her mind more than once. "I would never let anything so dreadful happen. But I'm truly grateful he happened upon us."

"He is very handsome, is he not?" Hetty gave her a dreamy smile and took another sip of her brandy. "So tall and broad-shouldered, yet not oafish in the least. I wager he's a marvelous dancer. And more than that, I imagine."

Selene was torn between laughter and dismay at Hetty's sudden frankness. She'd no idea strong spirits would make her companion so forthright. In the four years Hetty had served their family, the woman had never let an improper word slip from her lips. And now she was imagining...

Well, Selene was not precisely certain what thoughts were going through Hetty's head. She, herself, had been kissed a time or two. And there was the memory of certain embraces before her ill-fated betrothal... but no. She would not dwell upon the past.

"Don't you think so?" Hetty asked.

"I had not considered it," Selene lied.

In truth, she had spent much of the frozen ride recalling the moment Sir Kendrick had caught her in his arms as she slid down from the coach. His blue eyes had flecks of indigo in them, and she had not quite decided if his dark hair had undertones of mahogany, or the burnished black of a raven's wing.

His lips were well-formed, neither too fleshy nor too thin. Rather like all the rest of him.

"Come now." Hetty gave a brief laugh. "Of course you noticed —for you seemed to linger overlong in his arms. And I cannot blame you for that one whit."

Discomfiture flushed through Selene. Her tongue tangled upon excuses, but she was unaccustomed to defending her behavior to Hetty. To her family, yes—she had perfected the art of speaking her mind. Perhaps the brandy had befuddled her senses more than she thought.

A knock at the door spared her a reply.

"Hello?" Sir Kendrick called. "Are you settling in?"

"Yes," Selene said. "Please, enter."

He pushed open the door and strode into the sitting area of their suite. The lamplight flickered, picking out strands of auburn in his dark brown hair. Definitely mahogany.

"Join us," she said, indicating that he should pull up another chair before the small hearth.

"Gladly." He angled a chair near to hers and settled comfortably, one booted foot across his knee. "Are you warming up? How is the arm, Miss Miller?"

"It shall do," Hetty said. "As long as I don't move it, there's no pain."

Selene glanced at her, suspecting her companion of a bit of untruthfulness. Sir Kendrick's brows rose ever so slightly, as if he shared that suspicion.

"Sit quietly, then, until the doctor comes," he said. "I believe the landlady is fixing supper to bring up."

"Were you able to acquire a suitable room?" Selene asked. "There seemed to be some confusion when we first arrived."

He leaned back with a wry smile. "The inn is rather full, due to the storm. As a lowly baron, I had little recourse but to take the single room under the eaves."

"Pish," Hetty said. "A baron is nothing to sneeze at." She gave Selene a significant glance, her meaning clear.

Selene squirmed slightly inside. Where had this gossipy, matchmaking woman come from? She made a note to keep Hetty away from strong alcohol in the future.

"And my driver and footman?" Selene asked.

"They are settled," the baron said. "I saw to it myself. Even though they are in rooms over the stables, the accommodations are warm and comfortable."

"I don't know how we could have managed without you." A wave of gratitude washed over her, and she blinked back the sudden dampness at the corners of her eyes.

It was unlike her to lose control of her emotions, yet as she gazed upon Sir Kendrick, she felt quite overset.

His blue eyes fixed upon her, and she felt a flush of heat sweep from her toes up to the top of her head. Heavens—the brandy *was* affecting her senses. Although there was no denying he was one of the most handsome men she'd ever met.

"Where are you bound, Sir Kendrick?" she asked.

"I'm headed to my country estate in Lincolnshire," he said. "Although at the moment, neither of us are going anywhere."

She glanced toward the windows. Despite the drawn curtains, she could hear the wind whistling outside and the occasional spatter of sleet upon the glass.

"I wonder how long the storm will last," she said. "I would hate to miss the holidays with my family. Is yours waiting for you at your estate?"

It was a rather forward question, but she found herself consumed with interest. Was the baron married?

The affability in his expression faded, like a room darkened when one pulls the shutter closed. Had she not been watching him so carefully, she might not have seen the change. His smile did not falter, but stiffened about the edges, and he leaned forward in his chair.

"No, there is no one waiting for me."

"Well that's not right," Hetty said. "Have you no family at all?"

"Hetty!" Selene gave her a pained look.

She half expected Sir Kendrick to rise and excuse himself from such rudeness, but he remained.

"I have a sister, but she is recently married and has gone to the Continent for her honeymoon. London became rather... lonely, and I felt a change of venue might be in order."

Selene had the distinct impression he'd been going to say something other than *lonely*, but what it was, she could not fathom.

"Well, it is beyond fortunate that you happened upon us," she said.

"You seemed to have the situation in hand, Miss Banning." The dry humor was back in his voice.

"Perhaps. But I am not so certain I could have removed both myself and Hetty from the coach."

He leaned back, and the firelight pulled red highlights from his dark hair. "You strike me as a very capable woman—I've no doubt you would've managed something."

As far as compliments went, Selene did not think "very capable" was the most gratifying. But then, she had ever been accustomed to paltry praise, standing as she did so often in her sister's shadow. And in context, it was flattering that he thought her competent, and not some wilting flower unable to act.

What if he prefers the flowers? a small voice inside her asked. *Don't men favor beauty over such mundane things as capability?*

She gave a quiet sigh. Clearly the two times she had been in his embrace had addled her brains. Sir Kendrick was being kind, not flirting with her—and she should expect nothing more. She was not the type of girl whom men enjoyed flirting with. She was too forthright, too practical. Too *capable*.

The arrival of the doctor distracted her from her unproductive musings. He looked Hetty over in a gruff yet gentle manner, and, to their great relief, pronounced that her arm was only sprained, not broken.

"Still, it's a bad sprain," he said. "You'll want to rest—not that anyone's traveling in this storm. And I'll leave you something to help dull the pain. I'll come check again the day after tomorrow."

"The day after tomorrow?" Selene gave him an anxious glance. "Why, that will be Midwinter. Do you truly think we'll be trapped here that long?"

She ought to have been in London on the morrow, ready to celebrate the season with her family, not cooped up in some country inn with her injured companion and a too-handsome baron who, alas, had no interest in her.

"There, now." The doctor patted her shoulder. "Soon as may be, the weather will lift and you'll be off to your balls and parties and whatnot. But until then there's nothing you can do, except look after Miss Miller here, and bide."

Nothing was precisely what Selene feared—endless hours of nothing. Perhaps she would scour the inn for any books left behind by careless travelers that might help pass the time.

"We could play chess," the baron said to her, a sympathetic look in his eyes. No doubt he was equally nonplussed at the thought of their enforced stay in the small village of Pickwillow. "You do play?"

"Yes—that would be lovely." It would help, but she still felt the weight of disappointment settling on her shoulders.

She would miss helping Eliana prepare to take tea with the queen, and ice skating in Hyde Park, and caroling about Mayfair with Eliana's ever-present and enormous group of friends. Midwinter leading up to Christmas was Selene's favorite time of year, and she did not want to spend it snowbound away from her family.

But it could not be helped.

The doctor took his leave after seeing that Hetty's arm was well braced and she was comfortably settled. Selene fluffed up her pillows, and within moments Hetty was asleep.

"I'll bid you a good evening, as well," the baron said, moving toward the door. "I hope you have a restful night, after the taxing events of the day."

"I imagine I will," Selene said. "Thank you again for your assistance."

He gave her a wry smile. "I will not say it was my pleasure, since fighting several miles through a blizzard is hardly a delight, but it does please me greatly that I was there to help."

Their eyes met, and she could not look away from the warmth in his gaze. Her cheeks flushed, and she felt unaccountably dizzy.

"Careful there, Miss Banning."

He strode forward and caught her elbow, and Selene realized with some chagrin that she had been swaying on her feet.

"I am rather fatigued," she said.

Not to mention tipsy from the brandy. It would be a relief to don her nightgown and slip between the sheets. She hoped the inn bed was comfortable. Hetty seemed contented enough, judging by the snores emanating from her sleeping chamber.

One hand still at her elbow, Sir Kendrick guided her to the door of her own bedroom and halted at the threshold.

"Good night," he said, turning to go.

"Oh, wait one moment," she said, a sudden realization spiking through her. "I... well, this is rather awkward to admit, but I need assistance in removing my boots."

They were the new ones with high laces, quite fashionable, but the times she had worn them before, Hetty had to tug mightily before the boots would come off.

"Of course." He followed her back into the sitting area. "As I said, I am here to serve at your hour of need, Miss Banning."

She gave him a sharp look. Why, it had almost sounded as if he was flirting with her, though his expression remained composed. She settled into one of the armchairs and bent to undo her laces. It was not quite proper, asking for his help, but she could hardly wear her boots to bed.

"There," she said. "I think they're as loose as I can make them."

He knelt at her feet, which caused an odd little shiver to go through her. She restrained the most unladylike impulse to run her fingers through his thick dark hair, and gripped the arms of the chair instead.

"I beg your pardon," he said, "but do I have permission to grasp your ankle, Miss Banning?"

His words made heat flush through her body. His words—and the thought of his strong hands upon her, nothing but her stockings between his touch and her skin.

"Yes," she managed.

Oh dear. She had not thought this through at all. She should have asked him to send up one of the inn's maids. But she was so very tired, and a bit muddled, and...

He slid one hand beneath her skirts, and Selene nearly swooned at the feel of his palm on her calf.

"Brace yourself," he said.

She clutched the chair, despite the fact her body felt almost boneless from his touch. With a quick tug, he pulled off her left boot. It came fairly easily—but then, her left foot was slightly smaller than her right. The next boot would be more difficult.

Indeed, it did not come off with the first tug, nor the second, which only succeeded in towing the armchair forward a few inches.

"My apologies." He glanced up, a lock of hair falling across his forehead in a most appealing way. "Did I hurt you?"

"No." Her voice came out rather breathless. "Do try again."

"I think I'd best stand," he said, rising.

She nodded, trying not to stare at his broad shoulders, his trim waist... Never before had she been so *aware* of a man. Even during her brief betrothal she'd not felt her senses stirring so profoundly. It was thrilling and discomfiting all at once.

He bent and grasped her boot in both hands, tilted the heel, and, muscles bunching beneath his coat, pulled the offending footwear off.

"Thank you," she said, giving him a moment to regain his balance. "It would have been a rather uncomfortable night, had I been forced to wear one boot to bed."

He set the second boot beside the first on the flower-patterned carpet. "Is there anything else I can do for you, Miss Banning?"

The question carried an undercurrent of something dangerous that made her heart speed. He must know as well as she that her gown laced up the back. Yet it would be altogether too forward of her to request his help in undressing.

Boots were one thing, but a gown was quite another. And while she liked what she had seen of the baron so far, there was no guarantee he was a *perfect* gentleman. He might be a rake who would take undue advantage of her if she let herself slip into his clutches.

Although those clutches held a certain breathless appeal.

She felt her cheeks warm, and quickly turned her mind from such thoughts. Already they skirted the edge of impropriety. She was a young woman of good breeding, not the type of loose woman who would compromise herself at the first opportunity.

If that meant she must sleep in her corset, so be it.

"I shall manage," she lied. "Thank you. You must be tired."

His mouth curved up ever so slightly at the corner, as though he'd been following her thoughts.

"Then I'll bid you good evening, Miss Banning." He made her a very proper bow. "I'll see you and your companion tomorrow—

the innkeeper tells me there is a private parlor downstairs where we might take our breakfast."

"Excellent. And perhaps by then it will have stopped snowing."

"Perhaps." He moved to the door, gave her a last smile, then opened it and strode out.

The sound of the latch clicking as the door shut sent an odd, lonely pang through her heart.

Nonsense. She really must avoid hot toddies in the future—they addled her thinking beyond reason. Tomorrow she would feel completely restored, she had no doubt, and not prone to mooning about over the sparkle in Sir Kendrick's blue eyes, or the warmth of his smile.

JARED STRODE AWAY from Miss Banning's door, curbing the urge to go back and insist he help her with the laces of her gown. There was something endearingly stubborn about her. From their first meeting, when he'd glimpsed her attempting to clamber out of the tipped coach, the resilience of her spirit had struck him.

Perhaps that was why he'd lied about his true identity. Well, not *lied*, precisely—he was, after all, the Baron of Collingwood, in addition to his other titles. But he had not been entirely forthcoming.

Which explained why he was now climbing the stairs to a drafty room beneath the eaves, when he might have been enjoying a warm featherbed in the inn's second-best suite. When he'd made arrangements with the innkeeper, he'd chosen to remain simply Sir Kendrick. It had seemed simpler in that moment than having to explain his deception to Miss Banning.

He was not entirely certain he understood that deception, himself, beyond a deep weariness with the role he was forced to play in society, and the number of eager debutantes vying for his attention. It had been quite freeing to be simply a man of the lower gentry lending his aid to a lady in distress.

A charmingly determined lady, who did not flutter about helplessly and expect his title to be able solve every problem that might arise. Perhaps that was why he hadn't revealed it to her—though part of him suspected that Selene Banning would not have been overly impressed in any case.

The lamp outside his door flickered as he caught it up and carried it into his small room. There was not even a hearth, though the chimney of one of the lower rooms passed through, emitting a scarce warmth. Cold air pressed in through the tiny window, but at least the bed was mounded with blankets. He'd had sense enough to insist on that. No use waking in the morning to find his fingers and toes frostbitten.

Would Miss Banning succeed in undoing her own laces? Although part of him had wanted to demand she let him help her, he was wise enough to know where that road led. Already she had been warm and pliant from the brandy, her gaze lingering too long on his, her cheeks rosy with blushes.

He might have been able to steel himself against temptation—he did pride himself on being a gentleman, after all. Yet there was something devilishly appealing about Miss Banning. It would have been nigh impossible to keep from grazing his hand over the nape of her neck, stroking one finger along her bare shoulder...

Stop. Miss Banning was a young lady of Quality, not to mention the fact that he was acquainted with both her brother and her father. It was pure disaster to contemplate any type of seduction of the lady.

But if she doesn't know who I am...

He would know, however, and would not be able to face himself in the mirror if he besmirched the daughter of Viscount Blake.

Skin prickling with the cold, he quickly stripped down to his underclothes and slipped beneath the sheets. The wool blankets smelled of lanolin, and the storm still howled outside.

Despite Miss Banning's hopeful words, he did not think it would abate by morning.

Unfortunately, he did not think his attraction to her would, either.

"MORE SAUSAGES, MISS?" the serving girl asked.

"Thank you, no." Selene set down her cup of tea and smiled at the girl. "But if you would make up a tray for my companion, I'll take it up to her as soon as we finish breakfast."

Despite the inn being at full capacity, the server had done her best to keep Selene and Sir Kendrick well supplied with breakfast items as they dined in the back parlor. Hetty had been fast asleep, and Selene did not have the heart to wake her from her healing slumber.

It was a surprisingly pleasant meal. They commiserated on the continuing snowfall, then shared tales of growing up in the country. She confessed she'd foolishly ventured into the storm, after staying behind to help Star birth her foal.

"She's my mare, and a bit high-strung—not a docile expectant mother. After she nearly cracked the head of one of the stable hands, I insisted on helping with the foaling. Unfortunately, my sister was due in London. The Queen invited a select number of young ladies to attend her before Christmas, and of course my family could not refuse this singular honor."

Selene let out a breath. Perhaps she should have chosen her sister over the mare—but Eliana did not need her help. Mother and a bevy of doting friends and fellow debutantes were more than enough to carry her already-buoyant sister through. Indeed, Selene suspected she would have been relegated to the sidelines, watching her sister add yet another social triumph to her long string of accomplishments.

Better to be needed, even if it was by an irritable horse.

"I'm sure your family is worried about you," Sir Kendrick said. "They'll be happy to see you arrive safely—as will your numerous suitors, no doubt."

The comment made her stomach lurch, and she pushed her plate away, appetite fled. She'd made her choice, then discovered the bitter worm hiding inside the apple of love. *Supposed* love. But she'd been younger then, and had since learned her lesson.

"I have no suitors," she said. Not any longer, and probably never again. "But what of yourself? I'd think a gentleman with your..." *Oh dear.* Had she truly been about to reveal how handsome she found him? "Er, your title and... didn't you say you owned a townhouse in London as well as a county estate?" Mortification heated her cheeks.

Hadn't he said last night he was unmarried? If only Hetty were there to help steer the conversation to safer ground—provided she had not drunk too much brandy.

Or Eliana, who never made the types of gaffes Selene did, despite being four years her junior.

He regarded her, the spark of good humor in his eyes dampened. "Indeed. I must confess that in addition to my sister's absence in London, an overabundance of interested young ladies contributed to my departure. I currently have little appetite for social gatherings."

"I understand." And she did, completely. "If I did not have my family to spend the holidays with, I imagine I'd prefer to remain in the countryside with my horses. And books."

"Yes, well. I'm certain my horse Admiral and a copy of Poe's latest volume will prove to be adequate company this Christmas."

There was no mistaking the touch of self-mockery in his voice. She guessed he *would* be lonely, after all.

She studied him a moment, teetering on the edge of inviting him to spend the holidays in London with her family.

But that was absurd. He was a stranger to her, despite the fact of his gallant rescue. Her family would certainly look askance if she arrived with some unknown baron in tow—especially after the debacle three years ago.

The impulse passed, and the serving girl came in bearing a covered tray for Hetty. Taking it, Selene rose, and then gave in to an easier question.

"Would you like to come up for a game of chess?" she asked Sir Kendrick. "I discovered a board and pieces this morning."

His face brightened. "Indeed, that would be most pleasant."

She bit the inside of her cheek to keep from smiling too broadly. Once she beat him soundly, he might not find it quite so pleasant, after all.

JARED HAD THOUGHT at first to let Miss Banning have the advantage on the chessboard. However, after she neatly boxed in his pieces and almost caught him in a checkmate, he discarded the notion and played for all he was worth. The coal fire emitted a cozy warmth, and he enjoyed the look of fierce concentration on his opponent's face.

Miss Banning was unabashedly gleeful whenever she captured one of his pawns, and her smile transformed her features with light. She was pretty enough to begin with, and the animation in her face gave it an extra glow of beauty. It had surprised him to learn she had no suitors, but then a dim memory niggled the back of his mind concerning a failed betrothal.

When he'd asked last night, the fire behind her face had extinguished, and he vowed not to tread that path again.

"Checkmate!" she cried.

Dismayed, he glanced at the board to see that his musings about Miss Banning had led him to a fatal inattention.

"You're a very skilled player," he said. "Do you play chess with your family?"

"Yes." She began setting up the wooden pieces for a new game. "It's one of the few things I excel at that my sister does not. My brother is also a fine player, when his mind does not wander."

"Let me guess." He lifted the rook and polished it with his thumb. "You are the oldest sibling?" He remembered Viscount Blake's son entering Oxford, when he was an upperclassman.

She tilted her head at him, her brown eyes considering. "I am striving not to take your guess as a commentary upon my character, sir."

"Because you are clearly a leader, full of determination and unafraid to act?"

"Oh." Faint color washed her cheeks. "Well, if you put it that way, then yes, I confess I am the eldest child. While you, I suspect, are the younger. And furthermore, I guess that your sister is several years your senior."

Selene Banning was a perceptive young lady. He hoped she would not perceive his inconvenient attraction to her.

"You are correct," he said. "Alas, I've been coddled all my life."

She gave him a skeptical look. "Somehow I find that difficult to believe. Does your sister let you beat her at chess?"

"When I started winning every match, she declared herself finished and ceded the board to me," he said. "Still, she plays a fierce hand of piquet."

Miss Banning nodded. "I'm afraid you won't find me giving in quite so easily, sir."

"Of course not." He did not add that he found her determination—in chess, in snowstorms, and most likely in all things —endearing.

There was no point in being charmed by Selene Banning, although just at the moment he could not help it. While she studied the board with a look of concentration, he studied her. One might say she had brown eyes, brown hair, a pronounced nose, and a stubborn chin, but he thought her hair was the color of honey-dipped toffee, her eyes a lighter shade of caramel, her lips sweetly bowed and eminently kissable...

Blast. He must stop thinking of her in such a fashion. Jared cleared his throat and forced his gaze to the chess pieces. He was completely uninterested in entangling himself with a young lady of Quality. Hadn't he fled London to avoid that very thing?

As the game progressed, it was difficult not to notice everything about her: the faint scent of flowers wafting from her hair, the sparkle in her eyes as she laid an especially devious trap for him to fall into, the elegance of her long-fingered hands.

"Do you play the pianoforte?" he asked as she chased his king about the board.

"Yes," she said. "And the harp, and the mandolin. My family enjoys music very much. And you?"

"I am quite adept upon the drum," he said, making her laugh, which was his aim.

"Perhaps we might have a concert later," she said. "I noticed a piano in the back parlor. And the kitchen would certainly provide you a pot, and a spoon to bang it with. Since this dreary snow seems determined to continue all day."

She sighed and glanced at the window, where a haze of white filled the glass.

"Is it so terrible, to be trapped here with me?" He spoke the words without thinking, then cursed himself for a mooning idiot, and fixed a teasing grin upon his face.

Miss Banning blinked at him a moment, as though surprised at the notion he might be flirting with her.

"Not at all—your company is most pleasant." She blushed, ever so slightly, and scooted her rook forward. "Check."

"I would say the same, except for your deplorable habit of

beating me soundly at chess." This time he kept his tone light, and was rewarded as the corners of her lips turned up.

"You lack the proper concentration," she said.

He had to admit it was true. Something about her was deeply distracting. Part of him wished they might remain snowbound for weeks, so that he could discover more of her every day—and part of him wished to dash to the stables, saddle Admiral, and ride far away from whatever madness seemed to be overtaking him.

Surely it was boredom, and the fact of missing his sister. Those things must be conspiring to soften his brain. And soft it was—he knew the moment he slid his king out of reach that he had lost another match to the indomitable Miss Banning.

Although the delight in her face as she proclaimed checkmate once again helped ease the sting of his defeat.

Abruptly, he realized he'd been staring overlong at her, eyes tracing the soft curve of her cheek, the lift of her lips. Jared slid his chair back and stood.

"Thank you for the games," he said. "I must go and see that all is well with the horses—and your men, of course. If you will excuse me?"

The light in her eyes dimmed. "Certainly. Thank you for your company, Sir Kendrick. Please tell John and Benjamin to let me know if they need anything at all. It's my fault we're trapped here."

She looked suddenly so glum that he reached and caught her hand. The feel of her bare skin against his sent a jolt through his nerves, but it would be noticeably rude to release her too quickly. He must endure the sweet fire of her touch.

"Never fear, Miss Banning. I'll ensure your servants are cared for in every particular."

"Thank you." Still holding his hand, she stood. "And I must tend to Hetty."

He ought to let go, to turn and make for the door, but instead they remained there a long moment, hands clasped, eyes locked.

Then her companion called sleepily from the next room, and the spell was broken.

Flushing, Miss Banning tucked her hands into her skirts. "I shall see you at dinner, sir."

"Good day." He made her a bow, then strode out of the room, the blood rushing hotly in his veins.

He only hoped stepping into the snowy air would help cool that heat and dampen this most inconvenient interest he was developing in Miss Selene Banning.

SELENE RE-PINNED the wayward curl that kept trying to escape from her coiffure, surveyed herself in the looking glass, and sighed. It was foolish of her to worry so much over her appearance this evening. After all, a small midwinter party at a rustic inn was hardly a grand ball!

But with Hetty unable to do more than advise Selene on her hairstyle, she felt a bit unpolished.

Polish isn't necessary, she reminded herself. To be quite honest, she wanted to look lovely for one reason only—Sir Kendrick. He'd seen her at her worst; battling a snowstorm after a coach accident. Now she wanted him to see Miss Selene Banning, daughter of Viscount Blake, who might be too impulsive and outspoken for her own good, but was still good marriage material.

Oh heavens, she truly should *not* let herself think such thoughts. Selene closed her eyes and swallowed back the ridiculous notion.

After this one adventure, they would part ways and she would never set eyes on Sir Kendrick again. She certainly had never done so before, and she knew that he did not run in the same social circles as her family in London. She hadn't heard his name or title before, and she'd a memory for such things.

Their paths would not cross again.

Forcing herself to ignore the pang in her heart, Selene patted her hair one last time, then went to assist Hetty.

"I don't want you to overtax yourself," Selene said as she helped her companion don her gown.

"No dancing, certainly," Hetty said. "I'll leave that to you—and the handsome baron."

Despite herself, Selene felt a flush warm her cheeks. "The moment you feel at all tired, you must tell me, and we'll retire to our rooms."

Hetty raised her brows. "We'll see about that. You deserve a bit of fun after tending me so well. Not to mention being trapped here for nigh on two days, missing your family, and no doubt dozens of parties in Town."

"I'm not as inclined to the social whirl as my sister is. You know that."

"Yes." Hetty let Selene settle a shawl about her shoulders. "But it's good to hear you laugh again."

"What? I laugh often."

Her companion gave her a level look. "Sometimes I think you let yourself fall too far into your sister's shadow. She might be the sun, but the moon has her own brightness."

Drat her parents for giving their children such foolish, classical names. Selene had sometimes wondered why she, as firstborn, had not been named the daughter of the sun, instead of the moon. Far too often she felt as though her own light were, indeed, simply a reflection of her sister's radiance. At least where Society was concerned. After the broken betrothal, Selene's reputation had suffered, with words like *cold fish* and *harpy* bandied about by the gossips.

After all, who would choose the brown-haired, sharp-tongued sister so perilously close to being on the shelf when one could bask in the rays of Eliana's golden-haired beauty and sunny disposition?

But Eliana was not there, and perhaps Hetty was right that

Selene ought to enjoy herself. It was true she often found herself somewhat eclipsed by her sister. But here, Sir Kendrick's gaze would not stray to the lively, lovely Eliana as so regularly happened when Selene was in conversation with gentlemen at social gatherings.

She had drawn the line at delivering notes and poems to her younger sister, however. Once word had gotten out that Selene was not a secret conduit to Eliana, she found herself more in company with the dowagers than the young bucks.

"And drink some mulled wine," Hetty encouraged as they carefully traversed the stairs down to the inn's common room.

"Perhaps." As long as it didn't muddle her senses the way the brandy had.

Selene could not help scanning the assembled company as they descended. The common room was cheery and bright, lit with oil lamps and a fire on the hearth. The tables had been moved to the side, and held food and drink from the inn's stores, while the benches and chairs lined the walls, leaving the center open for dancing. Swags of greenery decorated the room, bringing the scent of evergreens to mingle with the smell of cinnamon and apples wafting from the fresh-baked pies upon the table.

The innkeeper had moved the pianoforte into the room, as well, and a young man was playing serviceable Bach upon it. Selene spotted both John and Benjamin in conversation with two ladies, who blushed and smiled. Perhaps they were maids at the inn, dressed now in their Sunday best, or villagers, or fellow travelers. It didn't matter, as the mood was convivial, the chatter bright. Everyone was there to celebrate Midwinter, no matter their current circumstances or station in life.

It only took her a moment before she spotted Sir Kendrick among the merrymakers. His mahogany hair caught the light, and he wore a russet coat that no doubt would make his eyes seem the color of the twilight sky.

The moment her gaze landed upon him he looked up and

smiled. By the time she and Hetty had reached the bottom of the stairs, he was there, offering Hetty his arm.

"Miss Miller, Miss Banning, you are both looking well this evening." He turned his gaze to Hetty. "May I see you to a chair, and bring you something to drink?"

Selene could not begrudge his kindness to her injured companion. Indeed, he was such a gentleman that it sent a bittersweet dart through her heart. If only they had met a few years earlier, before she had been disillusioned by love, then perhaps...

"That would be lovely," Hetty said. "I hear there's to be mulled wine, and dancing."

"Are you intending to skip a measure?" he asked, a teasing note in his voice.

"Had I a fan, I'd bat you with it," Hetty said. "Of course not—can't you see my arm's still in a sling?"

"Then perhaps Miss Banning will honor me with a dance. Or two."

He looked at Selene, and her breath caught at what she saw in his eyes. No echo of golden-haired sisters or thoughts of using her to gain prestige—only admiration. She felt truly *seen* for the first time in a long while.

"I would be delighted." She hoped her voice did not reveal the trembling in her blood.

Late into the night she had lain awake in the inn's slightly lumpy featherbed, calling up the memory of his strong arms about her. Not once, but two times he had held her. And, most delicious of all, she savored the recollection of his hand upon her calf, touching her heated skin through her stocking as he assisted her with her stubborn boot.

Then, that very afternoon, she had daydreamed away the better part of an hour recalling how they had stood overlong, hands clasped, eyes locked.

What did it mean?

Selene gave herself a mental shake. There was no doubt he was simply flirting with her to pass the time. She was a fool for thinking anything more would come of it. Had she not learned her lesson three years ago?

Still, she would indulge in a dance. Or two.

They settled Hetty comfortably in a cushioned chair where she could enjoy the party without danger of anyone jostling her arm. Sir Kendrick went to fetch mulled wine, and the lad at the piano switched to a lively tune.

"Ladies and gentlemen!" The innkeeper's wife strode into the center of the room, clapping her hands together. "Though it be cold and dreary outside, we'll celebrate this long night with warmth and good cheer. Now, who's ready for a bit of dancing?"

A chorus of assent answered her question, and two lines quickly formed. Selene noted with a smile that John and Benjamin stood across from the ladies whom they had been chatting with earlier.

"Here we are." Sir Kendrick arrived, bearing two goblets. He deftly deposited them on the table beside Hetty's chair, then turned to Selene. "Would you like to dance this next set, or wait a bit?"

"The floor is rather crowded at the moment. Perhaps the next dance, if you don't mind?"

"I am yours to command." He swept her a bow.

Although he was simply teasing, her heart gave a thump before settling back into a faster rhythm.

"Most gallant of you, sir," she said, ignoring Hetty's significant look and busying herself with her goblet of wine.

It smelled of cloves and oranges, and the first sip she took warmed her throat, though not nearly so strongly as the hot toddy had.

"This is delicious," Hetty said, drinking from her own cup. "I think we ought to be frequenting country inns far more often, if the quality of the food and drink here are typical."

"The fare here is rather above the norm," Sir Kendrick said.

"We're fortunate to be stranded here, as opposed to, say, a certain establishment in Lincolnshire that's infamous for weak ale and horrid beef pies."

"The apple pies smell wonderful," Selene said, which of course prompted the baron to go fetch them two pieces at once.

He returned with three slices, each upon a serviceable china plate, and they proved to be as delicious as they smelled. With the taste of apples still upon her tongue, she watched the dancers skip and turn over the floor. She was conscious of Sir Kendrick standing beside her, as though the air between them was vibrating slightly. When he turned to smile at her, she felt it like the heat from an open flame.

A curious sensation folded about her, and it took a moment for her to identify it. Pure happiness, unsullied by any cares. This evening was a sweet instant in time, suspended like a flake of gold inside amber, shining and perfect.

The current dance came to a close, and a white-haired fiddler pulled up a chair next to the piano, ready to power the next set of tunes. Selene gently took Sir Kendrick's plate, empty of everything except his fork, and set it atop hers on the side table.

He grinned at her and extended his arm. "Would you care to dance, Miss Banning?"

"I would." She tipped her head up at him and slipped her hand through the crook of his elbow. From the corner of her eye, she could see Hetty smiling broadly as they stepped onto the wide planks of the makeshift dance floor.

The piano player called out a quadrille, the other dancers applauded, and Selene took her place next to Sir Kendrick in the set. He proved to be an accomplished dancer, which did not surprise her, considering his natural agility. Anyone who could clamber about so handily on tipped coaches ought to be able to step the measures of a quadrille with equal grace.

They met, circled, parted, their eyes locking until the other couples disappeared in a blur of color and gaiety. By the fourth dance of the set, Selene felt as though the two of them had been dancing together for weeks, for years, their bodies constellations pivoting through the night.

At last the quadrille ended, to much applause and a general rush toward the refreshments. Selene caught her breath, and only then realized she was still holding the baron's hand. His touch was firm and solid through the fabric of her glove. Reluctantly, she let go, but he did not allow her fingers to escape.

Instead, he lifted their clasped hands. "You are wonderfully light on your feet, Miss Banning. Would you honor me with a waltz?"

"Are they playing one?" She glanced at the fiddler, who was leaning over chatting with the young man at the piano.

"They are about to," Sir Kendrick said, flashing her a smile.

On cue, the musicians looked up. The pianist caught the baron's eye and nodded, and the opening strains of a waltz sounded out over the lively conversation. Had Sir Kendrick arranged that in advance, or was it merely a fortuitous guess? Selene gave him a look, but his only response was a quick smile as he led her into the middle of the room again.

As quickly as the dance floor had emptied, it filled again. Even the innkeeper left his post at the bar to take his wife in his arms.

Sir Kendrick pulled Selene close, and she felt a rushing from her toes to the top of her head, as though her body was filled with bright air. She smiled up at him, so full of joy and thankfulness she could scarcely speak.

"Sir Kend—"

"Please," he said, an odd look crossing his face, "I'm not entirely at ease with that title. Would you do me the favor, just for tonight, of calling me Jared?"

She blinked up at him. It was quite improper—but then again, he did act as though the title of Sir Kendrick sat uncomfortably upon his shoulders. Once or twice she'd noticed he answered rather belatedly to that name, as if unaccustomed to people using it. He truly must not move in social circles very often, and a pang of sympathy went through her.

"Very well," she said. "But it's only fair that you call me Selene."

As she spoke, a flush warmed her cheeks. Yes, it was forward of her, but if he were lowering the barriers to formality, she would follow. After all, they were at a country inn, miles from any gossips. No need to be baron and viscount's daughter—at least not this evening.

"Selene."

Her name sounded mysterious and beautiful when he said it, and she felt her blush deepen. Averting her eyes from his mesmerizing gaze, she concentrated on the dance, dipping and turning as he spun them about the floor.

But every inch of her was aware of him, attuned to him, so that at times they seemed like one body dancing, breaths matching in time.

She was a fool, but for this one night she would savor her folly.

The waltz ended, the dancers applauded, and the innkeeper's wife exhorted them all to eat their fill.

"Mustn't let this food go to waste!" she cried.

The guests thronged to the tables, but Selene, slightly breathless, hung back near the corner. She was excruciatingly aware of Sir Kendrick—Jared's—arm still about her waist.

"My dear Miss Banning," he said, amusement warming his voice, "are you aware we're standing beneath a kissing bough?"

"I am not," she breathed, knees suddenly weak. He had not called her Selene, but he had called her *dear*.

She looked up to see the greenery above them, decorated with sprigs of holly and the white berries of mistletoe. She did not move away, did not step out of the curve of his arm and scurry to safety. Instead, she glanced to where Hetty sat. Her companion's eyes were closed, her chest rising and falling in the even rhythm of sleep.

Slowly, Selene turned to face the baron. Jared. The strength in that name fitted him well.

He met her gaze, then put both hands at her waist and drew her close. Small fires trembled through her body, sparks that blazed up into flames as he lowered his lips to kiss her.

Warm, and firm, and tasting slightly of cinnamon, his mouth pressed gently over hers. She sighed and parted her lips, and his tongue swept into her mouth. Behind her closed eyes, stars whirled, and she felt as though she were flying through the night sky.

Her heartbeat pulsed through her veins, and every inch of her body felt alive, as though she had woken from some long, dreamy sleep, to find a world full of light and vitality. She gave herself up to the sensation, her hands tightening over his shoulders.

When the kiss ended she drew in a deep, unsteady breath and opened her eyes.

"My pardon for taking liberties," he murmured, though he did not sound at all contrite.

She smiled at him. "I forgive you."

Although she was not entirely sure she ever would. She had never been kissed like that, never felt such a storm rushing through her. That kiss had opened a door to a room she could not enter, and the knowledge of it was searing. Soon—all too soon—they must part.

Or must they?

"I hope that you might consider calling upon me," she said. "Perhaps once the holiday season is over."

"Perhaps." He pulled back slightly, a note of caution in his voice, and she felt her hopes plummet.

Before she could question him further, had she the heart for it, the door of the inn was flung wide.

"It's stopped snowing!" a red-cheeked lad cried, borne in by a waft of chilly air. "The bonfire's about to be lit."

Selene pulled out of Jared's embrace, the memory of his kiss still warming her lips, though her heart was heavy. "Will you watch after Hetty while I run upstairs and fetch our cloaks?"

"Of course." He pressed her hand and gave her a rueful smile, as if in apology.

But she could not force him to make her promises. It was one kiss. She should not feel so overset by it.

Before he could read the yearning on her face, she turned and rushed up the staircase. Gaining the peace of her room, she poured a measure of cool water into the basin and splashed it on her cheeks, then made herself take long, steadying breaths. Going out in the cold was a splendid idea. If she were fortunate, it would freeze the tender shoot of emotion she felt springing up in her chest.

She had no business forming an attachment to a man she had just met! One whom, after tomorrow, she would never see again. With the cessation of the storm, they would go their separate ways—her toward London, him to his quiet country estate, which she did not even know the name of.

And she would not ask. If Baron Kendrick wanted her to know more of him, he would tell her. Though she might be a fool, Selene Banning was not one to beg for scraps.

Arms full of cloaks and gloves and mufflers, she went back downstairs and busied herself with helping Hetty bundle up. Jared excused himself to do the same, and she gave him a distant smile.

"We shall see you at the bonfire, then," she said.

He paused, giving her a close look, then shook his head and slipped away up the stairs.

"He's such a handsome fellow," Hetty said with a sigh. "You could do far worse."

"I shan't do anything at all," Selene replied. "Take my arm. We don't need you slipping on the ice."

It was not icy outside, however. The men had cleared a path from the inn, and the thin layer of snow crunched beneath their boots. The chilly air snatched at her breath until she pulled her fine wool muffler up over her mouth, then helped her companion do the same.

Overhead, the stars shone brightly in the velvety night sky, a sickle moon poised as if to reap that wintry light. The inn guests and villagers carried lanterns, the flames spilling warm orange light over the snow. In the middle of the road a wide circle had been trodden down, and in the center of that stood a black heap of branches.

Selene and Hetty joined the crowd standing around the unlit fire, conversation and laughter sending white plumes of breath into the air.

"There you are." Jared drew up beside them, carrying a blanket, which he quickly draped about their shoulders. "Until they get the fire lit, it's a bit too cold out here."

"Thank you," Selene said, and her companion nodded in agreement.

As if his words had been a signal, a tall man approached the pile of sticks, a flaming torch in his hand. He bent and thrust the torch into the center, until bright orange and yellow began to climb and leap upon the wood.

"Stand back!" the innkeeper cried. "I've a bad batch of spirits to coax this blaze along."

The man left his torch imbedded in the pile and moved away. Grinning, the innkeeper heaved a small cask into the fire.

For a moment, nothing happened. Then, with a *whump*, the fire burst free, the bonfire suddenly ablaze with flames leaping into the air. The crowd cheered, and Selene felt the warmth like sunlight upon her face.

The innkeeper's wife went around with small cups of mulled wine. Selene took one, inhaling the scent of cloves. The fiddler pulled a chair up near enough to the fire to play without his fingers freezing, and was joined by a drummer and a girl with a tin whistle. Soon a joyful tune wove about them, a ribbon of music twining with the fire, the night, the taste of spices on her tongue.

Sparks jumped from the bonfire into the clear sky, as if they wished to leap high enough to become stars, themselves. Despite herself, she felt her spirits lift. It was rustic and fierce, and Selene felt that the old gods might be stirring across the land on this, the darkest night of the year.

"I feel as if we've been thrown back in time," Jared said, coming to stand close beside her. "The modern world is eons away."

"I was just thinking the same." She smiled at him. "Would you like to share some of this blanket you so kindly fetched out for us?"

He gave her a look that heated her more warmly than the mulled wine. "As I gentleman, I must refuse your kind offer."

Selene rather wished he'd be less gentlemanly, but before she could say anything that might be misconstrued, Hetty gave a sniff.

"Nonsense," her companion said. "We'll only be out here a short while longer. Might as well not freeze yourself if it can be helped."

"As you command," Jared said to Hetty, a glint of humor in his eyes.

Selene lifted her right arm, holding the edge of the blanket out to the baron. The loss of heat was quickly offset by his presence at her side. Her pulse sped when he slipped his arm about her waist, snugging her against him. Perhaps he'd sensed her thoughts about being too much a gentleman. The fact that no one could see the embrace beneath the draped blanket made it even more daring.

A blush blazed up in her cheeks, and she dared not glance at Hetty.

"Warm enough?" Jared murmured in Selene's ear.

"Quite," she managed, trying not to lean into him.

She felt almost as dizzy as when they'd kissed. Her senses hummed, aware of his presence as if they shared a heartbeat, their breaths pluming into the air together.

This moment—she wanted to capture it, a perfect golden droplet of existence. Fire and snow, music and the vast silence of the night, woman and man. Everything.

Then the music ended, and Selene felt Hetty shiver.

"We must get you back inside," she told her companion. "Enough of this gallivanting about in the cold."

Jared withdrew his arm from her waist, and she could not help the small sigh that escaped her lips. He stepped forward and offered his arm to Hetty, who took it. Gently, Selene slipped from beneath the blanket, letting her companion enjoy its full shelter.

"Sir Kendrick," Hetty said, "I know I speak for Miss Banning as well when I say we are so grateful for your presence and aid on this journey. We shall be sorry to part ways with you when we leave for London tomorrow."

It was true, and Selene was glad that her companion had said as much. She was not certain she could have voiced the words without revealing too much of what was in her heart. Her foolish, dreaming heart.

"Indeed," he said, leading them back toward the golden-lit windows of the inn.

It wasn't much of a response, and Selene hurried to fill the silence.

"That supposes our coach is repaired," she said. "And that Hetty feels well enough to travel."

"I can sit inside a coach," her companion said. "As long as it doesn't overturn again."

"The roads should be passable, and safe enough." Jared held open the door and ushered them inside. "And I believe the innkeeper will send several men at first light to assess the damage to your vehicle and make what fixes they can. I know you want to reach London as soon as possible."

Selene nodded, although it was not entirely true. The past day had brought her a peace and lightness of spirit she hadn't realized she'd been missing. Somehow, the prospect of living once more in

Eliana's shadow—especially during the whirl of the holidays—held less appeal than ever.

But it was the way of the world, and useless for her to yearn for something so far out of reach. Might as well ask for the moon as a bauble to wear about her neck.

Banishing such thoughts, Selene busied herself with taking the blanket from Hetty and folding it. She resisted the urge to bring it to her face and inhale deeply of Jared's scent.

"I'll escort you ladies upstairs," he said, taking the folded blanket from her.

They ascended the staircase, Selene helping Hetty while Jared followed. At the door to their suite, she put a smile upon her face and bid him good night. She wanted to linger, to press her palm to his cheek, to daringly brush her lips against his once more…

But Hetty was a bit pale and clearly taxed by the evening's festivities. She needed rest, and Selene to tend to her.

"Good night, Selene," Jared said, taking her hand and bowing over it. "I'll see you at breakfast. Rest well, both of you."

Hetty's raised brow meant she'd heard the baron use Selene's given name, but she made no comment as they went into their suite.

After her companion was tucked into her bed, Selene sat awake, listening to the shouts of revelry outside. It seemed that the lads and men were encouraging one another to leap over the bonfire. She rose and peeked out the window, but Jared was not among them.

The fire was smaller now, only a few flames licking up from the embers. Beyond, the windows of the cottages glowed golden from the inside, the village a small, shining jewel set in an expanse of pure and silent white.

THE SNOW beside the road was nearly gone, reduced to muddy

lumps by the time they reached the outskirts of London. Jared rode beside Miss Banning's coach until the buildings hemmed in the road and he was forced to follow behind.

He noticed how often she glanced out the coach windows, and how often her gaze met his. Of course, he was watching her as much as she looked for him. Even more, perhaps—his eyes tracing that firm profile, memorizing the line of her nose, the curve of her lips.

"You will escort us back to London?" Selene had echoed his pronouncement at breakfast, her lovely brown eyes wide with surprise. "But... hadn't you just left Town?"

"Yes—but the roads will be muddy, and you'll need an extra shoulder to help free the coach when it gets stuck. Besides, I want to see that you arrive safely. No use in rescuing you from a blizzard only to abandon you partway along your journey."

She'd blushed and dropped her gaze to her plate of eggs, a smile playing about her lips.

"That's very kind of you, sir," Hetty had said, giving him a knowing look. "I'm sure we're both delighted by your offer."

"Indeed!" Selene said. "Of course we are. Thank you. I'm so glad to hear that the coach was able to be repaired."

She didn't need to know how much he'd paid the servants to go out at dawn and retrieve the coach, or the town carpenter to mend the axle, or the innkeeper for re-provisioning the basket of supplies and providing dry blankets and warm bricks as foot-warmers for the interior of the vehicle.

It might be a miserable, mud-filled day for him, but he was strangely content at the thought that Selene would be comfortable.

Of course, being Selene, she'd insisted on leaving the coach and helping push the two times they'd gotten badly stuck. Heedless of the condition of her skirts and boots, she'd added her small weight to their efforts. Both times—to his surprise—the combination of her lightening the coach by not being inside and the extra force of her efforts had been enough to dislodge the vehicle from the muddy ruts.

Selene Banning's determination blazed as brightly as her intelligence, and he could not help but be drawn to that light. Here was a woman unafraid of whatever life might bring her. Faced with adversity, she would roll up her sleeves and, regardless of her station in life, do what she could to fix matters.

As they passed Hyde Park and entered Mayfair, Jared pulled his hat low and dipped his face into his muffler. The last thing he wanted was to be recognized and hailed by name.

When they were a few blocks from the Banning's townhouse, he spurred his mount up to the coach and motioned for Selene to lower the window.

"Jared—Sir Kendrick," she said, resting her gloved fingertips upon the sill and giving him an open smile. "I've been thinking. We'll arrive soon, and you must come in and meet my family. In fact, I wanted to invite you—"

"I'm sorry, but I find myself most eager to resume my journey home," he lied, hating to see the happy light fade from her expression. "As soon as you reach your doorstep, I must turn about."

"Must you?" Selene asked, her voice tight.

Hetty leaned forward and peered out the window at him. "Are you quite certain?"

"I am. My apologies, but I ask you to indulge me in this."

"Of course we shall." Selene blinked a few times, her eyes suspiciously bright. "We've asked so much of you already, you must do as you see fit."

Ah, gods. What he really wanted to do was escort her up to her front door and kiss her upon the lips. A long, lingering kiss that would sear him upon her soul.

Then he would ask her to wait for him... though that was not a thought he was willing to pursue any further at the moment.

And truly, he could do no such thing. His deception would be made clear in a heartbeat, and he would not be able to bear the look of betrayal on her face when Selene discovered who he really was, and how he had deceived her.

She will find out eventually, the wiser part of himself said.

It was the truth. He couldn't remove himself from London forever. But he needed time to think on how to unravel this unexpected tangle—and coming face-to-face with Selene's family at this juncture was not a solution.

"I won't forget you, Selene Banning," he said. "You may be sure of that."

She gave him a forlorn look, and it was all he could do to remain true to his resolve.

"You know she is Viscount Blake's daughter, do you not?" Hetty demanded. "I expect you *will* call upon her at some point."

"Hetty! Sir Kendrick is under no obligation—"

"I will," he said. "Until then, I'll wish you both farewell, and Merry Christmas."

Selene looked at him, her expression strained. "The blessings of the season to you as well, Jared."

The sound of her speaking his name was something he would never tire of. Damnation, he wished he had something to give her —a pretty trinket or necklace she might wear and remember him by.

But he had nothing.

"That's Banning House up ahead," Selene said. "The red brick with the greenery above the door."

He forbore to ask if there was a kissing bough inside. Instead, he tipped his hat and bowed from the saddle.

"I'll leave you here, then. Farewell, Miss Banning."

"Goodbye." The word seemed to stick in her throat.

He could not bear the look in her eyes any longer, so he wheeled Admiral and headed for the far end of the street. The clatter of the coach wheels over the cobblestones receded, then stopped as it arrived before Banning House.

Despite himself, he turned in the saddle to watch. The

footman set the steps, and Selene disembarked, then assisted Hetty from the coach. A moment later, the front door of the townhouse flew open and a young lady with golden hair dashed out. She pulled Selene into an embrace, and even at that distance Jared could hear her bright laughter, the inflection of her voice raised in a question.

Selene turned and gestured to where he sat, and Jared quickly bowed again, hoping to conceal his features from the young lady's curious gaze. It was past time he made his exit. Raising one hand, he faced forward again and nudged Admiral into a trot.

This time he was truly departing London, and would not return until he must.

PART TWO

Selene sat in the warm drawing room at Lady Haversham's musicale, the mingled perfumes in the air clashing in a cacophony of scents. Only two days back in London, and she already felt as though she were wilting. Eliana was the hothouse flower of the family, thriving on the gaiety of the social whirl, while Selene was a hardy shrub, more suited to the outdoors. But it was worth it to be with her family.

And tomorrow was Christmas Eve, which they always celebrated with a small family gathering. Hetty had departed that morning, her arm much improved, to spend the holiday with her sister and nieces and nephews in Epsom. She would return in two days, but in the meantime William had been pressed into service escorting his sisters about Town.

After Christmas would be another inevitable round of parties, where Selene would run the risk of encountering Lord Finch. Edward Tottingham, Viscount Finch, whom she might have married and lived with unhappily ever after. Luckily—or perhaps unluckily—she'd overheard him boasting to his friends about their betrothal.

It had been at a garden party, and she, upon hearing his voice, was about to round the hedge and greet him warmly—he was, after all, the man she loved—when his next words stopped her cold.

"Aye, it's the leg-shackle, but the silly chit's so besotted with me I'll be able to do as I please once we're wed."

"Taking up with the lovely Melisande again, I imagine?" one of his friends asked. "Won't Viscount Blake take it ill, if his daughter dislikes you having a mistress?"

"I'll explain to my *wife*—" Edward said the word as though it were something slimy and disgusting, like *toad* or *newt*, "—that in order for me to fully function as a man, I must find proper outlets for my appetites. After all, I'll hardly want to be bedding *her* every night."

They all laughed then, and commiserated with him on Selene's unfortunate lack of womanly charms.

"At least her dowry and connections make up for her plain face and sharp tongue," Edward said.

He thought she had a sharp tongue? Selene had been hesitating, torn between shame and anger, but this tipped the balance. Lifting her chin, she stormed around the corner of the hedge.

Edward looked startled, but quickly composed his features into a welcoming smile. "Darling! How unexpected."

She could scarcely speak past her rage. With trembling hands, she stripped off her gloves, then tugged off the opal engagement ring he'd given her. Opals were bad luck, anyway. She wanted to fling it at him, but instead held it out, the metal pinched between her thumb and forefinger.

"I am breaking off our engagement," she said. "I hope you find that equally unexpected."

His smile dropped from his face. "You heard? We were simply—"

"You, sir, are a cad. Take your ring, for you'll have no part of me."

"Are you quite certain about this, Selene?" He narrowed his

eyes. "Your name will be worthless after this, should you break off our engagement and refuse me. I'll make sure the word goes out what a harpy you truly are."

"I'd rather have my reputation dragged through the mud than wed you. A momentary slur on my family is far better than a lifetime of misery at your side."

"Brave words. You'll live to regret them." He held out his hand, and she let the ring fall into his palm.

Her disgrace would not, of course, be momentary. She was trading one kind of unhappy future for another, but at least it was her choice, made with her eyes wide open. Not blinded by stupidity and maudlin emotion.

She forced her tears back, holding onto the shield of righteous anger, turned her back on Edward and his friends, and stalked away. Only when she'd gained the musty safety of the garden shed had she allowed herself to dissolve into weeping.

In the span of one afternoon her dreams of a golden future had tarnished beyond repair.

True to his threats, her former betrothed had taken every opportunity to besmirch her name. Fortunately, Selene's family had stood with her, and in the face of Viscount Blake's cold stares and Lady Blake's unflappable demeanor the gossip died down. Somewhat. Three years later, however, it was still quite widely known that Miss Selene Banning was fit for nothing but spinsterhood.

At least Eliana was considered free of her sister's taint. No doubt she would make a fine match that would erase a multitude of sins for the Banning family—not that Selene thought she would suddenly find herself upon the marriage mart again.

Her treacherous mind called up an image of Jared's face—his blue eyes smiling at her, the husky tones of his voice. She cherished it a moment, then banished the memory, heaping a bulwark of everyday cares between herself and her own foolish heart.

Perhaps this year she would cringe less when she encountered

Lord Finch. She might be plain and sharp-tongued, but she was still attractive enough for a baron to find kissable.

The musicale was about to begin, and as she waited for Eliana to leave her clot of friends and sit with her, Selene could not help overhearing the ladies gossiping in the next row.

"Did you hear that the Duke of Ashford is in London?" one asked.

"I thought he'd departed for the holidays," the woman beside her said. "What brings him back to Town?"

"There's a rumor he's formed an affection for a particular young lady." This was spoken with conviction by a matron wearing bright purple satin who looked vaguely familiar—the mother of one of Eliana's friends, perhaps. She flicked her fan open and made her listeners wait a moment, then smiled. "I have it on the best authority that he is considering leaving bachelorhood behind."

Gasps of amazement followed her pronouncement, accompanied by a clamor of questions concerning who the young lady might be that had snared the heart of the most eligible—and elusive—bachelor of the *ton*.

"I can't say. I learned this information in the strictest confidence." The woman snapped her fan closed. Then, very obviously, she turned her head and stared at Eliana, who was making her way over to where Selene sat.

"The Banning girl?"

"Heavens!"

"She's scarcely out of the schoolroom—but she's a beauty, there can be no denying."

Selene studied her sister, brows drawing together. Surely Eliana would have told her if she were entertaining suitors— particularly someone as sought-after as the Duke of Ashford.

Then the music began, and Selene gave herself up to the melding of violin and harp. She had to admit, when it came to music London had its benefits.

In the carriage on the way home, however she quizzed her sister.

"What's this I hear about the Duke of Ashford?" Selene asked as the iron-bound wheels clattered over the cobblestones. "The gossips believe you have formed an attachment. Do you even know the fellow?"

William, seated across from them, gave his younger sister a curious look. "Ashford? We were at Oxford together, briefly. He seems an agreeable fellow. Have you set a date yet?"

Eliana laughed. "Goodness, word travels quickly, does it not? But no, we have no understanding between us. I only met the duke a fortnight past, and we merely exchanged pleasantries at a ball. As you say, William, he knows both you and father. But I had not seen him again until this morning, when I encountered him in Hyde Park. It was while you two were off on your gallop. Had you been a bit more demure, Selene, and stayed with me, I would've introduced you."

"But is he courting you?" Selene batted away the dart of jealousy trying to prick her. If Eliana had caught the interest of a duke, that was good fortune worth celebrating.

"He's not courting me—not at all." There was an undercurrent in Eliana's voice that Selene could not quite decipher.

"Still, a duke—"

"Did you hear about the most delightful holiday custom Prince Albert has introduced from Germany? They bring a large evergreen tree inside and decorate it with candles and gilded nuts and little bags of candy—it's the most glorious sight. They have one at the palace, and I think I've convinced father that we need one, as well."

"A tree, inside?" William crossed his arms and leaned back on the bench seat. "I don't think father will agree to it."

"It's not that different from bringing greenery in," Eliana said. "Just—more. And if it's good enough for the queen, it's good enough for us. I expect we'll have one tomorrow, just in time for Christmas Eve."

"You have more faith in father than I do," Selene said.

Then again, Eliana had always been the favorite, able to talk their parents into supporting many of her wild schemes over the years.

The carriage drew up in front of Banning House. William handed his sisters out of the coach, clearly relieved his escort duties were at an end, and the three of them went to join Lord and Lady Blake in the parlor.

Their mother asked if they'd enjoyed the musicale, and their father, after offering William a glass of port, cleared his throat.

"Eliana," he said. "After much thought, your mother and I have agreed to your request for a Christmas tree. I've arranged for our footmen to go out and procure us an evergreen at first light."

With a squeal of delight, Eliana threw her arms about him. "You are too, too good—but you'll see. It will add so much to the celebrations."

Lady Blake gave her a fond smile. "However, Eliana, *you* are in charge of all the details and decorations."

Eliana kissed their mother's cheek, then skipped over to Selene and took her hands. "You must help me—oh, this is going to be so much fun! We'll have to make sure we have enough candles, and set the maids to making paper chains, and go to the confectioners…I must start a list."

Lord Blake held up his hand. "There is one other thing. We'll have a guest tomorrow, who'll be staying for dinner."

The import of his tone gave Selene pause, a premonition of change blowing about her like a cold wind.

"But it's always just the family on Christmas Eve," she said, knowing she sounded ungracious, but unable to keep silent. "I've barely been here two days, and I missed you all. I don't want some interloper joining us for dinner."

"Oh my," Eliana said, somewhat breathlessly. "Did he send word to you and mother? Is it…"

"The Duke of Ashford," Lord Blake said.

"Marvelous!" Delight shone from Eliana's eyes as she turned and smiled at Selene.

Selene tucked her hands beneath her elbows, trying not to begrudge her sister's radiance. Clearly Eliana was smitten with the duke. Their courtship was progressing quite rapidly if he were joining the Bannings for Christmas Eve dinner.

"Doesn't the man have other obligations? Family?" Selene asked, though she recalled how the gossips had said he was a bachelor.

"He does not," Lady Blake said. "Where's your sense of the season, my dear? It behooves us to be generous and open-hearted. I'm happy to welcome the Duke of Ashford to our table."

"Of course." Selene gave her mother a contrite smile. "It will be lovely to host the duke, I'm sure."

As for her heart, she'd left it behind in a small country inn during the longest night of the year. Or perhaps Jared Kendrick had ridden away with it, a tall figure on a dark horse disappearing into the snowy streets of Mayfair. She doubted she would see it again.

Oh, but now she was being maudlin. With a mental shake, Selene linked arms with her sister. Her own mood should not cast a shadow on Eliana's delight—or her impending betrothal.

"Tell me more about decorating this tree," she said, giving herself up to her sister's enthusiasm.

CHRISTMAS EVE DAY dawned bright and cold. Selene's thoughts of remaining nestled in her bed—much more comfortable than the one at the inn—were dashed when Eliana came in to wake her up.

She forgave her younger sister, though, when Eliana produced a cup of hot chocolate and a freshly baked sweet bun.

Selene sat up and enjoyed her breakfast in bed while Eliana opened the curtains and chattered nonstop about her plans for the tree.

"And then our special guest will arrive, and then dinner," Eliana said, smiling broadly. "I'm thinking I'll wear my new peach satin dress—and you should most definitely wear your periwinkle gown. One ought to look one's best for a duke."

There was no doubt Eliana would shine, and out of respect for her sister, Selene would do her best to rise to the occasion. And speaking of the duke...

"We'll need to procure presents for our guest," she said. "It would be too unkind to exchange our own gifts and have nothing for him."

"Of course!" Eliana perched on the side of the bed. "What does one give a duke, I wonder?"

"I wonder the same." Not only a duke, but a prospective brother-in-law. "How much do you know of his tastes?"

"A surprising amount." Her sister's eyes sparkled with secrets. "I don't think he cares overmuch for appearances."

"So a diamond-studded snuffbox wouldn't be advisable? Or a peacock-feather coat?"

Eliana let out a laugh. "A jade chamber-pot."

"A life-sized marzipan coach."

After a few more ludicrous suggestions, Selene burst out laughing, and Eliana fell back onto the bed, giggling madly.

"I'll miss you, rather dreadfully," Selene said, once they'd recovered their composure.

"Oh." Eliana sat bolt upright, her blue eyes wide. "You already know?"

"I've guessed."

Her sister pressed her lips together. "I'll miss you too—but I'm sure married life will be wonderful. Come now!" She bounced up and began rifling through Selene's wardrobe. "There's so very much to do today."

Clearly Eliana wanted to speak no more of her impending engagement, and Selene didn't have the heart to pursue the matter. She supposed everything would become official after the duke's visit. It seemed rather a whirlwind—but permission to court, and even an actual betrothal, were no guarantee of a wedding.

As she knew, to her own shame. Likely her damaged past was why Eliana wanted to spare her the details of her own courtship, and Selene told herself she was grateful for the kindness.

Besides, there was little time to dwell on such things, as her sister insisted they visit nearly a dozen shops before noon. Selene made her stop and enjoy a paper of roast chestnuts from a street vendor in the midst of their shopping frenzy, but soon enough Eliana was dragging her into a nearby bookstore.

"Perhaps we can find something for the duke in here," Eliana said.

Or at the very least for themselves. The library at Banning House was well stocked, but the entire family shared a love of reading, and new books were always welcome in their home. Selene picked up a treatise on the navy for her father, who enjoyed reading about all things maritime, though he preferred to stay on dry land, and a magazine of the latest Paris fashions for Eliana, when her sister's back was turned.

There was a new volume of Poe's tales displayed on the front shelf, handsomely bound in black leather with gold accents. She leafed through, somewhat enjoying the melancholy, macabre tone, and on impulse added it to her stack. Perhaps William would like the book—or she would keep it for herself.

A bit of cheery holiday reading. A wry smile twisted her lips. What a gloom cloud she was! She was beginning to tire of it, herself.

She made her purchases and the shopkeeper packaged them

up, waiting for the Banning's servants to come fetch within the hour. They'd have a number of parcels and packages to collect from a great many stores, for Eliana had not stinted in her preparations.

"Ready?" Eliana linked her arm through Selene's. "I think the tree must have arrived at Banning House by now, don't you?"

"Indeed." Selene was more than ready to regain the quiet of their parlor, have a cup of tea, and let Eliana direct her in the proper trimming of a Christmas tree.

The scent of pine filled the air as soon as they stepped in the front door. The butler took their cloaks and hats, then nodded as Eliana told him which shops the servants needed to visit to claim their packages.

"Very good, miss," he said.

"Is the tree in the front parlor?" Eliana asked, clearly ready to dash away and see for herself.

"Indeed."

Selene smiled at their butler. "Be so good as to send in some tea."

He nodded, and then Eliana took her arm and towed her into the parlor.

Before the bow windows stood a tall evergreen that nearly brushed the high ceiling. The trunk was buried in a tub of sand to keep it upright, and the furniture had been moved back to give its branches room.

"Well. We have a tree in our house," Selene said.

"Just wait." Eliana grinned at her, then rang for the maids.

Two of them bustled in, arms full of paper chains, while a third brought the tea trolley. Under Eliana's direction, they began draping the loops of white around the tree.

"It's rather pretty," Selene had to admit. "Reminiscent of snow."

"Yes, but we need more color." Eliana frowned, then sent one of the maids to the kitchen for a bowl of cranberries, and another to fetch her sewing basket.

Soon, the sisters were each stringing long garlands of cranberries. The servants came in with their packages, and shortly gilded nuts and bags of candy joined the decorations.

"We'll have to wire the candles onto the branches," Eliana said.

"And make sure to have a pail of water nearby." Selene eyed the tree. "It would be a terrible thing to burn the house down."

"We'll be careful." Eliana grinned at her. "Wait until it's lit. You've never seen anything so lovely."

A candle-filled tree couldn't match the winter stars on the darkest night of the year, but Selene simply nodded.

"We'd best start making ready for our guest," she said. "You'll want to look your best, I imagine."

"As will you, of course," Eliana said.

"Of course." A pretty dress and a dab of lip color couldn't erase Selene's marred past, but it was sweet of her sister to think so, and want her to make the effort.

They each repaired to their rooms, leaving the maids to finish decorating the tree. It was a pretty sight, Selene had to admit. There was something quite festive about all the colorful decorations. Perhaps this notion of a tree at Christmas might even spread through England. Certainly everyone was eager to follow Queen Victoria's lead.

Though where they'd find enough trees, year after year, she couldn't imagine. Perhaps it was a silly notion, after all.

AN HOUR LATER, while her maid was still curling her hair, Selene heard the front door knocker. Their guest must have arrived.

"There you are, miss." Her maid twisted one last curl about the iron. "You're a picture."

It was kind of the girl to say so. Selene scrutinized her reflection in the looking glass. The periwinkle gown did bring out the golden highlights in her hair—if one were looking for such things.

Which their guest would certainly not be, as Eliana would be radiant as the dawn.

With a sigh, Selene rose, dismissed her maid, and headed downstairs. She took the long way, and as she passed her father's study, she heard his voice through the partially open door.

"Yes," Lord Blake said. "I give you my blessing to ask for my daughter's hand. Provided, of course, that she accepts you. Now, I believe the rest of the family is awaiting your appearance in the front parlor."

Selene gathered up her skirts and dashed down the hall. She did not want her father to think she'd been intentionally eavesdropping.

So, it was true then, despite Eliana's denials. She would be marrying the Duke of Ashford. It made the season even more bittersweet, to know that after this year Eliana would be celebrating Christmas with her husband's family.

"There you are," Lady Blake said, holding out her hand as Selene rushed into the parlor. "Come stand by me so that I might introduce you to our guest."

Eliana perched on the settee, looking nervous, but smiled at her sister. "I'm so excited for you to officially meet the duke."

"He's just a man," William said, plucking a bag of sweets from the tree.

"Put that back this instant," Eliana cried, rising.

"Come fetch it, then." William held it up, taunting. He always had a knack for enraging his little sister.

"I'll keep him from escaping," Selene said encouragingly, stepping toward the door. "Leap upon him, quickly."

"Children." Lady Blake shook her head. "Do you really want the duke to see you behaving like wild creatures?"

With that, Lord Blake arrived, their visitor by his side, and Selene froze at the sight of the man standing there.

Jared.

Her heart thumped out his name. Jared Kendrick.

Gladness rose up in her like a flame, quickly doused by icy realization. *Dear heavens, no.* Jared was the Duke of Ashford—and he was going to marry her sister, Eliana.

His blue eyes met hers, a warm spark in them that faded when she did not smile back at him. How could she, when her soul was about to shatter?

Lady Blake stepped forward, unaware of the undercurrents threatening to pull Selene down into blackness, and extended her hand to Lord Ashford.

"Your grace, I'm so glad you could join us today. Allow me to introduce our eldest daughter, Selene. I believe you have met the rest of the family."

Jared—*she must stop thinking of him by that name*—bowed over her mother's hand. "As you may know, I had the good fortune to make your daughter's acquaintance last week."

"Yes," the viscount said. "Ashford has performed us a great service, as he was the fellow who rescued Selene upon the road."

"That's a jolly thing," William said, coming up to clap Lord Ashford upon the back. "Well done, sir."

She had spoken of him, of course, had told her family the entire tale of her winter adventure. Well, *almost* the entire tale. They did not need to hear about the kisses.

Eliana had thought it quite romantic, and Lord Blake had determined to seek out this Baron Kendrick fellow and reward him handsomely.

As it turned out, being the Duke of Ashford, there was nothing they could give him as a reward—except, apparently, their beautiful youngest daughter.

"Sir Kendrick." Selene made him a stiff curtsey as pain sliced her to shreds inside. "Or rather, your grace. This is quite a surprise."

The most horrible surprise of her life; even worse than overhearing what Edward had really thought of her.

Jared smiled at her again, the expression coming so easily to his face she could hardly bear it. How could he carry on with such ease while she was breaking apart?

"We thought you'd be stunned." He glanced at Eliana, his smile deepening. "Your sister is quite a conniver."

Oh, she was. She was indeed.

But how could Selene blame her? She had never confessed she'd lost her heart to Baron Kendrick—and even if she had, there was no reason to think that he and the Duke of Ashford were one and the same.

"I suppose you are a baron, in addition to being a duke." The words fell like stones from her lips. Why? Why had he deceived her so?

He gave her a curious look. "I am also Baron Kendrick, yes. I suppose you are angry with me for not telling you the complete truth—and I offer you my sincere apologies."

Selene stared at him a moment. She could not forgive him, ever.

"She forgives you, of course," Eliana said, taking Selene's arm. "Or she will, once she has a moment to think it over."

"Let us adjourn to the music room," Lady Blake said. "A bit of song is just what we need."

They always sang before dinner—the carols of the season, the jaunty wassailing tunes. But Selene's voice had dried in her throat, just as the blood had shriveled in her veins.

She let Eliana tow her down the hall, while William fell back and chatted with their guest. The two of them fell into conversation about their school days, and Selene concentrated on moving her feet forward without tripping. Without collapsing in a heap on the oriental runner, or dashing upstairs and locking herself in her room.

She must put up a good front for Eliana. She must pretend that her heart was not breaking anew each time she looked at Jared.

They arranged themselves around the piano, and she gratefully slid onto the bench. She would not have to look at him, but could instead concentrate on the music and try to imagine that he was not there. Only her family, singing *We Wish You a Merry Christmas*.

But he had a deep, rich baritone that she could not help listening to. Each song was a sweet torture. She wished he would propose to Eliana and take her sister away immediately.

Instead, Selene must endure.

Endure the laughter of her family. Endure sips of too-sweet Madeira. Endure sitting across from Jared at dinner and hearing the story of the "daring rescue," as Eliana now termed it.

The only way to manage was to shrink down inside herself, until she felt she was a tiny puppeteer, operating the strings of a body called Selene Banning. Cue the smile—pull the mouth up just so. Pass the pudding—lift the arms and turn to the right. Eat a bite of roast goose—move the jaw up and down, the taste like sawdust on her tongue.

Laugh at her brother's jokes—that one was a bit more difficult, and she feared her mirth had a brittle sound. Indeed, Eliana gave her a concerned look, and Jared often glanced her way, a confusion in his eyes that she did not know how to answer.

Did he imagine she would *welcome* his upcoming nuptials to her sister?

The connection she thought they had forged was meaningless. Her sister was the sun, and Selene the dark moon, invisible.

After dinner, Eliana proudly led them once more to the front parlor. While they had been eating, dusk had fallen and the servants had lit the candles on the tree. Even through her numbness, Selene could appreciate the glowing sight—as though a hundred stars had floated down to alight upon the branches.

"It is beautiful," Lady Blake said, a smile in her voice. "This could be a lovely new tradition."

She linked arms with the viscount, and he looked fondly down at her. Eyes blurring, Selene turned away. The tree was a smear of light in her vision.

"Let's open the presents," Eliana said. "I've been waiting all day for this."

She moved to a chair, Lord and Lady Blake took the settee, and Selene sank down upon the nearest piece of furniture, which turned out to be the sofa.

In addition to lighting the tree, the servants had arranged a pile of gifts beneath its spreading branches, including a number of gold-wrapped presents decorated with red velvet bows.

"Since I'm the guest, I think I should distribute mine first," Jared said, coming to stand next to Selene. He gave her an intense look. "Who should we start with?"

"Eliana," she managed.

It was time to end the torture. No doubt he would bestow some beautiful, extravagant piece of jewelry upon her sister, then declare of his intentions—since he now had the viscount's blessing.

Eliana would accept, the family would cheer, and then Selene could plead a headache and escape to the blessed privacy of her room. She dug her fingernails into her palms, steeling herself against the pain of seeing the man she'd fallen in love with proposing to her younger sister.

"Very well." Jared gave a small shake of his head, then went and fetched one of the smaller packages. With a flourishing bow, he presented it to her. "Miss Eliana, please accept this gift."

Eliana laughed sweetly. "My dear Duke of Ashford, you are too kind."

Selene bit the inside of her cheek, so hard she nearly winced from the pain.

Quickly, Eliana undid the bow and unfolded the bright paper to reveal a small wooden box inlaid with mother-of-pearl. She opened the lid and pulled out two hair combs decorated with topazes set in a starburst pattern.

Selene blinked at the sight. She had not thought Jared would be so parsimonious toward the woman he loved and wished to marry. The combs were pretty, certainly, but nothing above the ordinary.

She shot him a glance, the first tendril of doubt winding through her. Did he love Eliana, or was he like all the rest—false to the core?

Of course he was.

And there her sister sat, smiling and oblivious as she ran her fingers over the bright gemstones. Selene swallowed her cry of dismay. Eliana could not marry him—she would not allow it. At any moment now he would go down on one knee and say the words.

What could she do? Rush over and push him away from her sister? Rise and scream that the tree was on fire? Heart racing, she reviewed her options.

Jared glanced over at her, as if he could sense her agitation. Instead of kneeling at Eliana's feet he moved to the pile of gifts and selected another small present.

"Selene's turn next," he said.

"Oh, yes!" Eliana cried, and their parents nodded agreement. William, standing beside the tree, folded his arms and grinned.

The world was tipping and slowing, and Selene's mind scrambled to make sense of it. Why was everyone smiling at her? Why hadn't Jared asked Eliana to marry him? She drew in a shallow breath. It was very warm, as if the candles were heating the air to the temperature of a summer's day.

The Duke of Ashford seated himself beside her on the sofa. She could not bear to have him so close, the sparkle in his blue eyes, the secret red strands in his hair—and she could not bear to look away.

"Selene," he said, "please don't be angry with me any longer. I know I deceived you, and I am sorry for it. I thought... I'd hoped..." He thrust the present at her. "Open it?"

Once again her body was a puppet, although this time she had no idea who was controlling her hands as they untied the ribbon and peeled back the paper.

Another jewelry box, smaller than the one he'd given Eliana. She raised the lid, then froze as the light glimmered off the pendent nestled within. A large blue moonstone shone up at her, diamonds ringing it like stars. With trembling hands she lifted the pendant by its black velvet ribbon, dimly aware of Eliana's gasp of approval.

"It reminded me of Midwinter night," Jared said softly. "A memory to treasure. Will you wear it?"

She stared at him a long moment, the moonstone dangling between him. The look in his eyes was full of hope and worry. And—did she dare to imagine it?—love.

Mutely, she nodded, turning so that he might fasten the pendant about her neck. If she spoke, she feared she would shatter the fragile dream that had spun itself about her.

The silver-mounted stone was cool against her skin. The brush of his fingers at the back of her neck made her tremble. When he leaned forward to drop a kiss against her cheek, she felt as though a brand had been laid against her heart.

Slowly, she turned to look at him, fearing he could read everything in her eyes—all her secrets, her hopes and desires, her crippling doubts. Hoping he could see all the way into her soul.

"Jared," she said.

Just his name, but it was enough to ease the tightness in his face.

Slowly, he slipped off the settee, going to one knee on the carpet before her. Behind him the tree glowed like a promise. Like redemption.

"There's a ring to match," he said, drawing a small silk bag from his pocket and shaking the diamond-studded moonstone band into his palm. "I greatly hope that you will wear it, too. Selene Banning, will you marry me?"

"Why?" The word dropped ungracefully from her lips.

She still could not believe he meant to propose to her. How could he not notice that Eliana was the better match? The room stilled, even the candle flames ceasing to flicker.

That familiar smile crossed his face as he reached and took her hand. "Why? Because I didn't get more than five miles out of London before I realized I had to return. I'd left something very important behind, you see."

"What was that?" she asked, struggling to breathe.

He squeezed her hand lightly, his fingers warm and strong.

"My heart," he said. "Will you marry me?"

She swallowed, an enormity of emotion rushing over her as she realized she'd been wrong—foolishly, blindly wrong all evening. Jared had never intended to propose to Eliana! The knowledge was an anvil lifted from her soul.

He was there for *her*, Selene. He had been, all along.

"Must I ask you a third time?" There was a teasing note in his voice, but she could hear the hint of anxiety beneath.

Slowly, she smiled at him. "Yes."

"Very well then." He held her gaze. "Miss Selene Banning, will you—"

"My dear Sir Kendrick, or whatever title you are going by this evening, yes. I will gladly marry you."

The room exhaled. The candle flames began to dance once more. Eliana let out a gleeful cry, and William echoed her with a quieter hurrah. The viscount handed his wife the spare handkerchief he'd brought along for the occasion.

"I'm glad to hear you say it, my determined, beautiful fiancée." Jared slipped the moonstone ring onto her finger. It fit perfectly.

She wanted to laugh like a child, she wanted to weep until the storm of emotion inside her had passed. Instead she held his hands tightly in hers and let the turbulence slowly subside.

"You forgot *capable*," she said.

"That goes without saying. It is one of the things I love best about you." He smiled at her, and there was no mistaking the honesty in his face.

"Let us give the happy couple a moment alone," Lady Blake said, beckoning to her other children, then leading her husband to the door.

A few seconds later, Selene and Jared were the only ones in the salon.

Still grasping her hands, he rose to sit next to her. The candle flames reflected in his eyes, and a great sense of peace moved through her—the solace of that Midwinter night, coming to rest next to her heart.

"I must tell you something," she said.

"Yes?" He leaned close.

"I don't care if you're a baron, or a duke, or king of the world. That doesn't matter to me one whit."

"You gave me a bad turn this evening," he said. "I feared I'd lost you, after all. That you were so angry at my deception, you'd never forgive me."

"I..." Her face heated. "I was not precisely angry with you. I made a mistaken assumption." He raised his brow, encouraging her to continue. She took a deep breath, feeling even more foolish as she confessed. "I thought you had come to court Eliana."

"Your sister?" He gave a short, surprised laugh. "She's a dear girl, but how could you possibly think that? She doesn't hold a candle to you."

Hot tears pricked her eyes, and one spilled down her cheek. Gently, he smoothed it away with his thumb.

"Goose," he said. "For a highly intelligent woman, you were rather blind."

"I suppose I was." She drew in a wavering breath. "I'm sorry for it. This was a miserable evening."

"Until now."

"Won't Hetty be surprised when she comes back."

"I rather doubt it." He slid his hand down her cheek, then tipped her chin up.

"I love you," she whispered.

For a moment they sat there, faces inches apart, eyes locked. Everything that needed to be said passed between them in that moment.

Then their lips met. Selene closed her eyes and inhaled—pine and candle wax and the taste of her beloved. The kiss deepened, a fire winding through her veins. Outside the window a gentle snow began to fall, and down the street a group of carolers lifted their voices: *And heaven and nature sing, and heaven and nature sing, and heaven, and heaven, and nature sing.*

High above the clouds covering London, between both heaven and nature, the full moon shone, as it always shone—bright and perfect in the winter sky.

Ready for a longer tale? SONATA FOR A SCOUNDREL is a RITA-nominated, *USA Today* bestselling full-length Victorian Romance. Enjoy!

A PRINCE FOR YULETIDE

CHAPTER ONE

The scent of fresh spruce filled Banning House, wafting from the tree taking up the entire bow window in the parlor. Miss Eliana Banning hummed under her breath as she tied small bags of sweets to the branches. The family—with much urging on Eliana's part—had adopted the tradition last year, when Prince Albert and Queen Victoria had installed the first Christmas tree in Buckingham Palace. Indeed, many noble families had been quick to embrace the Germanic custom. All up and down the street, trees graced the windows of the Mayfair town houses—but the Bannings had been among the first.

"William," she said to her older brother, who was assisting her in the tree trimming, "there's a bare spot near the top. Do fill it."

"Hand me a gilded almond," he said, mumbling the words around something in his mouth.

She narrowed her eyes. "You beast! No wonder it's empty. You stole the bag of candy that was there."

William hastily swallowed. "A man must have sustenance during these difficult times."

"If I were any taller, you'd be banished from the room."

"A pity you have such stubby arms," he said. "But truly, I must be off soon. I'll send in the maids and footmen to help."

Eliana picked up a rustling length of paper chain, then set it back down again, her mood dimming. "I miss Selene. We had such fun last year."

Her older sister was married now, with a house—and Christmas tree—of her own. And while Eliana did not begrudge her sister her happy new life, in the months since Selene had married and left Banning House, a strange discontent had settled over Eliana.

She sighed, very softly. If she were perfectly truthful, perhaps she was a bit jealous. After all, Eliana had always been the very model of a pretty, agreeable, and sociable young lady. Yet plain, serious Selene had been the one to make a brilliant match.

Certainly, Eliana had gentleman callers aplenty, and good friends both male and female, but increasingly, she felt as though she were holding up a mask that no one cared to look behind. It felt as though all the gentlemen she associated with only seemed interested in pursuing fun and jollity, and nothing more. Everyone was so very merry and witty, and, in truth, it was becoming a bit exhausting.

And speaking of masks...

"We might as well finish up for the day," she told her brother. "I must prepare for the Midwinter Masque."

William shot her a look. "Is that tonight? Hetty is accompanying you, I hope. Don't get up to any mischief, Eliana."

She swatted him on the shoulder. "You sound like Father. Yes, of course my companion is coming—what do you take me for? And Selene and Jared will be there as well."

"That's the Duke and Duchess of Ashford, you impertinent girl. Make sure you curtsey appropriately."

She rolled her eyes, then went on the attack. "And when will *you* marry, sir? You've a title to inherit and pass down to your sons. You'd best get busy."

He frowned and gave a mock shudder. "Leg shackled so soon? I'm young yet. Don't you think *you* should be the next in the family to go?"

"I'm younger than you by six years!"

"Yes, but you're a girl. You grow stale much sooner."

Grinning, William ducked away from her threatening hand. "I'm only teasing, Ellie. You're a pretty girl, and you have plenty of time."

"Of course I have." She sniffed at him, but the words echoed hollowly inside her.

Selene had narrowly avoided being a spinster, and Eliana feared she was headed for that same fate. Was she doomed to be always the merry companion, and never the bride? It was all very well to have a pretty face and sweet nature, but not if she only attracted empty-headed buffoons for suitors.

Increasingly, she wanted something more—wanted to *be* something more, herself. If only she knew what that was. It was as though she were living in a cocoon, wrapped up in expectation and habit, unsure if she even had wings. What if she broke out and discovered she was only a worm, and not a butterfly at all?

"Give my love to our esteemed parents," William said, heading to the hall to fetch his coat and hat. "I'm planning on Christmas Eve dinner next week, of course."

"And our annual caroling," Eliana reminded him. "We'll gather here this coming Thursday at two o'clock. Don't look so doubtful —we need your voice more than ever, now that our best baritone is out of Town for the holidays."

"Alas, you must settle for second best." William pulled on his gloves, then bent to kiss her cheek. "Enjoy your ball tonight, and—"

"Yes, yes. Stay out of trouble. I don't know why everyone thinks I'm such a scapegrace. I'm actually quite a proper miss, you know."

William merely arched one brow. The butler opened the front door, and out her brother went, letting in a chilly blast of air.

"My, it's cold." Eliana rubbed her arms. "I wonder if it might snow."

"It might," the butler agreed. "What time would you like the carriage brought around this evening?"

"Eight, I think." With a shiver, she retreated from the hallway and went upstairs, where Hetty waited to help transform her into Red Riding Hood for the Midwinter Masque.

It took well over an hour to finish fitting the red velvet cloak Eliana had chosen. She'd kept the mask a simple affair, however, just a plain red satin half-mask over her eyes, unlike some ladies of her acquaintance. Her best friend, Lady Peony Talbot, was going as a swan, and her elaborate headpiece included sequins, satin, and a ridiculously tall plume of white feathers.

Now Eliana sat quietly, trying to be patient as Hetty curled her hair into careful ringlets.

"You look a trifle melancholy," Hetty said, pausing in her pursuit of the perfect curl. "Is anything the matter?"

Eliana smoothed her palm over the silver skirts of her gown and cast about for a reasonable answer. She wasn't about to admit that she felt a bit adrift, not to mention lonely for some gentleman she had yet to meet.

"I miss Selene," she finally said. "Now that she's married, we hardly see her anymore."

Hetty smiled. "Being a duchess is keeping your sister busy, indeed. But I'm sure she misses you as well."

Eliana frowned. "I think she's too happy being wed to the Duke of Ashford to pay us any mind."

The moment the words left her mouth, she regretted them. Jealousy was unbecoming in a lady, and it was not like her to be so petty.

Hetty gave her a sympathetic look. "You'll find your own

happy ending, Eliana, of that I'm certain. Now, turn your head a bit more so I might fix this last curl properly."

Eliana was not nearly so sure. Had someone asked her a year ago if she'd any doubts about making a match, she would have laughed at them quite merrily. But something had changed. She had grown up a little, perhaps—no longer quite the flighty girl she had been. Even more than that, she'd seen the depth of the bond between Selene and Lord Ashford, and realized that she could settle for nothing less than that for herself.

It was unfortunate, in some ways, that her standards had risen so high. Several gentlemen of her acquaintance whom she might have found satisfactory a year ago now failed to come up to the mark her sister's husband had set.

She let out a sigh, and Hetty gave her another look.

"No more moping about, miss. Aren't you looking forward to the Midwinter Masque? It's only the most anticipated ball of the winter season. I'm sure you'll have your pick of gentlemen."

A pity she didn't want her pick of them. She only wanted the *right* one—but as of yet, he was nowhere to be found.

"After last year's scandal, I'm sure the masque will be a horrid crush. Perhaps I shouldn't attend."

"Nonsense." Hetty set the curling tongs down. "You look particularly pretty tonight, and besides, you can't disappoint Lady Peony. She needs her friends' support tonight, more than ever."

Eliana glanced at her reflection in the wardrobe mirror. She supposed she looked well, with her golden hair perfectly coiffed and the gauzy silver of her gown complementing her complexion. And Hetty was right. Peony was one of her dearest friends and could not be left to face the gossips alone.

"It's very brave of her to go," Hetty added. "After what happened with Prince Sebastian..." She trailed off and began sorting through Eliana's jewelry box.

"The Ice Prince." Eliana spoke the name all of London had begun calling the nobleman after he'd so coldly and publicly spurned Lady Peony at last year's Midwinter Masque. "I'll never forgive him for breaking Peony's heart."

"Then make a point of refusing him a dance tonight," Hetty said. "Here, I think the pearls will go very nicely, don't you?"

It was hardly a satisfactory revenge, to spurn the prince, but it would have to do. Perhaps, if all the other ladies in London followed her lead, he might feel some shame and run off back to his ancestral family in Sayn-Wittgenstein.

Righteous indignation still glowed through her when she thought of the prince's despicable actions last year. It was plain the barbaric blood of the Visigoths ran in his frost-ridden veins. England would be better off without him gracing their shores, that much was certain.

CHAPTER TWO

Prince Sebastian Nikolai Sayn-Wittgenstein-Hohenstein glanced at his dye-blackened fingertips and frowned.

"Don't fret, your highness," his valet, Reece, said, clearly noting the direction of Sebastian's gaze. "We'll scrub your skin clean enough. Besides, you'll be wearing gloves during the ball. No one will notice."

"I hope not." Sebastian looked up to study his reflection in the tall looking glass at the end of his dressing room. It was strange to see his normally pale hair turned jet black. His light blue eyes seemed very intense in contrast. "Are you certain this will fool people?"

"Of course it will. With the addition of your mask, and if you adopt an accent, no one will suspect you are Prince Sebastian. Already the servants are putting it about that you've taken ill and won't be attending the Midwinter Masque."

"Much to the relief of certain ladies, I've no doubt." He narrowed his eyes, his reflection glaring back at him.

Last year had been a debacle, and he'd yet to shed the ridiculous nickname the *ton* had saddled him with. The Ice Prince. A heart made of frost, they said, with a demeanor to match.

"Make sure you laugh often," Reece said, as if reading his mind. "It will throw them off the scent, if anyone suspects."

"I have very little to laugh about."

The past fourteen months he'd spent in London had not gone particularly well. His mother wanted him to find a suitable English wife—not that she herself had been a good match for his stern Prussian father. As soon as Sebastian was old enough to be sent off to boarding school, she'd left the palace at Berleburg and returned to her noble family in England, taking Sebastian's sister with her. Unfortunately, Sebastian's father was in agreement, and so it was decided—quite without Sebastian's input—that he was to wed an English heiress.

Unfortunately, his mother's wishes were no secret to the nobility of London. At every social gathering he had to contend with an endless stream of eligible young ladies and their title-hungry relatives. Every potential bride looked at him with the hope she might call herself a princess. None of them bothered to look any deeper than that.

He had thought there might be one, but Lady Peony Talbot had proved as shallow as the rest. Sebastian let out a low breath that was not a sigh of discouragement. Of course not. Royals never voiced their emotions openly.

Reece gave him a wry smile, nonetheless.

"Don't fret, highness. I'm sure you'll find plenty of young ladies who'll want to dance with you."

"They would, even if I were not in disguise. Every eligible lady in London thinks she'll be the one to melt the heart of the Ice Prince." Sebastian's lip curled as he said the words. Damnation, would he ever be free of that nickname?

"Not *every* lady." Reece coughed and busied himself with brushing out Sebastian's coat.

It was as black as his newly dyed hair, and would help him blend in better than his signature cobalt blue.

"True," Sebastian said. "Lady Peony certainly does not like me. Nor her dear friend, Miss Banning."

"Then I think you ought to try and be particularly pleasant to Miss Banning. Since she never seeks you out, she won't suspect your disguise."

"As long as she isn't keeping close company with Lady Peony, I admit I find that idea refreshing." And rather ironic.

Miss Banning had been, briefly, under his consideration as a potential wife—but she was a flighty, empty-headed young lady, always the center of attention, and clearly quite content to be nothing but a preening flower beneath the sun of her many admirers. If anything, she was *too* charming. He needed a certain steadiness in a prospective wife—a fortitude he strongly doubted Miss Banning possessed.

Reece gave him a speculative look. "If there *are* any young ladies you're planning on courting, this would be your opportunity to find out what they really think of you. And who they are when not putting on airs for the prince."

"I think not. One revelation a year is more than enough."

He had thought, last year, that Lady Peony might be the one lady he could stand to marry. The daughter of an earl, she had an excellent pedigree, and she had not made herself an utter fool over him. As a result, he'd let down his guard and begun the first stages of a cautious courtship.

Only to have the lady immediately put the rumor about that he was planning to ask for her hand at the Midwinter Masque.

When he'd stepped into the ballroom last year, all eyes had turned to him, and a speculative buzz had risen. He took his first dance with Lady Peony, who'd been uncommonly subdued, before the rumor reached his ears that everyone was waiting for him to go down on one knee and make the grand gesture.

At that moment he supposed he'd earned his nickname, for an icy fury had gripped him. He had stalked out of the ball, enough

ANTHEA LAWSON

shreds of his dignity left to depart without publicly confronting Lady Peony and making the scandal even worse.

Instead, he'd written her a cold note, telling her precisely what he thought of rumor mongers and ladies who imagined he was so easily manipulated, and informing her that their brief association was at an end.

The *ton* was abuzz, and he was scorned for a time—but a prince never fell far from grace. A handful of his acquaintances knew that Sebastian hadn't intended to ask Lady Peony to marry him; not immediately, and certainly not at the Midwinter Masque. But his reputation could take the blow better than hers if it was known that she was a scheming, grasping liar, so he'd said little on that score. Only kept his distance.

"What name will you take?" Reece asked, pulling Sebastian out of his unpleasant memories.

"I need to choose something I'll answer to." Sebastian tilted his chin up so that his valet could tie his silky white neck cloth.

"Your middle name, perhaps?" Reece suggested.

"Indeed." Sebastian thought a moment. "I'll be Count Nikolai, a minor lord from Russia."

He'd be able to manage the accent; one of his companions at boarding school had been the son of a Russian grand duke.

"Well then, Lord Nikolai, I believe you're ready to attend the Midwinter Masque. Don't forget to enjoy yourself."

Reece held out his coat, and Sebastian shrugged into it, then swiped his wolf mask from the dressing table and held it in front of his face.

It was wearying, always and ever being Prince Sebastian, which was, he supposed, why he'd agreed to Reece's ridiculous scheme that he attend the Midwinter Masque as someone completely different. That, plus the fact that he wanted to prove to himself he was man enough to return to the scene of the crime, as it were. Even if he were in disguise.

126

The man looking back at him from the mirror bore little resemblance to the aloof and pale-haired Ice Prince. Instead, a mysterious stranger stood there, ready for a night where, for once, he could take off the mask of nobility and simply be himself.

CHAPTER THREE

"Did you hear?" Eliana leaned close to Lady Peony, trying to avoid inhaling the fluffy white feathers edging her friend's mask. "*He* won't be here tonight. Apparently the prince has been taken ill."

With an attack of conscience, perhaps, though she doubted it. Preferably it was something painful and debilitating, like gout.

"Oh, that's a relief." Peony's fan, which she had been waving back and forth in an agitated manner, slowed. "I almost couldn't come tonight, after what happened last year."

Her voice hitched, and Eliana patted her friend's gloved hand. Peony was sweet and a bit meek, and the debacle last year had wounded her deeply.

"It wasn't your fault," Eliana said. "Prince Sebastian was an utter cad to you, breaking things off without a word, when everyone knew he was supposed to propose at the ball."

Peony nodded mournfully and said nothing.

"But the Ice Prince isn't here, so cheer up! Is your dance card full?"

"Not entirely."

"Mine either." Eliana glanced about the crowded ballroom, her gaze obscured by the eyeholes of her mask.

It was not quite as impractical as Peony's, being made of paper and silk and sitting closely against her face, but it was still hot and a little scratchy.

At last she glimpsed the familiar dark hair and blue gossamer dress she'd been searching for.

"There's my sister. I'll make her relinquish her husband for the quadrille. Once you take a turn with the Duke of Ashford, the men will be lining up."

Peony did not deserve to be a wallflower, and her reputation, though bruised, was recovering. If only she would stand up for herself a bit more...

But Peony's kindness had shored Eliana up during her low points, and she would not abandon her friend simply because Peony lacked a backbone of steel.

"Wait here, and I'll send Ashford over," Eliana said. "It's quite a crush."

Indeed, it took her several minutes to maneuver past the clumps of people in conversation. She amused herself as she sidled past by trying to identify the lords and ladies. Some she knew by their laughs, others by their tone and mannerisms. Having often been at the center of such groups, she was well aware of the individual quirks of the members of the *ton*.

It was rather amazing, though, how the masks made it difficult to recognize a person. Hair color and stature were excellent clues, of course, but Eliana found herself wondering how many of the people she passed were known to her. The sensation of moving alone through an unknown crowd was a bit odd, accustomed as she was to counting so many people as friends and acquaintances.

"Lady Ashford," she said, fetching up with relief beside her sister. "How inspiring you look tonight."

Selene turned, her gossamer blue skirt catching the light. Eliana could tell her dark eyebrows were raised behind her mask.

"You shouldn't say my name," Selene said. "This *is* a masked ball, after all."

"Don't be silly—you know as well as I that the gossips revealed the Duke and Duchess of Ashford were going as 'a Poet and his Muse.' Terribly romantic of you."

Selene smiled. "Jared is regretting having to carry around a book and a pen all evening, though I did warn him it would be cumbersome."

"Then he ought to set them down and dance. In fact, if you might prevail upon him to take a turn with Lady Peony, it would be much appreciated."

"Of course. The poor girl. I suppose you've heard that Prince Sebastian will not be in attendance tonight?"

"Thank heavens. The Ice Prince would certainly bring a certain chilling effect to the occasion."

Selene tapped her blue lace fan against her hand. "I hope he isn't terribly ill. Perhaps he chose to stay away for Lady Peony's sake. That would be gallant of him."

"Marriage has made you see the good in everyone, however improbable," Eliana said. "At any rate, do ask the duke."

"Of course. And I'll have him dance with you as well. Make your suitors take notice. I'm surprised you're not surrounded by your usual coterie of admirers."

"Perhaps they don't recognize me."

Or perhaps she had already dissuaded several of her would-be paramours, telling them she felt unwell and preferred to sit quietly with Lady Peony for a time. It was easier than pretending to a cheer she did not feel.

"Now you're being silly." Selene poked her in the arm with her fan. "Go off and chat with your admirers, and don't fret too much about Lady Peony. She needs to stop feeling sorry for herself, and you hovering over her doesn't help."

"As you say, oh Muse." Eliana ducked away from another poke.

Her sister's quiet laughter followed Eliana as she wove back through the crowd. And although she was smiling, Eliana felt a twinge of discontent.

She didn't actually want to return to Peony, nor did she want to circulate and be witty and bright and charming. The thought, which used to fill her with energy, now only made her tired. Whatever was the matter with her?

Drawing up her red hood to cover her hair, Eliana let the flow of the crowd push her to the edges of the room. She fetched up beside a decorative column and caught her breath. She just needed a moment to herself, and then she would be the usual merry, animated girl everyone expected her to be.

Surely she would.

Before she achieved that state, however, her quiet was intruded upon by a black-haired gentleman wearing a wolf mask. His eyes were very blue behind the white fur covering his mask, and the nose protruded out so far that she could barely see his mouth or the line of his jaw.

"Good evening," he said in an accented voice. "I beg your pardon, but when I saw a beautiful maiden in a red cloak, I knew we must meet. I am Count Nikolai of Kiev."

Her pulse accelerated as she looked at him standing before her, tall and a bit forbidding. Despite the confidence in his voice, there was a wary set to his shoulders, as though he were inclined to flee back into the dark forest from which he'd emerged.

"Perhaps it is better if we do not become acquainted," she said. "After all, the tale does not end well for the maiden."

He brought his hand to his heart. "You wound me. In some versions of the story, it is the wolf who is the unfortunate one, after all."

"Then either way, we oughtn't to meet."

Despite her words, a strange shiver went through her. Perhaps a Russian count with melancholy eyes was just the antidote she was looking for.

His teeth flashed white in the shadows beneath his mask. "On the contrary. One might say it is fated. Would you tell me your name?"

Eliana hesitated. It was not the done thing, of course, for a man and woman to meet without an introduction. Yet the rules of a masked ball were different, and besides, it was clear that Count Nikolai was a foreigner, unaccustomed to the customs of England.

"You may call me Mademoiselle Red," she finally said.

If he turned out to be a pleasant fellow then she might gift him with her name, but she was not entirely certain. The wolf mask gave him a dangerous air.

"It is my pleasure, Mademoiselle Red." He made her an elegant bow. "But why do you lurk here behind the colonnade? A beautiful young lady such as yourself should be out dancing and laughing and breaking all the young men's hearts."

"Even the most sociable of ladies needs a moment to herself," she said.

"And I have intruded." He dipped his head. "You must forgive me. But will you also promise me a dance later if I go away now and leave you alone?"

He made her smile with his boldness, and for some reason her entire mood lightened. This was a masked ball, after all, and what could be more amusing than Red Riding Hood dancing with the wolf?

"In truth," she said, "I suspect you're a better companion than my own lonely thoughts. I will dance with you now."

He held out his arm, his blue eyes serious, and led her to the dance floor. The small orchestra on the balcony struck up a waltz, and Eliana let out a half sigh, half laugh. Of course, it would be nothing so simple as a quadrille or country dance. No, she must step right into the wolf's embrace.

"You see?" he said in his Russian accent. "Fate conspires with us."

"Or against us."

She placed her left hand on his shoulder and let him clasp her right hand. His other arm slipped about her waist with a strong, sure touch that made her suspect Count Nikolai was an accomplished dancer.

Two bars into the music, her suspicions proved correct. He guided her deftly about the floor, neatly avoiding the other couples, and then whirled her into a series of spins that made her red cloak billow out behind her.

She laughed, she could not help it, and he sent her a reluctant half-smile in return. Eliana had the impression he was not one to smile easily, and decided that would be her goal for the evening. After all, they were at the Midwinter Masque, and despite the debacle last year, it was supposed to be a cheery event.

"You are very light on your feet, Mademoiselle Red," he said.

"And you are quite skilled yourself, my lord."

"Pruss—that is, we Russians are taught the same social graces as other European nobility." He stiffened slightly.

"Take no offense, please. I meant no slight upon your nationality."

He deftly pushed her out into a spin. When she was back in his arms, he lowered his voice.

"That might be, but I hear you English have been rude to a certain visiting prince, calling him unkind names."

Eliana studied him, trying to read the features behind the mask. Was he truly offended?

"That has nothing to do with the fact he's a foreigner," she said, "and everything to do with his behavior. We call him the Ice Prince because he has a heart impervious to kindness or love."

"He sounds a most unpleasant fellow." The wolf mask rose as Count Nikolai scanned the crowd. "Is the prince here? Point him out to me, so I might avoid him."

"Luckily, he has been taken ill and is not in attendance this evening." She could not help the edge in her voice.

The count looked down at her once more. "What did he do, to make you dislike him so?"

"Last year, at this very ball, he made a fool of my dear friend

Lady Peony. He was supposed to propose to her, and instead they exchanged words and he departed, leaving her standing alone in the middle of the dance floor. The next day she received a note that their courtship was at an end."

"How unfortunate." The count's lips pressed into a rigid line. "Perhaps this prince of yours did not know he was supposed to propose that evening."

"Not know?" She blinked up at him. "He'd been courting Lady Peony for weeks. Everyone knew the prince was going to ask her to marry him very soon."

"Did they?" There was something dangerous in the count's voice.

"Don't side with him, just because you are both foreigners," she said. "And there's no need to turn rabid, either. If a gentleman courts a lady and makes certain promises, he ought to stand by his words, and not leave her to be the laughing stock of the *ton*."

His jaw clenched, but he bent his head in assent. "You are correct, of course. You seem a very good friend to the young lady in question."

"Friendship is important. Our connections with other people help make us better, in turn." It was one of the simple truths of her world, though she realized she'd never spoken it aloud.

"I know little of that." There was something stricken in his eyes.

"My lord—"

He stopped her by whirling them into a series of turns, but her heart ached at the loneliness she'd glimpsed in his expression.

When they returned to a more sedate pace, she caught her breath and vowed to steer their conversation onto safer ground.

"How long will you be in London? Will you be able to enjoy some of our English holiday traditions?" She was half tempted to invite him to come caroling.

"I fear I must depart tomorrow." There was something forbidding in his tone that kept her from asking further questions. They had already clashed once—and that was one too many times for what was supposed to be a happy evening.

"A pity you can't stay longer." She meant the words, a bit to her own surprise.

There was something about Count Nikolai that made her wish they could become better acquainted. He intrigued her, and it was refreshing to speak with a gentleman who was not afraid to disagree with her.

As the waltz came to a close, she cast about for a reason to remain in his company. It certainly was more interesting than making jokes with her companions about the various masks and costumes on display. Not to mention her private crusade to make him smile more.

"Have you tried English mulled wine?" she asked him. "They're serving some in the refreshment room. Perhaps you have something similar in your homeland."

"I believe we do," he said, "though I will not know until I taste it."

"Will you join me in a glass?"

"With pleasure." His solemn voice held none of the light flirtation she was used to from gentlemen. Which, of course, made him all the more appealing.

She took his arm and steered him through the crowd. Their passage elicited laughter and comments concerning Red Riding Hood and her tame wolf, and Eliana could not help smiling in return. No doubt they made quite a sight together—as if they'd planned their costumes from the start.

They reached the parlor off the ballroom, where the refreshments were laid out. Like the ballroom, this room, too, was packed with people, elbow to elbow.

"Allow me to fetch our wine," Count Nikolai said. "There's no need for both of us to fight through the crowd."

"Thank you, my lord." She glanced about for a place to wait, and spied an alcove on one side of the room with a low bench, miraculously unoccupied. "I'll sit over there."

She expected him to leave her and go jostle for a place at the tables, but instead he gently took her elbow and escorted her to the bench.

"What nice manners they have in Russia," she said, taking a seat. Her red cloak pooled about her, a little too disconcertingly like blood.

He tipped his head. "Some foreigners know how to treat an English lady. I shall return shortly, my lady."

To her surprise, he bent and took her hand, pressing a kiss upon the back of her glove. It sent a jolt of heat through her, though surely she could not possibly have felt the warmth of his lips through the fabric.

She blinked, and then he was gone, smoothly slipping through the crowd.

What a curious man Count Nikolai was. A foreigner with a touch of melancholy, though perhaps that was because he was far from home. Indeed, it was a sad time of year to be alone. She would be quite downcast if she were spending the holidays away from her family and friends.

Her own discontents seemed rather small in comparison. Eliana took a deep breath and resolved not to mope any longer about her romantic prospects. The right man would come along, and she must simply trust the fact.

After all, look at her sister. A year ago Selene had been headed for certain spinsterhood, when a carriage accident and a chance meeting had transformed her life. Certainly the same thing could happen to Eliana.

"My lady."

The sound of Count Nikolai's low Russian accent made her blink. He stood before her, a glass of mulled wine in either hand.

She took the glass he held out, admiring the gold filigree about the rim.

"Please, sit." She patted the bench beside her. "There's room for two."

Barely, but it would be rude to make him stand there and drink his wine.

"As you wish." He sat beside her, and once again she was struck by the edge of elegance in his movements.

His leg pressed lightly against hers, and a strange heat washed over her, as though she sat too near a blazing fire.

"Tell me about Kiev," she said, in an effort to distract herself from the sensation. "I know very little about Russia. What do you do for fun at the holidays?"

"We enjoy the snow. We go ice skating. Do you like to skate?"

She could not help the little shiver that went through her. "Not at all. I fell into a pond when I was a young girl and nearly drowned, so I stay far away from water whenever possible."

"I did not mean to distress you." His blue eyes were sympathetic, as though he, too, bore childhood scars. "Shall we sample this mulled wine of yours?"

"Certainly."

It was a welcome distraction from the old fear, and she raised her glass to her nose. The scent of cloves and oranges wafted up, along with the briny smell of warmed inferior wine.

"Alas," she said, "I'm afraid our host has not used the finest of vintages."

One side of his mouth quirked up, and he glanced about the crowded room. "If you had to serve several hundred people, would you bring forth the best wine from your cellars?"

"I like to think that I would. But then, my family is not one to host large balls. They generally prefer quieter gatherings to a monstrous crush."

"But you do not? You strike me as a quite sociable young lady."

"Because I wear a red cloak and hood? That's rather presumptuous, my lord."

"Not at all." He tilted his head, his eyes very blue behind the white fur of his mask. "You are an accomplished dancer, able to converse and waltz easily. You're adept at wending your way through large crowds. And you are a charming companion."

Eliana felt a blush rise.

"Thank you." To cover her confusion—for normally such compliments did not unbalance her—she took a sip of mulled wine.

Then instantly regretted it, as sour citrus filled her mouth. She swallowed, trying not to cough. At least their host had added a bit of brandy, as was customary, and the liquor warmed the back of her throat.

Count Nikolai took a drink from his own glass, his Adam's apple bobbing as he swallowed. He had a strong throat, and she liked the line of his jaw, what she could see of it behind the mask. She wondered what the rest of his features looked like, then an instant later scolded herself for such shallow musings.

The worth of a person was not in their looks, after all, but in their hearts and minds, in their conduct and humor.

She should know.

How many men had fallen in love with her, declaring she was their perfect muse, all because of her pretty face and smile? In fact, she felt increasingly sure that none of her suitors had cared to dig much below the surface to discover who Miss Eliana Banning truly was. Why bother, when she would look so well as a wife upon their arms?

Sometimes she wished she had not been born quite so cheerful and outgoing—not to mention pretty—but was instead more like her sister, whose quiet competence had carried her into a brilliant match.

"Why so pensive?" Count Nikolai asked. "I agree the wine is dreadful, but surely there is a cure for such a terrible taste."

"I believe there's a table with sweets at the other end of the room," she said.

"I find our conversation sweeter still," he said, then let out a short laugh. "You must forgive my flattery. It seems the wolf has been quite tamed by Mademoiselle Red."

She blushed again, hoping her red silk mask concealed the reaction. Heavens, this wolfish lord made her feel like a starry-eyed debutante, not a young lady with two Seasons' worth of flirtations behind her.

"I'm not sure what I would do with a pet wolf," she said. "It's probably better to set you free in the woods, instead."

His eyes flashed. "Is it better to live tame and cared for, or free and lonely?"

The question pricked at her, echoing as it did her recent dissatisfactions.

"Can't one have both freedom and contentment?" she asked.

"One might, but perhaps not in this society." His voice had turned from teasing to thoughtful. "There are always expectations, as you know."

Yes, she did. Every year she found herself more hemmed in by those expectations: to make an excellent match, to be a companionable wife, to remain cheerful and bright no matter her mood. To be the Eliana that society had branded her.

Who was she truly, outside of that cocoon? Who did she want to be? She feared that if she ran away to the woods to find out, she would die of exposure. Or loneliness.

Eliana shook herself and gave the count a wry smile. "I did not mean for our conversation to become quite so sober. Normally I'm more pleasant company, I assure you."

He tilted his head, regarding her. "Sometimes the cover of anonymity allows us to speak the truth most clearly. You needn't hide who you truly are, or what you feel."

He was too perceptive, and her own thoughts were too muddled to speak clearly of.

"What are you hiding, Lord Nikolai?"

For a moment he said nothing, his pale blue eyes studying her intently. "At this moment, I am hiding only the fact that I would like to kiss you."

She would have taken it as flirtation, except for the seriousness of his tone.

"Now that you've spoken it, it's hardly a secret." She flipped her scarlet fan open and began fluttering it before her face.

"It is our secret, between the two of us. But I see I've offended you, Mademoiselle Red. My apologies. Despite my costume this evening, I am not a wolfish gentleman."

Still fanning herself, Eliana glanced at him. She was not sure she believed him—there was something dangerously masculine in the way he looked at her. Though perhaps it was the Russian way. At any rate, her heart was beating far too quickly for comfort.

CHAPTER FOUR

Their gazes locked, and Eliana felt herself falling into the blue of his eyes. What was happening to her? This reserved wolf was not at all the type of gentleman she'd envisioned meeting this evening. Or, perhaps, ever.

A commotion at the doorway of the refreshment room made her blink and look away, both relieved and disappointed by the distraction. A maskless fellow had rushed in, cheeks flushed and hair damp.

"It's snowing!" he announced. "Nice, big flakes, too. Perfect for wishing upon. Come out, everyone."

"Lord Whitcomb," Eliana said. "Always looking for the fun in everything. No doubt he and his cronies have started a pile of snowballs to pelt the unwary."

Count Nikolai's lips twitched up in a smile. "If it just started snowing, then I doubt he's been able to gather sufficient ammunition. Now is the perfect time to venture outside and watch the snow fall. Shall we?"

He set his mostly untouched wine aside, rose, and offered his arm.

Should she accept? Slowly, Eliana put down her own glass of

wine. The count must have sensed her hesitation, for he leaned closer and lowered his voice.

"Mademoiselle Red, despite my appearance, I assure you I do not bite. Nor will I attack you with a snowball or attempt to stuff snow down the back of your cloak. But I would like to see the snowfall. It will remind me of home."

The wistfulness in his tone, more than anything, prompted her to rise and slip her arm through his.

"How long has it been since you've been in Kiev?" she asked.

"A very long time." His voice held a wry note.

She wondered what had sent him from his home, but she was too much of a lady to pry. They barely knew one another, after all.

"I take it you've been traveling about Europe?" she asked instead.

"I've been living abroad for some years, yes. Would you care to fetch your pelisse before stepping outside?"

She glanced at the drawing room where the butler had taken charge of everyone's outer garments, and shook her head at the line already forming.

"We won't be out long. Unless you're worried about your fur?"

"I believe wolves are used to the snow. But what of your cloak? Will the snow not mar the velvet?"

She paused at the side door leading into the garden and untucked her hand from the crook of his elbow.

"Simple." She untied the cloak and whirled it about, a flutter of bright red, then resettled it inside-out upon her shoulders.

The lining was more durable than the silk velvet, which brushed softly against her bare arms. The cloak began to slip, and he caught the edge, his fingers grazing her shoulder. The contact made heat flare under her skin. Seemingly oblivious to how his touch affected her, he pulled the cloak closed and helped her fasten it.

"You are a resourceful woman," he said.

The compliment warmed her, and distracted her from her

giddy reaction to his nearness. No one ever said she was resourceful or clever—they reserved those words for her sister. No, Eliana was beautiful and charming and witty, and she was growing rather tired of it.

The count held the door open, and a gust of cool air blew in. One or two snowflakes drifted past the threshold, melting immediately in the overly warm, perfumed air of the town house. Eliana could hardly wait to step outside.

The babble of voices and strains of music from the dance floor quieted as Count Nikolai closed the door behind them. As Eliana had suspected, they were not the only guests to slip out to enjoy the sight of the snow. She need not fear for her virtue—not when nearby was a gaggle of young ladies dressed like flowers, and a shepherdess and shepherd a little beyond them.

She and the count walked a few paces into the garden. The bushes wore a dusting of snow like powdered sugar on a cake, and the peculiar silence of snowfall descended about them. Even the giggling young ladies' voices were muffled, though Eliana could still see them lifting their hands to the sky and sticking out their tongues, trying to catch the huge, fluffy flakes drifting down.

It felt as though they'd stepped into a different world, far removed from the whirl and expectations of London. A world where she could listen to her own thoughts, her own heartbeat, and make her own choices.

Something cool and soft landed against her cheek, just below the edge of her mask.

"Make a wish," Count Nikolai said. "Quickly, before it melts."

"I wish—"

He set his finger to her lips, the heat of his touch like fire against her mouth. Startled, she glanced up at him.

"Don't speak it aloud, or it won't come true. Hurry." Count Nikolai removed his finger from her mouth. The sensation of his touch lingered, like a drop of brandy burning on her lips.

I wish I might find someone who loves me, Eliana, for who I could be and not who they assume I am. She put all the recent fierce longing of her soul into the wish.

His gaze still fixed on her face, his eyes widened. "That looked like a fearsome wish, indeed. I would not want to be your enemy."

The blush heating her cheeks surely must have melted the snowflake. "It was not that kind of wish."

Even behind the mask, she could see his brows rise. "In that case, I think I would want to be your friend."

"It wasn't *that* kind of a wish, either," she said tartly. Though perhaps it was. Not that it was any of his business. "Aren't you going to wish for something?"

"What makes you think I didn't?"

She pulled her cloak closer about her shoulders. "What good is this game if you don't know what the other person wished for?"

He let out a breath, a puff of white in the snowflake-crowded air. "Very well. I'll tell you mine, but then it will not come true."

"You can't know that. Wishes are magic." The snow gently swirling about them seemed to dance in agreement.

"You'll see I'm right." A self-deprecating tilt to his lips, he leaned forward and lowered his voice. "I wished to kiss you."

She should bid him a curt good evening and whisk herself back into the house. Miss Eliana Banning would certainly do so. But she was weary of being the vivacious yet proper Miss Banning. For just this night, this moment, she could be Mademoiselle Red.

She could be daring, and serious, and a tiny bit wicked.

The bouquet of young ladies had gone back into the house, and the few other people in the garden were blurred shapes, concealed by the thickly falling snow.

She took a step forward, until she could feel the heat of his body brushing against hers. Oh, she was reckless, but she didn't care.

"I told you, wishes are magic," she said, tilting her face up. "I grant your wish."

He sucked in his breath, as if he might argue. Then, before either of them could reconsider, he bent and pressed his lips to hers.

Her hands went to his shoulders and she leaned in, her senses whirling like the snowflakes. Gently, she parted her lips, and his tongue dipped inside. She tasted cloves and oranges, heat and desire.

In a sudden movement, he gathered her close against him. The nose of his mask bumped against the side of her face, but she didn't mind. It was a small nuisance balanced against the extraordinary sensation of his kiss.

Sparks raced through her, flaming mirror-images of the snow falling around them, but contained—barely—within her body. Fire, and the taste of his tongue, and a dizzying whirl inside her head that made her clutch his shoulders for balance.

He was kissing her. *Her*. Not merry, pretty, sometimes shallow Eliana Banning, but the girl inside. The one who was now emerging, who wanted to make her own decisions instead of going along with Society's expectations.

The one who had spent the best evening of her life dancing and conversing with a masked man who didn't even know her name.

He held her tightly against him, and every inch of her said *yes*, over and over, lost in his arms. Their breaths mingled, and their hearts seemed to settle into the same rhythm. Nothing else mattered but this endless moment, a perfect rushing of heat and cold, of light and dark, of man and woman.

They could have stood there, kissing, until they were covered with snow, until the night wore into dawn and the last invisible stars set. But the door opened, loudly disgorging Lord Whitcomb and his boisterous group of friends into the garden.

Count Nikolai pulled back, and the rush of cold air against her lips made Eliana want to weep with a sudden sense of loss. His mask was dislodged, and she caught a glimpse of his handsome face; the planes of his cheeks descending to a strong jaw.

"Have we met, sir?" she asked, peering up at him through a sudden flurry. "You look familiar."

"I don't believe so." He let her go and adjusted his mask, bringing the wolf's face down over his own once more. "Certainly I would have remembered a woman of your particular wit, Mademoiselle Red."

There was something in his tone that didn't quite ring true, and her heart beat faster with hope. Had they somehow, impossibly, met before? She almost told him her name, just to be certain, but the rowdy fellows began pelting one another with snowballs. She and the count were not in imminent danger, but the air felt suddenly much colder.

Eliana shivered, and he was instantly beside her, slipping one arm about her shoulders.

"Time we went in," he said. "It's ungentlemanly of me to have kept you outside so long."

"It was worth it." Somehow, she felt transformed, as though that kiss had been the key to unlock the door to her new self. She smiled at him and tried to keep her teeth from chattering.

He raised his hand to her cheek, then frowned when she shivered once more.

Somehow, in the space of just a few minutes, he'd whisked her inside and installed her in a comfortable armchair before a fire in a parlor he'd commandeered for her use.

"Fetch the lady a drink," Count Nikolai said to the footman he'd waylaid on their way inside. "And none of that wretched mulled wine, but something palatable."

"Very good, my lord." The man bowed and hurried away.

The old Eliana would have protested that it was improper to be alone in the parlor, then made some kind of bright remark to take the sting from her words. But she trusted Count Nikolai and the improbable, yet undeniable, connection she felt between them.

"I apologize for freezing you half to death," he said, going to poke up the fire. "I hope you don't catch a chill. Now, remove your slippers."

"You're quite imperious," she said, nevertheless bending to undo the laces of her footwear. Her toes *were* rather cold.

He dropped to his knees and gently drew off her slippers, and the feel of his hands on her feet made sparks tingle through her once more. He pulled a nearby footstool over in front of the hearth, then gently positioned her feet before the flames.

That a wary wolf would treat her so tenderly made her nearly swoon back in the chair.

"Thank you," she said, trying not to sigh the words.

Count Nikolai took the second armchair set before the hearth and gazed into the fire. His mouth set into a tight line beneath the mask, as though his thoughts had taken a grim turn.

"I hope you're not regretting that I granted your wish," she said.

"I don't regret that kiss in the slightest." His voice held a touch of coolness, however, that made her doubtful.

"You must think me rather forward, I suppose."

Although she had shared illicit kisses in shadowed corners with certain suitors, it never went further than that. None of those kisses, however, had made her feel the way Count Nikolai's had—as if her body were the wick of a candle, with a bright flame dancing upon it.

He turned to face her, and she wished she could pull off his mask and read his face.

"I'm only sorry that our brief acquaintance must end tonight," he said. "Under other circumstances, I believe we might have been friends."

His words were like a blow to the chest, and she sucked in a wounded breath. "Must it end?"

ANTHEA LAWSON

"Yes. I'll escort you back to the ballroom, and then I must take my leave."

Before she could ask why, or implore him to stay, the footman returned with a small glass of brandy.

"I hope this will suitable to your needs," he said, handing it to Eliana. "Will there be anything more?"

"Nothing more," she said. "You may go."

The footman bowed and left the room. She watched him leave, then turned to the count.

"What if the servants say something?" she asked.

"We are incognito," he said. "Almost no one in London knows me, or that I am currently visiting. Finish your brandy, and I'll escort you back to the ballroom in plenty of time to preserve your reputation."

"And then it will be farewell?"

"Yes." There was an implacable note in his voice.

For a mad moment, she thought of lifting her mask and introducing herself, of asking him to call upon her and see if, indeed, they could be friends.

But that was a fruitless notion. He'd already said he was leaving on the morrow, and that their time together that evening was at an end. She had enough self-respect not to throw herself at him, pleading that he stay a little longer. And how foolish was that impulse? She hardly knew the man.

Instead she took a quick swallow of brandy, then pulled her now-warm feet from the footstool and fished about for her damp slippers.

"When will you be returning to Town?" she could not help but ask. Maybe it would be soon, and they might further pursue their acquaintance.

"Never."

"Oh." She straightened and met his gaze. "I am very sorry to hear that, Count Nikolai."

Sorrow crept in under her ribs. Why did this man, who

148

seemed to enjoy her company without the knowledge of her name and reputation, have to leave London, never to return? The knowledge was a stone in her chest.

It wasn't fair.

"Life seldom is," he said, and she realized she'd spoken the words aloud.

"Well," she said, tying the laces of her slippers. She ducked her head so that he wouldn't see the foolish brightness of tears lurking in her eyes. "It was a pleasure to make your acquaintance, my lord."

"It was." He held out a stiff arm to help her rise and escort her from the parlor. "I won't forget you, Mademoiselle Red. Or this night."

"Neither will I."

Already the memory of him and their kiss lodged, bittersweet, against her heart. She feared it would haunt her for years.

CHAPTER FIVE

Damnation, he was an idiot. Sebastian escorted Miss Eliana Banning back to the ballroom, made her a low bow, and then left her there. He could feel her gaze burning his back, and he ruthlessly smothered the impulse to return and take her into his arms, to spend the rest of the night dancing with her, making her smile. Talking with her, which had revealed a deeper and more curious mind than he'd ever guessed.

What had he been thinking, kissing her in the garden? She'd nearly recognized him, and only the thick snowflakes had saved him from embarrassing discovery.

He clenched his fists and stalked down the hall to retrieve his coat and hat. The experiment of the masquerade was over, and it had cost him more than he wanted to admit to let his true self out for the evening.

"Good evening, my lord," the butler said, opening the door for him. A scatter of snow whirled into the entryway. "Would you like me to send for your carriage?"

"No need." He gave the man a nod, and stepped out into the snowy night. Only when he was well away from the house did he remove his wolf mask and replace it with his top hat and muffler.

In fact, he did not have a carriage waiting. The only one at his disposal was decorated with the royal Sayn-Wittgenstein coat of arms, so instead he'd paid for a hansom cab to bring him to the ball.

He could hail another one, but it was satisfying to be out in the snow. His greatcoat kept him warm, and his boots crunched through the thin coating of snow on the ground.

The gaslights were fuzzy blobs lining the street, and the sky held a luminous glow. He squinted up into the snowfall, which seemed endless, and a sudden wave of homesickness washed over him.

Not a yearning for the palace in Berleburg, though, but for his childhood, when life was uncomplicated and the winter holidays were a time of sheer delight. Before he'd been sent away to boarding school, and learned that showing joy—or any emotion— was a weakness worthy of pummeling.

Tonight, he'd let his guard down. He hadn't expected to, yet wearing a mask and shedding his title had allowed that boy inside him to peek out. To smile a little, and converse openly, and dance.

And kiss Eliana Banning.

If only he'd realized earlier that she was more than the empty-headed beauty she appeared, he would've attempted to make her acquaintance. But after the unfortunate mess with Lady Peony, it was far too late. Her opinion of Prince Sebastian was set, and if she learned how he'd deceived her tonight, she'd despise him even more.

He let out a frosty breath, a plume of frustration into the snowy night.

So, he'd had one night of stepping outside the shackles of princedom. It had been an enchanted fairy tale—one where the wolf sheltered in the warmth of Red Riding Hood's smile, and then let her go and went back to living wild and lonely in the forest.

The muffled clop of hooves alerted him, and the dark shape of a cab emerged out of the snow. Sebastian hailed it and climbed inside. No use tromping about in the snow any longer. The fairy tale was over.

Back in his rooms, Reece took his coat and hat, and shook his head over the condition of the mask.

"The damp is making the glued seams come open. What were you doing, your highness? Wearing the thing out in the snow?"

"Yes." Sebastian did not explain further. "Fix it up as best you can. And bring me a brandy. I'll be in my study."

He could tell that his valet wanted to hear more about his adventures at the Midwinter Masque, but Sebastian did not want to talk.

"Stop brooding," his sister used to say. "Really, Sebbie, you are such a lump of coal."

Then she'd tease him out of his mood, calling him all kinds of ridiculous names until he couldn't help but laugh.

But Mother had taken Margret and moved far away. And although he'd now been in London for over a year and saw both of them once a week at dinner, he'd never been able to reclaim that closeness. His sister mostly stayed quiet, while his mother let him know the constant, small ways in which he disappointed her.

Reece brought his brandy, and Sebastian took a drink, staring into the fire.

"She must be quite the woman," his valet said.

Sebastian glanced up. "What makes you think my mood has anything to do with a lady?"

"I know the look, your highness." Reece gave him a wry smile. "I've worn it myself a time or two. The question is, what are you going to do about her?"

Nothing, was his first impulse.

And yet, he'd give much to see Eliana Banning again. She made him feel simultaneously at ease and on fire with desire to know her better—body, mind, and soul. No other woman had ever elicited such a reaction from him. It had confused him into fleeing the ball—and confused him still—but perhaps he might have another chance.

Brandy burning in his throat, emotion like coals in his heart, Sebastian swallowed. "How long will this dye stay in my hair?"

His valet's smile deepened. "The color will hold another day or two before it begins to noticeably fade."

"Well then. I believe Prince Sebastian is going to remain ill for another day at least. See to canceling my appointments."

He wasn't certain what he was going to do, or how another day would matter in the end. All he knew was that if he let the sweet fire named Eliana Banning slip out of his life, he would regret it forever.

CHAPTER SIX

The next morning, Eliana blinked at the light filling her bedroom. She rose and went to her window seat, pushing the curtains wide.

Brightness covered the world. The snow had stopped, leaving a thick layer of white over the streets and shrubbery. Sunlight sparked off the frost crystals scattered on the snow, like diamonds stitched over the gauzy skirt of a ball gown. The sky was a bright blue—almost the color of Count Nikolai's eyes.

She leaned forward and sighed, her breath misting the glass. Must everything remind her of him? The more she tried not to think about the man, the more she could not put him from her mind.

As the snow sparkled outside her window, she considered what she knew of Count Nikolai.

He claimed to be from Kiev, though in retrospect she realized he'd never told her anything about his home. He had long-fingered, strong hands, and a certain way of carrying himself—an almost regal bearing. A wary, melancholy tone in his deep voice. Blue, blue eyes, and black hair. Tall enough that she had to tip her face up to kiss him. Sensual lips, and an embrace that simultaneously made her feel safe and dangerously alive.

Oh dear. This would never do. She could not spend the rest of the holidays pining away for a gentleman she'd met only once— and never really known at all.

"Good morning, Miss Eliana." Hetty bustled in, carrying a tray. "Heavens, back in bed with you! Your toes must be freezing. Here's your morning chocolate."

"It's not that cold in here," Eliana said. "The maid was in earlier to stir up the fire."

Still, she obediently climbed back between the sheets. Really, what could be better than a cup of hot chocolate in bed on a snow-filled morning?

Seeing Count Nikolai again, her traitorous mind whispered.

"I hope you enjoyed the masque last night," Hetty said. "I fear I was perhaps not as vigilant a chaperone as I ought to have been. I confess I lost sight of you for a time."

"I danced and tried the mulled wine and went into the garden with a few others to watch the snow fall," Eliana said.

"That wine!" Hetty made a face. "Really, Lady Entwhistle's cook needs to find a better recipe. Who did you go out into the garden with?"

Eliana took a sip of her chocolate to postpone answering. Hetty was too perceptive, despite her claims of being an unmindful companion.

"A group of young ladies," Eliana said. "And a gentleman named Count Nikolai."

Hetty's brows went up. "I don't believe I've met the man."

"Nor will you. He's leaving London today." No doubt he was already gone.

"Don't look so downcast, my dear. Perhaps he'll return soon. Now, what gown would you like today? The green wool?"

The next half-hour was spent in dressing and arranging her hair, and when Eliana went down to breakfast she felt somewhat restored.

The scent of freshly baked dough and cinnamon filled the

breakfast room, along with sunshine streaming through the windows. The warmth of the scene—her mother and father sitting at the table, cups of tea at hand, their hound Beatrice lying near the hearth—helped ease the tightness around Eliana's heart.

"What a fine day," her mother, Lady Blake, said. "Cook was inspired to make sweet rolls."

"A pity it doesn't snow more often," Lord Blake said, patting his stomach.

"Perhaps that's a good thing." Lady Blake gave her husband a look. He was overly fond of Cook's baking.

"A letter came for you early, my dear." Her father nodded to her place, where a cream-colored envelope sat beside her breakfast plate.

Miss Eliana Banning was written in bold handwriting, followed by their address.

"I don't recognize the hand," Lady Blake said.

"Neither do I." Eliana picked up the envelope.

Could it be from Count Nikolai? Her pulse sped at the thought.

She slit the paper open and drew out the short letter.

Mademoiselle Red, it began, and her heart pounded so loudly that Eliana was certain her parents would hear.

I admit I could not put you from my thoughts last night, and prevailed upon Lady Entwhistle to reveal who the lady in the red cloak was, along with your address.

I am writing to say that I am staying in London another day, in the hopes that we might meet again. Might I take you for a sleigh ride in Hyde Park this afternoon?

Regardless of your answer, I will call upon you at 1pm. I cannot depart town without laying eyes upon you once more, even if it is simply to have you send me on my way.

Yours most respectfully,

Count Bastian Nikolai

Eliana felt as though she'd swallowed a shard of sunlight—hot and bright and sharp. She re-folded the paper, her fingers trembling slightly.

"What is it, my dear?" her mother asked. "Is everything well?"

"Yes. I've received an invitation to go sleigh riding this afternoon."

"From whom?" Her father's voice held an edge.

"Count Nikolai of Kiev." Eliana cleared her throat. "I was introduced to him last night, at the ball. He seemed to be a respectable gentleman."

More or less. Rather less, if one counted the kiss in the garden.

Her mother's eyes widened slightly, as if she suspected Eliana was not being entirely truthful. "Do you want to go?"

"Oh, yes." Eliana suspected she'd spoken too quickly. "That is, it's a lovely day to go out, and the count is pleasant company. I believe. From what little I saw of him."

Blast it, she could feel her cheeks heating. She busied herself with pulling her sweet roll apart, though she did not think her parents were deceived.

Her mother let out a little cough that sounded suspiciously like a laugh. "If you say so."

"The gentleman in question will introduce himself to me immediately upon his arrival," Lord Blake said. "And Hetty will go out with you, of course."

"Of course," Eliana said, relieved her father wasn't making a bigger fuss about an unknown gentleman coming to call upon his daughter. Perhaps her mother was gently kicking him beneath the table. "I'm sure Hetty will enjoy the sleigh ride as well."

"From Kiev, you say?" Lord Blake let out a harrumph. "I fear the Russians are not the most trustworthy of allies. They're in thick with the Ottomans."

"I agree that the situation in the Bosporus is likely to turn unstable," Lady Blake responded, "but perhaps we might refrain from political discussion at the breakfast table."

"Don't mind me," Eliana said, and took a last bite of her sweet roll. "I need to make ready for Count Nikolai's visit."

It wouldn't take her three hours to prepare, of course, but she needed to escape before her parents thought up any more awkward questions that she could not answer.

CHAPTER SEVEN

"You're taking rather a chance, your highness," Reece said as he helped Sebastian into his greatcoat. "What if someone recognizes you?"

"I'll keep my hat low and my muffler high," Sebastian said.

Indeed, the very recklessness of it made his mind feel clearer than it had in months. He'd become mired in routine and expectation. It was beyond refreshing to break out, to feel like he was living life on his own terms, even if it were only for the space of one evening and one day.

He'd spent a restless night, unable to put Miss Eliana Banning out of his mind. At first light, he'd penned her a note and sent Reece to make sure it was delivered. Only then had he been able to sleep—a deep, revitalizing slumber that had left him feeling ready to face anything.

True, so far their interactions had been based on deception. But there was something more there, something he'd be a fool to ignore.

Or perhaps he was simply deluding himself.

Either way, he had to meet her once again, to be sure. He couldn't spend the rest of his life unhappily moldering away in

London. It was time for a change—and if Eliana Banning wasn't the change he needed, then he would bid his mother and sister farewell, and go back to Berleburg. He and his father disliked one another immensely, but surely there was something a royal prince might do, even if he was in the wrong line of the family to actually inherit the throne.

"The sleigh is waiting for you a block over, your highness," Reece said, following him to the back door. "I wish you well on your adventure."

Sebastian nodded his thanks. Perhaps he was acting like an idiot, but at least his blood was flowing, his steps strong and sure. His boots crunched over the snow as he strode to the gate set in the snow-encrusted brick wall and let himself into the alley.

As promised, the brightly painted sleigh waited at the end of the next street. A groom stood beside the horse, holding the reins and looking a bit chilled.

"I am here on behalf of the prince," Sebastian said in his Russian accent. "Please inform Lord Ramsey the sleigh will be returned by dusk, with his highness's due thanks."

"Good to see the contraption get some use, now that milord's children are grown and gone," the man said. He thumped the gray mare on the shoulder. "Be gentle with Belle. She's got a sensitive mouth."

"I will take good care of the horse and the sleigh." Sebastian gave the man a handful of coins, still warm from his pocket.

"Very good, sir." The groom bowed, then headed briskly back down the street, hands tucked in his armpits for warmth.

"Well then, Belle." Sebastian stripped off his glove. He let the mare snort her warm breath into his palm, then patted her soft nose. "Let us go courting."

Less than a quarter hour later, Sebastian pulled to a stop outside Lord Blake's town house. His heart thumped uncomfortably beneath the heavy wool of his greatcoat, but he took a deep breath of frost-scented air and willed himself to remain calm as he dismounted from the sleigh.

That fragile balance tipped the moment the front door opened and Miss Eliana Banning stepped out. Her golden curls spilled from beneath a winter hat of white ermine that matched her muff, and she wore a bright red pelisse, glorious scarlet against the white snow and subdued bricks of the buildings.

Without the mask, she looked less mysterious, and even more beautiful. It would be easy to believe there was little more to her than a pretty face—in fact, until last night, he had. Yet there was far more to Miss Banning than met the eye. And perhaps more than even she herself suspected.

"Good day, Mademoiselle Red." He swept her a low bow, then nodded at her scarlet coat. "You are living up to your name, once again."

"Hello, Count Nikolai," she said. "You found me out easily enough. Please come inside. Father wants to meet you."

"Ah." This was a complication he'd not expected. "Of course. Will someone—"

"One of the footmen will come out to tend the sleigh." She glanced at it, her eyes bright with anticipation. "It's lovely. Wherever did you get a sleigh on such short notice?"

"An acquaintance of my mother's is in possession of a number of unusual carriages and other vehicles. I thought of him this morning, and he was kind enough to lend me his sleigh."

"I thought you had no family in London?"

"She met him some time ago." Sebastian skidded over the truth. "Tell me, is your father a dragon that I must appease to win your company this afternoon?"

Her cheeks blushed a soft pink. "I believe most fathers are protective of their daughters. He wants to ensure that you are not a wolf, waiting to gobble me up."

Damnation. Her words made him want to scoop her off her

feet, toss her into the sleigh, and dash off through the snow in search of a secluded place where he might kiss her again.

"I told you last night, I am quite tame."

"Then you do not deny it."

"You are deliciously attractive, Mademoiselle Red, of that there is no doubt. But I am a gentleman."

The groom arrived at that moment, allowing Miss Eliana to turn away to hide the color in her cheeks.

"You ought to call me Miss Banning," she said, leading him up to the front door. "I told Father we were introduced last night. Did you truly pester Lady Entwhistle until she told you who I was?"

"I did indeed, until she revealed that the lady in the red cloak was a certain Miss Eliana Banning, youngest daughter of Lord and Lady Blake."

"What if she'd been wrong?" Miss Eliana flashed a smile at him. "You'd be in a bit of a pickle by now."

He feared he already was. There was no point in trying to conceal himself from Lord Blake, who was reputed to be a perceptive fellow. Any attempt at subterfuge would result in instant mistrust, and there would be no hope of driving out with Miss Eliana that afternoon.

Of course, revealing he was Prince Sebastian could well have the same result.

Assuming that she would not recognize him the moment he removed his hat and muffler, which he rather feared she would. Miss Eliana's intelligence was one of the reasons he was drawn to her, after all.

The butler opened the door, and Sebastian halted, catching her arm.

"I must make a confession," he said, dropping his faux-Russian accent. "I'm afraid I've deceived you, Miss Banning, and for that you have my deepest apologies."

The smile faded from her face, and her dark blue eyes

searched his. "What are you saying, my lord? You are not actually Count Nikolai?"

"I'm afraid not."

The butler cleared his throat and pulled the door a little wider. "Do come in."

He did not need to mention how rude it was to keep Miss Eliana standing on the front step in the chilly winter air.

Regret washing over him, Sebastian released her and gestured her to step inside. Well. He'd been a fool twice over, and now was about to pay the price.

He silently followed and removed his hat, handing it to the butler. The door closed, but the cold remained as Sebastian unwound the soft woolen muffler concealing his features. He was conscious of Miss Eliana staring at him, but could not meet her gaze.

He pulled his scarf away, and the silence was broken by her quick gasp.

"Prince Sebastian." Her voice was hard. "I don't know what games you think to play with me, but they are not welcome. Nor are you. Please take your leave, your highness."

"Miss Banning, please." He looked at her then, hoping for a glimmer of warmth in her eyes. "Let me explain."

Her gaze was frosty. "After making a laughingstock of Lady Peony last year, you thought to do the same with me? Were you hoping we would be discovered—"

"Ah, the mysterious Count Nikolai," a man called.

Sebastian looked up to see Eliana's father, Viscount Blake, stepping into the foyer. His jovial expression transformed to concern as he looked from Sebastian to Eliana.

"What is going on here?" Lord Blake asked. "Prince Sebastian, I'm not certain black hair suits you. Eliana, endeavor not to look so fearsome. Please, come into my study and explain."

Miss Eliana took a step back. "I have nothing to say to this man."

Her father's brows rose. "Even more reason I'd like you both to come. Now."

Feeling more like a chastised child than a prince, Sebastian followed Eliana and her father down the hall, catching only the briefest impression of wood paneling and gold-framed landscapes before Lord Blake ushered them into his study.

"Now," the viscount said, moving to stand before the hearth fire, "explain. Eliana, you may begin."

"He deceived me." She whirled and pointed at Sebastian. "How dare you attend the Midwinter Masque in disguise!"

Viscount Blake muffled something that sounded suspiciously like a laugh. "Isn't that the point of the ball?"

Sebastian squared his shoulders. "I knew the Ice Prince would not be welcome. In truth, I am weary of my own company of late. I did not intend to upset you today, Miss Banning. It is only that I wanted to see you again, without any unfortunate history between us."

"So you thought you'd just keep up the charade?" Her eyes flashed with anger. "That it was perfectly acceptable to continue to dupe me in order to enjoy my company? That, sir, will not stand."

"You are correct. It was very poorly done of me. Although revealing myself to you was bound to end badly—as this meeting amply demonstrates. Do you blame me for wishing to postpone that unhappiness a bit longer?"

She drew in a breath, ready, no doubt, to heap more scorn upon him, but Lord Blake stepped forward.

"Do I understand correctly, that you wish to court my daughter?"

"I did, sir."

"Well, I want nothing to do with you." Eliana sent Sebastian a narrow-eyed look.

"Lord Blake." Sebastian turned to the viscount. "May I beg a moment alone with Miss Eliana?"

"I don't believe you may." Lord Blake folded his arms, then looked from Sebastian to his daughter, then back, a thoughtful expression on his face. "But I think the two of you ought to gather up Eliana's chaperone and take that sleigh ride."

Eliana gave him a stricken look. "Father, how could you? I don't want to be seen consorting with Prince Sebastian under any circumstance."

"I'll wear my hat and muffler," Sebastian said. "Everyone believes Prince Sebastian is currently laid low by illness. As far as the *ton* is concerned, you'll be riding with Count Nikolai."

"But—"

"I wished to go out and enjoy the snow with a young lady whom I found to be both interesting and intelligent. Miss Eliana, even when you're angry, I believe I will still enjoy your company."

He gave her a deep look, trying to remind her that they'd shared more than just conversation the night before, but a kiss full of heat and passion.

She paused, and the color in her cheeks was not, perhaps, all due to anger.

"If I go sleighing with you, do you promise never to call upon me again?" she asked.

His heart clenched at the thought, but he made her a conciliatory bow. "Miss Eliana Banning and Prince Sebastian have never met. And after today, Count Nikolai will depart London forever."

"Very well." She swallowed. "I agree to a *short* sleigh ride."

"Then it's settled," Viscount Blake said. "Eliana, go fetch Hetty. I'll just have a private word with the prince."

She pressed her lips together and darted Sebastian a warning look. He responded with a small shrug. Whatever Lord Blake wished to speak to him about, he would not argue with the man, but of course he would not reveal their secret kiss, either.

As soon as Miss Eliana left the study, the viscount cleared his throat. "I can't say that I want to know any of the particulars, but it's clear my daughter has developed a fondness for you."

The words surprised a short laugh from Sebastian. "I'm sure you're mistaken. Miss Eliana clearly holds me in the lowest contempt."

"She'll come around, as long as you don't disappoint her any further." Lord Blake moved to stand before Sebastian, and fixed him with a penetrating look. "But that leads me to the point. What are your intentions concerning Eliana?"

Throat suddenly dry, Sebastian swallowed. He was unused to being so off balance. For the second time in a handful of minutes, Lord Blake had made him feel like a bumbling young man, not a confident prince. But unlike his own father, the viscount did not seem interested in grinding Sebastian into the dirt because of it.

"Well?"

"I had hoped to further my acquaintance with your daughter," Sebastian said warily.

Damnation, how could he explain himself to Lord Blake when he himself was not certain of his motivations? Acting on impulse was never a good idea—which was why he so very rarely did so.

"To what end?" The viscount raised his brows. Though his expression remained mild, his voice had taken on an edge. "I trust that you are acting as an honorable gentleman, your highness."

"Of course. I am not attempting to lead your daughter astray, Lord Blake, I assure you."

At least, not much. Sebastian wouldn't say no to another kiss from Miss Eliana, but the chance of that was about as small as a snowflake surviving the heart of a fire.

"Or break her heart in attempted revenge?" the viscount asked.

Sebastian blinked at the man. "I don't follow you, my lord."

Lord Blake leaned forward. "Surely you're aware that Lady Peony Talbot is Eliana's good friend. Perhaps you still harbor some ill will toward that young lady."

"You are more devious than I, to think of such a scheme," Sebastian said. "While I'm unhappy for the misunderstanding last year and am not overly fond of my subsequent nickname, I am not bent on revenge."

"Then you forgive Lady Peony?"

Sebastian blinked. Did the viscount suspect the truth about Lady Peony's lies? "How much do you know of what transpired? Was your daughter—"

"No. Eliana thinks the best of everyone. I don't think it occurred to her to question her friend's version of events. But others have, your highness, and draw a slightly different conclusion."

Sebastian let out a deep breath—one he felt like he'd been holding for the better part of a year. He hadn't looked for understanding from anyone, and his respect for Lord Blake's perceptiveness rose yet again.

"I could not make any accusations, of course," Sebastian said.

"I understand." Lord Blake reached over and thumped his shoulder. "You have my permission to court my daughter. Now, let us not keep Eliana and her companion waiting. This snow won't last forever."

CHAPTER EIGHT

Eliana could not believe how terribly Count Nikolai—that is, Prince Sebastian—had deceived her. The nerve of the man, to invite her for a sleigh ride, and think he could keep up his foolish pretense!

And she had kissed him.

Mortification heated her cheeks, even as the cold air swept over her face. The sleigh glided smoothly over the snowy streets, the horse's bridle jingling merrily, its hoofbeats a muffled thud over the hidden cobblestones.

Eliana had tried to insist that Hetty sit between herself and the deceitful prince as they went out to the sleigh. Her companion had shaken her head and pushed Eliana ahead of her to mount the low step into the vehicle.

"Think how it would look, miss," she'd said. "People will remark, to see you sitting on the outside, and you don't want that."

No, Eliana didn't. The less attention anyone paid to them, the better.

So here she was, settled uncomfortably close to the prince,

with Hetty on her other side. Taking up far too much room, in Eliana's opinion.

She'd told her companion everything—well, leaving out the kiss—and to her dismay, Hetty had found it very romantic.

The prince glanced down at her as they neared the gates of Hyde Park. "Will a quick turn about the park be amenable?"

"Certainly," Hetty answered, before Eliana could decline. "I imagine the trees look lovely, all covered in snow."

Eliana jabbed an elbow into her companion's side, and the older woman gave her a serene smile.

"I'll wave at all your friends," Hetty said, a pleasant note of warning in her voice.

Eliana blew out an annoyed breath. Her gloved fingers twisted tightly together, hidden in the warm recess of her ermine fur muff. She would endure this ride, bid "Count Nikolai" farewell, and then do her utmost to steer clear of Prince Sebastian for the rest of her life.

"Is it because of Lady Peony?" she asked the prince as he turned the sleigh down Rotten Row. "Is that why you perpetrated this lie?"

He glanced down at her, his eyes a paler blue than the sunlit sky above. "Only inasmuch as I knew Prince Sebastian would not be welcome at the Midwinter Masque, and I wanted to attend."

"So you could trick and entrap unsuspecting ladies." She did not blunt the edge of bitterness in her tone.

"I wanted to meet you," he said, the honesty in his voice taking her aback. "And I knew Miss Eliana Banning would never pass the time of day with the Ice Prince."

Hetty let out a little sigh, and Eliana was tempted to elbow her again.

"You are correct," she said to the prince. "I cannot condone what you did to my friend. She is only now beginning to recover from the heartbreak, and you damaged her prospects terribly."

He set his jaw, and did not speak.

To either side, the sun glittered off the snowy blanket covering the grounds. The bare tree branches were edged with diamonds. A few tracks from other sleighs and the pockmarks of bootsteps marred the path, but overall the park was very quiet. For several moments, there was nothing but the sound of the sleigh runners hushing through the snow.

"I regret that things fell out so badly between Lady Peony and myself," he finally said.

Eliana's anger flared once more. "Regret? You should feel far more than that, your highness. You should be ashamed and deeply remorseful. Indeed, you are well named, Ice Prince."

"Do you think so?" There was steel in his voice. "Did you find me so cold, last night?"

Oh, unfair. Despite herself, the memory of their kiss sparked through her.

"You were playing a part," she replied, trying to believe her own words.

"No. Last night I was myself, Sebastian Nikolai. It is all other days that I am playing a role." There was a depth of weariness in his voice that moved her, despite her irritation.

For a fleeting moment, she imagined how it must be, to always wear the mantle of a prince, an unwilling disguise few people cared to see beyond.

Last night, beyond their flirtation, Eliana had felt a true connection with Count Nikolai. Had he felt it too? He must have, for he'd risked his disguise to see her again

A cloud moved over the sun, and the air cooled. Another sleigh passed them, the laughter of the occupants ringing through the air.

Eliana did not feel like laughing. Weeping, perhaps, for what she'd glimpsed. For what could never be. Even if she'd seen the true Sebastian last night, that was only part of the man. The rest was still the Ice Prince, who had abandoned Lady Peony and thought nothing of deceiving Eliana. Such a man was not the kind of person she could imagine courting her, let alone sharing a life with.

"Turn around," she said, her throat tight. "I'm ready to go home."

SEBASTIAN KEPT his emotions clamped down as he turned the sleigh past the iced-over water of the Serpentine. His experiment was at an end, and it was abundantly clear Miss Eliana wanted nothing more to do with him.

Whatever connection he'd felt between them was gone, melted away as the snow would soon melt, to become just a damp memory of a single evening. He glanced at the white-laced trees, the frozen water boasting several skaters, the unbearably bright sunshine. Increasingly, it seemed time for him to leave London.

The thick silence that had fallen around them was broken by a shrill scream, followed by a woman's panicked cry.

"Help! Please help!"

"There." Eliana pointed to the bank, where a woman was waving wildly at them. Beyond her, a short distance out in the Serpentine, a small figure struggled.

"A child," Mistress Hetty gasped. "Fallen through the ice."

At the first cry, Sebastian had already turned the horse and slapped the reins. The snow churned under the mare's hooves as they raced to the water's edge. There were places where the Serpentine was not deep, but here, at the bend, it would be well over Sebastian's head.

Eliana glanced about, her eyes wide as the sleigh careened forward. "We are the nearest help, by far."

"How will we rescue him?" Hetty asked.

"I... I will go out on the ice to reach him." Eliana's voice shook. "Hetty, give me your cloak, and I'll throw it to the boy when I get close."

"No." Sebastian reined in the mare as they reached the distraught woman. "I'll go out."

"You can't." Eliana's face was very pale. "You're too heavy and will only break the ice further. I'm the lightest one of all of us. I must be the one to go out."

"Please, please save him," the woman said, tears glazing her face. "I told Theo not to go on the ice, but he's a willful boy."

"Don't fear," Sebastian said as he leaped from the sleigh. "We'll save him."

He turned to help Eliana, but she'd jumped out right behind him, Hetty's cloak bundled under one arm. Together they raced to the edge of the Serpentine, snow flying beneath their feet.

The boy was several yards out, his struggles growing feebler.

"We're coming!" Eliana called. "Keep your head above the water."

"Miss Eliana," Sebastian said, "I can't let you—"

"You must." Despite the terror in her eyes, she went to her knees and slowly began crawling out over the ice.

Damnation!

"Let me try." He took a step onto the frozen surface. It creaked menacingly, promising to plunge them both into the frigid water.

"No!" Eliana turned to him. "Please, Sebastian. I must go."

"Wait." He unwound the woolen muffler from about his neck. Disguise be damned. "I'll tie the end about your ankle, so that I can pull you back."

"Quickly." She scooted back onto the snow, casting an anguished look at the boy flailing in the small pool edged with broken ice. "We can't let him drown."

Part of him wanted to let the boy go, to selfishly hold her back and protect her from the dark, hungry water beneath the ice—but his better nature won out. Sebastian knotted the scarf around her boot, and a moment later she was crawling over the ice. He knelt, the end of the muffler wrapped about his fist. It went taut.

"I must go further," Eliana called back to him in a voice thick with fear. She was still at least two yards from the boy, who was gasping and whimpering.

"A moment." Grimly, Sebastian stripped out of his greatcoat and tied one sleeve to the end of the muffler. "You've more length now. Lie flat."

He took his own advice, carefully levering himself down and stretching forward on the ice. It was bitterly cold through the layers of his waistcoat and shirt. His chilled fingers clenched the tail of his coat.

Eliana scooted forward another yard, then lay down and slung Hetty's cloak out in front of her. It reached the jagged edge of the pool but was too far away for the boy to grasp.

Sebastian imagined he could feel the ice shivering with the strain of bearing their bodies. They did not have much time.

"Hurry," he said under his breath.

"I can't reach him," Eliana cried, panic in her voice. She shook her foot, where it was tethered to him by his clothing. "You must let me go."

Never.

If the ice broke, the water here was not impossibly deep. He'd have a few moments before the cold sapped his strength—enough time to haul Eliana back and throw her to safety. The boy too, fates willing.

His heart pounding with fear—not for himself, but for her—he slid out further over the frozen lake. She was so very brave.

"Here!" she cried, flinging the cloak forward again. "Yes, that's it! Hold tightly, Theo."

She began edging back, and Sebastian tugged his coat, trying to help speed her progress. They'd been on the ice too long, and it creaked loudly in warning. The boy slid free of the water, gasping.

Sebastian's boots slipped over the frozen surface as he tried to find enough leverage to pull them all back. His heart pumped frantically. A widening crack had formed from the hole Theo had made. It raced after the boy, as if the water would not let him escape.

Then someone caught his ankle and yanked, and he slid back far enough to get a toehold in the snow.

"Pull," Mistress Hetty said, yanking on his boot once more.

He did, scrambling backward and hauling on his coat sleeve. He prayed the muffler knotted around Eliana's ankle would hold.

It did, and she came sliding toward him, her hands clenched in Hetty's cloak. The boy clung to it, sodden and sobbing, but blessedly free.

The place she'd lain cracked into pieces, ice floating in the dark water. Sebastian caught Eliana about the waist, yanking both her and the boy to shore. Arms around her, he let them fall backward into the snow and held her tightly against him, trying to catch his breath, to calm his speeding pulse.

Mistress Hetty and the other woman grabbed Theo, and Hetty bundled him into her cloak. It was damp, but not as sodden as the boy himself.

Another hunk of ice shuddered free, licked by the cold waves of the Serpentine, but they were, all of them, safe.

Eliana shivered in Sebastian's arms, her face buried against his chest, her breath coming in short gasps. His heart was stunned with admiration at the courage it must have taken to face her fear and go to the boy's rescue.

And he had thought her flighty and vain.

"I've got you," he said softly into her hair. "It's all right."

"Oh, Master Theo," the boy's companion sobbed. "We nearly lost you. Whatever would your parents have said..."

"Hush now." Hetty patted the woman's shoulder. "We must get everyone warm. Prince Sebastian?"

He reluctantly let go of Eliana, whose breath was coming more easily now despite her shivers. Hetty helped her to her feet, and then he stood, brushing the snow from his sleeves and ignoring the murmurs from the crowd of bystanders who had gathered during the rescue.

If they recognized him, he no longer much cared on his own account. But he did for Eliana. They should be off as soon as possible, and not just because the lot of them were half frozen.

"Thank you." Eliana turned to him. "I couldn't have done it without you."

Tears glinted in her blue eyes, and he wanted to pull her close again. But now was not the time.

"You deserve all the credit," he said. "But we must get everyone inside. We could go to my mother's—it's closer than Banning House."

"My sister's is closer still," Eliana said. "Just off Hertford Street."

"We won't all fit in the sleigh," Hetty said. "I'll walk."

"You don't even have your cloak," Eliana said. "I will follow on foot."

"Everyone, to the sleigh," Sebastian said, glad to see that the mare had stood quietly through all the commotion. "No one is staying behind."

He caught up the cloak-wrapped boy, whose teeth were chattering so loudly that Sebastian could hear them clacking, and strode to the vehicle.

"Mistress Hetty, Eliana must perch on your knees," he said. "In you go. And then Theo's governess. What is your name?"

"Mrs. Pare," she said, sniffling. "My lord, my lady, thank you so much for rescuing him."

"He's not completely safe yet." Eliana climbed up to sit with Hetty. "We must ensure he doesn't catch a chill."

"All of us must take care," Mistress Hetty said. "Why, the prince is coatless, you were lying on the ice, I don't have my cloak, the poor boy is nearly frozen through... What a mess we're in."

Sebastian handed Theo up to his governess, then leaped into

the driver's side and took the reins. He had no notion how the Duchess of Ashford would take their arrival, but that didn't matter. Nothing did except getting the lot of them inside and next to a warm fire.

CHAPTER NINE

Eliana tried to control her shivering as the sleigh swept out of
Hyde Park. The aftermath of the rescue, and the danger she'd put
herself in, made her feel light headed.

The entire time she'd been on the ice, fear had been a fist at
her throat, choking her. But she'd made herself continue; one
hand, then the next, one knee, then the other. She could not allow
the boy to drown simply because she nearly had, years ago.

Though the moment she'd realized that she must be the one to
crawl out upon the frozen Serpentine had nearly paralyzed her
with terror.

Breathe, she'd told herself. *Don't think of the water waiting below.*

The only thing that had made it bearable was the solid, steady
presence of Prince Sebastian. He'd stripped off his muffler and
greatcoat without a second thought. If the ice had broken beneath
her, she knew he would've immediately plunged in to save her.

That knowledge had enabled her to move forward, gloved
hands slipping on the ice, air burning her throat, until at last she'd
been close enough to throw Hetty's cloak to the boy.

But the moment Sebastian had pulled her to safety, she could not stop imagining being trapped beneath the ice, with no air, and the dark water pulling her down...

"Turn here," Hetty said to the prince.

Eliana shook herself. The ordeal was over, and it was foolish to tangle herself into a useless knot of fear. She made herself take a deep breath—in, then out—and pay attention to their surroundings.

"It's the town house ahead, on the right," she told Sebastian. "That one, with the tree in the window." The sight made her feel a tiny bit better.

He pulled the sleigh to a stop, then jumped out and handed Eliana down. She wanted to cling to his strength. Instead, she turned and hurried up the walk, her boots slipping in the snow, and raised the lion's-head knocker on the front door.

It only took one rap before the butler opened the door.

"I'm sorry, Lewis," she said, "but it's rather an emergency. We pulled a child out of the Serpentine and he's chilled half to death."

Lewis, a staid old gentleman with a fringe of pure white hair, blinked at her a moment, then nodded.

"Of course, Miss Eliana," he said. "Come in. Take the boy to the front parlor. I'll notify Lord and Lady Ashford of your arrival, and send a groom out for the sleigh immediately."

"Thank you," she said, stepping into the house. The comforting smell of cinnamon and evergreens filled the air.

The prince followed, carrying an unconscious Theo, with Mrs. Pare close behind. Hetty brought up the rear, pausing a moment to speak with the butler.

"This way." Eliana led them to the first door on the left and held it open while Prince Sebastian strode through.

"Is he breathing?" Mrs. Pare hovered at the prince's elbow, gaze fastened on her young charge. "Oh, how I rue this day!"

Eliana followed them into the parlor and closed the door behind them. Thankfully, a fire burned warmly on the hearth. The tree in the window caught the afternoon sunlight. It sparkled with

bead ornaments and strands of silver tinsel, almonds wrapped in gold foil, and thin, creamy candles in polished tin clips, waiting to be lit.

The prince went to his knees before the fire and gently laid Theo on the rug. Eliana snatched a pillow from the nearby settee and tucked it beneath the boy's head, then smoothed his wet hair back from a forehead that was appallingly cold.

"Theo?" Mrs. Pare stripped off her gloves and took her charge's hands, rubbing them briskly between her own. "Wake up, my dear boy."

Eliana glanced at the tree, a glimmering blur behind the sudden tears in her eyes, and sent up a silent prayer to all the angels. *Please, let the boy live.* Next to her, Sebastian caught her gaze, his expression strained. The artificial darkness of his hair made his skin look pale.

"He's barely breathing," he said in a low voice.

She had no idea what to do. "Perhaps some spirits?"

"We must try."

She rose, then swayed as the room spun. Sebastian sprang to his feet, one arm going about her shoulders to steady her. Eliana let herself rest against him a moment, grateful of the support.

Of course, her sister would pick that moment to step into the room.

Her gaze went to Eliana, then moved to the prince, and her eyes widened. Eliana took a step away from Sebastian, but it was too late.

To her credit, Selene said nothing about that improper embrace.

"How is the boy?" she asked instead. "I've sent for the doctor. And his parents, thanks to Hetty discovering their direction from Mrs. Pare."

"He's not well," Prince Sebastian said. "Thank you for your hospitality, Lady Ashford. I know this was a bit sudden."

She waved one hand. "We're happy to be of assistance, your highness. Please, tell me what happened."

As Sebastian told her sister about rescuing Theo, Eliana moved to the sideboard. Hands shaking only a little, she poured out a measure of brandy and carried it over to Mrs. Pare.

"Come, love," the governess said, lifting Theo's head and coaxing him to take a sip. A bit of the liquid dribbled down from the corner of his mouth.

Eliana held her breath, hoping.

The boy swallowed, then coughed, his eyes flying open. He looked blearily around the parlor, then his gaze fixed on the sparkling tree.

"Did I die?" he asked in a weak voice. "Is this heaven?"

"No, my dear—you're alive, and in the Duke of Ashford's parlor," Mrs. Pare said, gathering him close.

Tears stung the corners of Eliana's eyes. Thank heavens. The angels had heard her prayers.

The doctor bustled in, followed by Hetty and the Duke of Ashford. After a brief commotion as their hosts took charge, Eliana found herself installed in an armchair by the tree, a cashmere lap robe draped over her knees.

Prince Sebastian sat across from her, his sleeves and waistcoat mottled with moisture. She realized they'd left his greatcoat and muffler at the edge of Serpentine.

Hetty joined Mrs. Pare on the settee, giving her comfort as the doctor knelt before Theo, making his diagnosis. The duke and duchess stood together, and Eliana noticed her sister's gaze resting thoughtfully on the prince.

"The boy will be all right," the doctor pronounced at last. "He needs to rest, and be kept warm, but already his color is better. I believe he will make a full recovery."

His governess let out a cry of relief, and Eliana sagged back into her chair.

Sebastian gave her a faint smile. "Well done, Eliana."

"We all did our part," she said.

"You risked the most," he said seriously. "I admire you a great deal for your quick actions and bravery."

Flustered, she turned her head to look at the Christmas tree. Now that she'd gathered her wits, she did not want Sebastian's admiration. And she most especially didn't want the warmth that his words brought.

"Prince Sebastian," Selene said, coming to stand beside Eliana. "Forgive my curiosity, but why is your hair dyed black?"

His mouth twisted. "A poor attempt at a disguise, I'm afraid."

Selene blinked at him. "In order to pay a call upon my sister?"

"Oh, heavens." Eliana grabbed her sister's skirt and gave it a warning tug. "Prince Sebastian is not courting me, so banish that notion from your mind."

Selene's eyebrows climbed.

"Even if I were," the prince said, "I fear Miss Eliana would not have me."

"That is correct," Eliana said. For some reason, her throat was tight. "I have excellent reasons for it, and for insisting you never call upon me again."

Sebastian's eyes darkened, and he gave a short nod.

"But—" Selene began.

"Shall we offer our guests some mulled wine?" the duke broke in.

"Of course." Selene shot Eliana a look that promised they would speak more on the subject. "Mulled wine is just the thing, and I had the kitchens prepare some right away. In fact, I think the footman is bringing it in now."

The air in the parlor filled with the scent of cloves and cinnamon as the man brought around a silver-chased tray bearing glasses of wine. Everyone took one, even the doctor, and Mrs. Pare shared hers with Theo, one arm wrapped about his shoulders.

Prince Sebastian glanced down at his cup, his expression set.

ANTHEA LAWSON

"Never fear, your highness," Eliana said in a low voice. "This is a superior version of the beverage you tried before."

Despite her attempt to remain unheard, her sister responded.

"Yes, it's an old family recipe. We use only the best wine and brandy, I assure you."

Eliana wrapped her hands about the warm glass and took a sip. The taste of the spices warmed her mouth, then spread, and she let out a low sigh. What an afternoon it had been. She wanted nothing more than to return home and crawl beneath the covers.

A doubtful cast to his expression, Prince Sebastian raised his glass and took a swallow. Eliana watched him closely. She had promised him it would not be dreadful, after all.

"What do you think?" the duke asked. "I confess I'm not a fan of the beverage myself, but the Banning family recipe is fairly palatable."

"Fairly?" Selene nudged her husband. "You used to tell me you found it delicious."

"It's the most delicious mulled wine I've ever had," the duke said. "Even if we were not married, I would take a cup."

Selene laughed, and even the prince looked amused.

"It is not unpleasant," Sebastian said, taking another drink.

"I like it very well," Theo piped up, and everyone smiled at him.

"The lad has a future as a diplomat," Lord Ashford said.

Near the edge of exhaustion, Eliana set aside her empty glass. Sebastian shot her a look, then rose.

"I believe I ought to take Miss Eliana and her companion home," he said. "Lord Ashford, if I might presume upon you to borrow a greatcoat? Mine seems to have been mislaid."

"Of course," the duke said. "We'll find something that fits."

"I should be going as well," the doctor said. "I'll call upon Master Theo tomorrow. At Plumley House, is that correct?"

"Yes," Mrs. Pare said. "I'm certain his parents will be here soon to collect us. Thank you so much."

"Good day to you all." The doctor bowed to the ladies.

Lord Ashford, accompanied by Prince Sebastian, ushered the doctor out of the parlor. Theo, now wrapped in a cozy blanket, went to admire the tree, while Mrs. Pare and Hetty conversed quietly on the settee.

"So, sister," Selene said, taking the chair Sebastian had absented, "whatever is going on between you and the prince?"

"Nothing." Eliana ran her fingers back and forth over the soft edge of her lap robe.

"It does not appear to be nothing. He looks at you like a man in love."

"That's a ridiculous notion!" Eliana shook her head sharply. "The Ice Prince isn't capable of such feelings. Remember what he did to Peony?"

Selene's eyes narrowed. "I know he appears to be in the wrong, but I thought the same thing of Jared. You must give the prince a chance to explain himself."

"There's nothing to explain."

"Eliana, I've never seen you like this. Are you quite certain you know your own heart?"

"Excuse the interruption," the butler said from the doorway. "Prince Sebastian wishes to inform Miss Eliana and Mistress Hetty that he waits upon their convenience."

"We can't leave him waiting in the cold." Eliana pushed the lap robe aside and stood, glad to end her sister's interrogation.

"This conversation isn't finished," Selene said.

Eliana ignored the warning note in her sister's voice. As far as she was concerned, there was nothing more to discuss.

"Thank you so much, Miss Banning!" Mrs. Pare rose and made her a low curtsey, tears still glinting in her eyes. "You saved Theo, and I'm certain his parents will call upon you to express their extreme gratitude. You certainly have mine, forever."

"I'm glad you were there to rescue me," Theo piped up, running over to hug Eliana around the waist.

She gave the boy a squeeze in return. "So am I—but it was a group effort. Prince Sebastian deserves equal thanks for pulling us to safety."

"Is he really a prince?" Theo blinked up at her. "Where's his crown?"

"You'll have to ask him that yourself, next time you see him. But for now, we must be going."

"I'll call upon you soon," Selene said, escorting them to the front door.

"I'm sure Mother and Father will be delighted to see you," Eliana said.

Her sister gave her a slightly exasperated look, while Hetty went to retrieve her cloak from the butler.

"You must forgive your prince," Selene said in a low voice. "Whatever he's done, you must discover if there was good reason for it."

"He's not my prince."

"And Jared wasn't my duke—but I forgave him his deception. Don't let this stand in the way of your happiness."

"There can be no happiness built on lies." Eliana turned to Hetty. "Are you ready?"

"Ready enough." Hetty brushed at her cloak, which still sported a large damp patch from its part in the rescue.

"At least it's not far to Banning House." Eliana, despite her irritation, kissed her sister on the cheek. "Thank you and Jared for your help."

"Of course." Selene clasped Eliana's hands. "Don't do anything irrevocably foolish."

Like kiss Prince Sebastian? Too late.

The air outside was cold enough to make Eliana's breath plume. Prince Sebastian waited at the curb to hand them into the sleigh, and soon enough they were off with a jingle of sleigh bells. She did not think she would ever find the sound particularly merry again.

As they glided through the streets of Mayfair, Eliana fought the temptation to lean against the warm solidity of Sebastian's side. Their adventures were at an end. And no matter what her sister might think, there could be nothing between them.

CHAPTER TEN

Sebastian was acutely aware of Eliana seated beside him on the sleigh bench. She held herself stiffly, and he wished, quite foolishly, that he might gather her against him.

But she would not welcome his attentions—she'd made that clear. For a short time, just after the rescue, he'd thought she was warming toward him, but that hope died when she'd told her sister he was unwelcome to call upon her. Her blue eyes had been frosty as he handed her into the sleigh.

"Well," Mistress Hetty said as they came to a stop in front of Banning House. Her voice held a note of forced cheerfulness. "Here we are. What an adventurous afternoon!"

"At least everything ended well," Eliana said.

Sebastian silently disagreed as he leaped down and went around to hand the ladies out. Yes, they'd rescued the boy, but he feared he'd lost his bid for Eliana's affections. How odd that not even two days ago he'd believed her to be a flighty, shallow young lady.

Instead he'd seen strength and bravery, and perhaps a touch of loneliness in her eyes that matched his own, strange as that might

be. And then there was the matter of that searing kiss, which had left him stunned.

A pity it had not appeared to affect Eliana equally in turn.

Mistress Hetty gave him a rueful smile as he assisted her from the sleigh. With a slight nod, she made her way up the walk, giving him a moment of privacy with Eliana.

"Miss Eliana?" He held his hand out to her.

She remained a moment in the sleigh, sunlight warm on her fair hair, her cheeks pink from the cold. He engraved that image in his memory—likely the last time he would ever be this close to her.

"Prince Sebastian, I trust you will be true to your word," she said. "I went sleighing with you and got rather more than I bargained for. Now you must honor your promise to never visit me again."

He set his jaw, biting back any words of entreaty. She'd made her choice, and he must abide by it. To ask her to reconsider would only make him appear even more the fool.

"Despite what you think of me," he said, voice clipped, "I will hold to our bargain."

She set her hand in his and stepped down from the sleigh. For a moment they stood there, hands clasped, gazes locked. His heart beat fiercely while words he could not say burned in his chest. Then she pulled away from him, chin high.

"Farewell, your highness."

"Goodbye, Mademoiselle Red."

Her lips parted, but she said nothing—only whirled and hurried into the house without looking back. The door closed with a solid thud behind her.

Sebastian folded his arms and stared blindly at the shrubbery beside the front door. So much for disguises, and adventure, and kisses. The day that had begun full of possibility had ended bleakly.

But not, he reminded himself, any differently than every other day for the past year. It didn't matter if he'd glimpsed a moment of light and warmth and acceptance in Eliana Banning's eyes. That was a mythic summerland where he did not belong.

He was, after all, the Ice Prince.

ELIANA HOVERED behind the curtains in the front parlor, watching Prince Sebastian as he stood unmoving before the sleigh. His expression was bleak, but she hardened her heart.

This was the man who had cruelly abandoned Lady Peony on the very night he'd promised to ask her to marry him. And, to heap insult upon injury, lied to and deceived Eliana. He did not deserve her sympathy, but her scorn. She was right to insist that he never see her again—no matter that her treacherous emotions tried to insist otherwise.

Still, she watched until the horse shook its bridle, rousing the prince from his thoughts. He lifted his head, his breath a plume of white in the air, then patted the horse on the shoulder and stepped into the sleigh.

Pulling the collar of his borrowed greatcoat closely about his features, he flicked the reins and was off. She tried not to sink into misery at the sight.

"Oh, my dear, what is the matter?"

Eliana turned away from the window to see her mother standing in the doorway. Lady Blake's blonde hair was swept up in an elegant coiffure, and she wore a blue brocade tea dress.

"I've had a taxing afternoon," Eliana said. "Not to put too fine a point on it."

Her mother went and settled on the sofa before the window, patting the cushion next to her. "Sit down and tell me. Does it have to do with the gentleman who called upon you today?"

Eliana sat beside her mother, trying to decide how much to reveal. Best that she begin with the most obvious event of the day.

"I must let you know that a Lord and Lady Plumley will be visiting at some point to thank me for helping rescue their son," she said.

"Heavens! What happened?"

Eliana recounted the events of the afternoon. Her mother gasped when Eliana described crawling out on the ice.

"It was extraordinarily brave of you," Lady Blake said, taking Eliana's hand and holding it tightly. "But you should not have risked yourself so."

"I had to. I was the lightest person there and had the best chance of reaching the boy without the ice breaking further."

"Your gentleman caller should have kept you from such danger. Count Nikolai—is that his name?"

"Yes," Eliana lied. "But he won't be calling again."

"He won't?" Her mother gave her a concerned look. "Your heart seems troubled by it."

"Not at all." Eliana's gaze went out the window, to the sleigh tracks disappearing down the street. "The gentleman in question isn't worth the heartache. Truly. I'm going up to rest now, Mother."

Lady Blake squeezed her hand, then let go. "I hope you trust your feelings in such matters. You know your father and I want only your happiness."

"As do I."

Mustering up a smile that felt merely painted on, Eliana left the parlor. She must believe that somewhere in the world was a gentleman who would love her. Not a wolf in disguise, or a deceitful prince, but a man of honor and integrity. Such a man she could give her whole heart to.

If he even existed.

CHAPTER ELEVEN

Sebastian leaned toward the mirror in his dressing room and turned his head side to side, examining his hair. The fair strands were overlaid with an ashen cast, the residue of the dye that his valet had assured him would wash out without a problem.

"My hair still looks odd," he said to Reece. "I'm not certain I should go out."

"You can't hide in your rooms forever," his valet said. "Look at the volume of correspondence you've received in the last three days."

"Mostly from my mother," Sebastian said dryly. "And you know very well I haven't been hiding in my rooms."

The day after young Theo's rescue, he'd visited the boy's family to make sure all was well. To be honest, he'd hoped to cross paths with Eliana, too, but she had already come and gone.

It wasn't breaking his word, he reasoned with himself, if he were to encounter her in the course of making social calls.

Nor was it breaking his word to stop at the finest jeweler on Bond Street and commission a pendant shaped like a delicate silver snowflake, set with a dusting of diamonds.

Don't be an idiot, the wiser part of him insisted. *She doesn't want to see you.*

He could not help but see *her*, however. She was constantly in his mind, waking and sleeping. His dreams ranged from heated recollections of their kiss to frigid nightmares where she plunged through the ice and he was helpless to save her.

"Perhaps another rinse with lemon juice will help, your highness," Reece said.

"If we must." Sebastian was due at the weekly family dinner soon, and if he did not make an appearance, his mother would be convinced he was on his deathbed. "I'll tell Mother the color is a lingering effect of the illness."

"I'll send down to the kitchens for more lemon juice and hot water," Reece said. "All in the name of your cure."

"Remind me not to trust you in matters of disguise again," Sebastian said.

With an inward sigh, he braced himself for yet another rinsing of his hair. He was beginning to despise the smell of warm citrus.

As EXPECTED, Sebastian's mother noticed his hair the moment he stepped into the foyer of her mansion and doffed his hat. He was not sure she believed his assertion that it was due to his supposed illness, but she did not dispute his claim, only narrowed her eyes and scolded him for being late.

At least he had the consolation of an excellent dinner—better than his own cook produced from the admittedly small kitchen of his bachelor's lodgings.

Sebastian might be a prince, but he did not see the need to occupy an entire three-story town house and keep a large staff—despite his mother's disapproval.

"Have you given more thought to taking other lodgings?" she asked as he escorted her into the dining room. "You must properly represent the monarchy of Sayn-Wittgenstein. There is a certain style royalty is expected to maintain."

"You do that well enough." He glanced up at the massive chandelier over the table, then at the rest of the gilt-encrusted dining room. "No one will think our family lacking in ostentation."

His sister Margret, already standing at her chair, sent him a sympathetic smile, but said nothing. Mother's opinions were impossible to sway.

As soon as they were settled at the table, the servants brought out the soup course; an excellent lobster bisque.

"What have you been up to this week?" Sebastian asked his sister—mostly to deflect the conversation away from his mother's constant critique of his life, but also because he realized he almost never asked her anything. Eliana would not approve of how distantly he treated Margret, of that he was certain.

His sister launched into a detailed report of the various balls and parties she'd attended, complete with impersonations that were quite good. Even Mother softened a bit when Margret did a fair impression of Lady Antwerp's rapid-fire monologues on the state of England.

"And did you go to the Midwinter Masque?" Sebastian asked.

"Goodness, no," their mother answered. "Not only is the company there too fast for Margret, that dreadful woman tried to entrap you there last year. No one in our family shall ever set foot at that event again."

She gave a delicate shudder, and Sebastian refrained from pointing out that she'd been most encouraging when he'd declared he was going to court Lady Peony.

An unfortunate choice, especially when a much better one had been standing next to her all along. He rued the day he'd dismissed Miss Eliana Banning as an empty-headed flirt and decided to pursue her friend, the supposedly dependable and worthy Lady Peony.

Throat tight, he took a swallow of his wine. There was no changing the past.

"Not to bring up too tender a subject," Mother continued, "but who are you courting now?"

"No one." He gave the same answer he always did.

It was still true—no matter that he could not banish the memory of Eliana Banning's smile. Not to mention her courage, and kindness, and beauty...

His mother sniffed. "Are there no ladies in London worthy of a prince?"

There might be one, but he would not say her name.

"Perhaps it's time for me to leave England," he said, partly to annoy Mother, but partly to say aloud what he'd been contemplating.

He could not continue on as he had been, that was certain. London held almost nothing for him except a disappointed mother and a sister he'd used to know.

And a young woman who might have been his future, had he chosen more wisely.

"Oh, Sebbie, don't," his sister cried. "We're finally getting reacquainted. I don't want to lose you again so soon."

Her words sent a pang through him.

"I'll return," he said. "I simply need a change of scene." And a town where he wouldn't be looking for Eliana Banning on every street corner.

"I'm sorry to hear it." His mother folded her napkin precisely and laid it on the table. "When you return, I hope you'll have grown up enough to take more responsibility in your station."

"I'm hardly a wastrel, Mother," he replied, stung.

"No." She fixed him with a hard gaze. "You are a prince and must act accordingly. Perhaps more travel will do you good. I see I was wrong to hope that you might wed an English lady and settle in London. You are not suited to it by temperament. Indeed, I'd venture to say you're as cold as your father."

"It seems so." He drew in a breath through burning lungs. "I will, of course, take my official leave of you before I go."

"I'd expect so." She rose and gave him a stiff nod. "You're excused from my table, Sebastian. I imagine you'd like to start planning your retreat from England as soon as possible."

Margret watched him dolefully, her eyes bright with unshed tears, as he pushed back his chair. Standing, he made them his most courteous bow, despite the anger simmering beneath his skin.

He did not feel cold. Rather the opposite.

"Good evening, ladies," he said. "I'll see myself out."

The butler was surprised by his sudden exit, and hastily sent for Sebastian's carriage to be brought round. Sebastian collected his coat, hat, and gloves, and declared he'd wait outside. He didn't want to stay a moment longer in his mother's mansion.

Once out in the fresh air, he took a deep breath, willing himself to calm. Overhead, the sky had softened to dove gray, and a few stars winked on the horizon. The gas lamps lining the street shed a cheery glow, illuminating the dirty snow and slush churned up by carriage wheels.

Yes, he would leave London. But he would not flee like a whipped dog, his tail between his legs. No matter what his mother said, he knew how to behave as a prince, and a man.

If Eliana could master her fear, then she deserved no less from him. Before he went, he would take his heart in his hands and tell Eliana Banning that he was in love with her, and the consequences be damned.

CHAPTER TWELVE

Although she usually enjoyed the yearly tradition of singing carols with her friends, Eliana was having a difficult time rising to the occasion. The only one who had seemed to notice that something was the matter was her brother, William, but she put him off by saying she had a touch of the stomachache.

After everyone gathered, they had sung at Banning House and, by special request, at the Plumleys', where young Theo looked to have made a full recovery. Now they were making their way to Lord and Lady Ashford's, where the afternoon of caroling would end with a small party.

"Did you hear?" Lady Peony said, her eyes bright. "Prince Sebastian is leaving London! Oh, what a blessed relief."

Eliana's heart clutched. "He is? Are you certain?"

"Yes. My lady's maid heard it from one of the servants at his mother's house. He announced it last evening at dinner, apparently. I suppose he thinks to leave on a heroic note, as some people seem to believe he was involved in rescuing a drowning boy in Hyde Park the other day."

"I've heard the same," Eliana said. "Do you think it was him?"

Peony waved her hand. "No, it was some gentleman with black

hair. But I heard you were there as well. Who is this mysterious fellow? You must tell me!"

"I shall, later." Eliana kept her voice light. "How soon is Price Sebastian departing, do you know?"

The news made her feel as though she'd swallowed a large stone.

Which was foolish, since she'd told Prince Sebastian to keep his distance. But with the prospect of his departure looming, she suddenly realized she did not, after all, want him to completely disappear from her life.

She was attracted to him, she could not deny it. Yet he was not worthy of her affections… was he? Could she possibly forgive him for what he'd done to Peony?

Yes.

The realization was like a bell rung inside her. She must.

Eliana's breath loosened in her chest, her thoughts unfurling like bright wings, ready to carry her dreams into reality. The cocoon had broken open, and she suddenly wanted to sing and dance in the middle of the slushy sidewalk.

Her sister had been right—it was better to forgive the man she suspected she loved than clutch bitterness to her heart and watch him sail away from her, forever.

"I believe the Ice Prince will be gone within the week," Peony said. "And I won't have to live with the fact that I… I mean, that he treated me so dreadfully."

Her words struck Eliana, pieces clattering together in her mind to make a picture she'd refused to see before. Yet she should have guessed.

She halted in the middle of the walk and grabbed Peony's arm.

Her friend gave her a concerned look. "Eliana, are you well?"

"No." Eliana let out a brief, mirthless laugh. Her entire perspective had tilted, and she did not like it one bit. "I must ask you something, Peony. Do you promise to answer honestly?"

"Of course." Peony set her hand over Eliana's. "We're bosom beaus. There are no secrets between us."

Eliana took a deep breath. "Did Prince Sebastian actually say that he was going to ask you marry him the night of the Midwinter Masque?"

Peony's face paled, and she dropped her hand from Eliana's arm. "How could you ask me such a thing, after everything I've endured?"

"I know it pains you, and I'm sorry. But I must have an answer. Did the prince promise you a betrothal?"

Peony darted a glance at their friends, who had paused at a chestnut seller's stand. The nutty aroma drifted through the air, mixing with the scent of smoke.

"We should catch up," Peony said. "Wouldn't a roast chestnut taste delicious?"

"You must tell me." Eliana dug her boots into the slushy snow.

The clues had been there along, and she suddenly felt like a fool for accepting what she now suspected were nothing more than lies. The truth loomed like a wave, poised to crash over her.

"He was going to ask me," Peony said, her voice strained. "I know he was."

Eliana closed her eyes briefly as the wave broke, drenching her with the cold, unavoidable realization that everything she'd believed about Prince Sebastian was untrue. She didn't need to forgive him—in fact, he should be the one to forgive *her*.

She'd treated him most unfairly, and he'd said not a word in his own defense—because to do so would have damaged Peony's reputation beyond repair. Instead, he'd taken the blame, withstood the barbed gossip, and endured being mocked as the Ice Prince.

Eliana had thought him a man of questionable honor, when all along he'd acted with the highest of motives. He was a gentleman indeed, and she had disdained him. The knowledge twisted inside her like a knife.

"So you lied?" she asked. "What did you hope to gain from it?"

"An offer of marriage!" Spots of color bloomed on Peony's cheeks. "And I did not lie, not precisely. I might have mentioned my expectation that the prince would soon ask for my hand, and wouldn't the Midwinter Masque be a romantic place to do so?"

"And who did you mention this to?" Eliana's patience with Peony was beginning to shred.

"Angelica Barrows." Peony shot a look at the young lady in question, who was currently accepting a roast chestnut from the vendor.

"She's a notorious gossip! Oh, Peony, how could you? It was very wrong to try and force the prince's hand."

"He led me to believe he was planning to propose." Peony's voice was thick with unshed tears. "It was not so *very* wrong of me. He could have seized the opportunity instead of leaving me to be the laughingstock of London."

Anger flared through Eliana. "He should have agreed to shackle himself to a woman who had just proved she was not above using lies and gossip in order to get her way? You ought to be ashamed of yourself."

"The prince behaved dishonorably," Peony shot back.

"No. *You* did." Eliana crossed her arms as the truth shook through her. "He could have denounced your lies and ruined your prospects forever. Instead he took the blame for 'abandoning' you, while refusing to give in to your manipulations."

Peony dropped her gaze to the dirty snow lining the street.

"I thought it would work," she said in a low voice. "Mother encouraged me to spread the rumor, so that I could call myself a princess sooner rather than later."

Her poor, weak friend. The misery in Peony's expression was unmistakable, and Eliana felt unwilling sympathy seep through her irritation. Peony's mother was a harpy, and Peony had never been able to stand up to her, even when she clearly ought to have.

Eliana unfolded her arms and caught Peony's hand. "I do

understand. I can see why you behaved as you did, though I can't condone it. But you must stop playing the poor, victimized lady. You see that, don't you?"

"I do. I meant to months ago, but…"

"It brings you too much sympathy." Eliana let out a sigh. She was deeply disappointed in her friend. And in herself, for believing the worst of Prince Sebastian when the truth had been in front of her all along.

It was little consolation that the gossips had not bothered to see past Peony's lies, either. They loved a good scandal, and the Ice Prince had been an excellent personage to fasten upon. It was a wonder he hadn't left London months ago.

"They're waving to us," Peony said, looking up the street to where their companions waited. "Please, don't say anything of this."

"I won't. But you should consider it. At the very least you might apologize to Prince Sebastian."

"I can't." Peony dashed a gloved hand across her eyes, swiping at her incipient tears. "Though I'll try to stop playing the wounded innocent."

"Good." Eliana squeezed her friend's hand. "Let's rejoin the others."

She dearly wished she could beg off singing at their last stop, but it was her sister's house. Despite the turmoil raging through her, she must make an appearance.

"I'm sorry, Eliana." Peony gave her a strained smile. "I felt terrible for lying to you for so long. And now I have a headache on top of everything."

"Do you wish to go home?" Eliana asked.

Peony shook her head. "Not yet. You need my voice to keep Angelica in tune. Though I imagine I'll leave the party early."

"Of course."

As they rejoined their friends and continued along the slushy Mayfair streets, Eliana couldn't stop thinking of Prince Sebastian.

He could not leave England! At least, not before she told him that she now knew the truth. If he wanted to depart after that, she would not blame him—but at least he would know that not every young lady in London held him in contempt.

Rather the opposite, on her part, though she would not confess the true depth of her feelings to him. He'd already been manipulated enough by the ladies of London. She didn't want him to feel as though she were attempting to entrap him into staying in England.

She would inform him that, should he ever want to return, he would be welcome to call upon her. That would be sufficient. And though her heart cried out for so much more, she stifled the impulse. She would not hold Sebastian back from his course.

These musings kept her occupied until they drew up in front of Ashford House. In counterpoint to the overcast afternoon, the candles on the tree were lit. It shone, magical and inviting, from the front parlor window.

Eliana and her friends arranged themselves in a semi circle before the door. William hummed the starting note, and they began with "Here We Come a-Wassailing." As they sang, she felt her spirits rise with the music. She could not remain wistful and melancholy while singing about love and joy.

Whatever happened now with Prince Sebastian, she must trust it would be for the best.

And so she sang, wholeheartedly, her clear soprano rising above the harmonies in the cool winter air.

CHAPTER THIRTEEN

Earlier that afternoon...

ONCE HIS MIND was made up, Sebastian tried to distract himself from thoughts of Eliana by throwing himself into his preparations to depart England. The prospect left him feeling half in sun, half in shadow, like a waning moon in the night sky.

On the one hand, it was high time for a change, to take his future in his hands and move forward. On the other, his heart was heavy with the mistakes he'd made in London, the might-have-been that had shone briefly in Eliana Banning's eyes.

At least he would see her once more. He hoped she would not spurn his gift of the snowflake pendant, though it now seemed a foolish gesture. Still, the necklace was finished and delivered, and he could not leave without some acknowledgement of what he'd glimpsed between them.

His first call of the afternoon, however, would be at Ashford House.

"The Duke of Ashford's greatcoat has been brushed out," Reece said, presenting him with the garment folded into a bulky bundle. "You could return it by footman, of course."

"I'll do it myself." Sebastian finished pulling on his gloves, then donned his hat.

"Very good, your highness." Reece's face was impassive, but his clipped words were disapproving. "Your carriage is waiting."

His valet was of the firm opinion that they ought to remain in London, and that Sebastian should court Eliana Banning until she agreed to be his wife. Sebastian had tried to explain why that was impossible. She'd made it abundantly clear she did not want to see him again. And when she did, he didn't expect her opinion of him to alter one bit.

"You ought to tell her the truth," Reece said. "Tell her you never promised to ask that other lady to marry you."

Ever since the debacle at last year's Midwinter Masque, Reece had refused to say Lady Peony's name aloud. It was both tragic and amusing to Sebastian.

"*That other woman* is Eliana's friend," he said. "Eliana would think I was defaming Lady Peony, and her mind would remain unchanged. The scene would be quite ugly, I assure you. It's better to say nothing of what transpired last year."

Under his valet's stony gaze, Sebastian pocketed the box holding the snowflake necklace, scooped up Ashford's coat, and headed out the door.

The sky was overcast, matching his gray mood as he stepped into his carriage. The driver set off for Ashford House, and Sebastian watched the streets of Mayfair pass outside the window. Now that he was leaving, he had to admit to a grudging fondness for the city. Where would he end up? Vienna, perhaps, or Paris? Or—he laughed bitterly to himself—Kiev?

He disembarked in front of the Duke of Ashford's town house. The tree in the window was lit, the candles glowing with warmth against the wan afternoon light.

The butler admitted him with a bow, accepted the return of

the coat, and directed Sebastian to wait in the parlor while he summoned Lord and Lady Ashford, who, it seemed, were both at home that afternoon.

The parlor was newly decorated with evergreen boughs and holly branches twined together with gold ribbons. A fire blazed in the hearth, and the air was suffused with the scent of cinnamon. A long table against the far wall held a warming bowl filled with mulled wine, and trays of sweets and candied fruits were set out to either side.

It appeared Lord and Lady Ashford were about to host a party of some kind. Well, Sebastian would give them his thanks and farewell, and be on his way.

While he waited, he inspected the tree. In addition to the beaded ornaments and gilded nuts, a few trinkets were tucked here and there among the branches. He spotted a tiny porcelain teapot, a miniature stuffed bear, and a carved globe, before his hosts made their entrance.

"Prince Sebastian," Lady Ashford said with a warm smile. "What a pleasant surprise. You're just in time for our party."

"I don't mean to intrude," he replied. "I only came to thank you both for your assistance the other day. And to tell you I'm leaving England."

"You are?" Lady Ashford's smile faded. "But what about Eliana?"

"I beg your pardon?" Sebastian blinked at her.

"You must forgive my wife," the duke said, slipping his arm around her shoulders. "She simply wants to see her sister happy, and somehow got the notion that the two of you would suit."

"I'm afraid we would not." Despite himself, Sebastian's fingers went to the small box in his pocket containing the diamond-set snowflake.

"Are you certain?" The duchess gave him a serious look. "I truly don't think you ought to leave London just yet."

"Darling, don't pester the man," Lord Ashford said. "If he feels he must depart, it's not for us to argue otherwise."

"Well." She gave her husband a look that Sebastian could not interpret, then turned back to him. "At least stay for a bit, your highness. We're expecting some carolers—it's one of our family holiday traditions. In fact, they should be arriving at any moment."

She moved to the window and looked out.

"I should take my leave," Sebastian said.

"Lord Ashford." His wife shot the duke a sharp glance. "Please presume upon our guest to remain a short while longer."

"Do stay," Ashford said with a wry smile. "Have a glass of mulled wine, at least. If I must endure the singing, then you should, too."

Sebastian let out a low breath. He was nervous about his next call, though he didn't like to admit it. But surely it would do no harm to tarry a little longer in Ashford's warm and cheerful parlor.

"Very well," he said.

Lady Ashford gave her husband a reproving look. "And really, my lord, the singers are not so terrible as that. It's the holidays! Where is your sense of cheer in the season?"

The duke went to his wife and kissed her on the forehead. "Standing right before me," he said. "I need nothing else."

She raised one hand and cupped his cheek. The raw emotion in the gesture made Sebastian's chest tighten, and he looked away.

"You've discomfited our guest, my dear," Lady Ashford said. "Give him that cup of wine."

"I'm afraid you're planning to discomfit him even further," the duke said, moving to the refreshment table.

Foreboding settled coldly on Sebastian's shoulders.

"Lady Ashford," he said. "Am I correct in thinking that your sister Eliana will be among the carolers?"

She cleared her throat. "Well, yes. And there they are now!"

The sound of singing rose in the air, and Sebastian glimpsed a half-dozen people gathered on the walk. Eliana Banning stood in the middle, her fair hair shining despite the clouds covering the sun. She wore her red pelisse, and Sebastian's heart thudded loudly in his chest.

"I promised Eliana I'd never see her again," he said tightly. Yes, he'd meant to break that promise, but not like this. "I would not want to upset her in front of friends and family."

"Selene," the duke said to his wife, a note of warning in his voice.

She firmed her lips, seemingly about to argue, then relented.

"Very well. Prince Sebastian, you may wait in the library until they are gone."

"Quickly." The duke inclined his head and led Sebastian out of the parlor and a short distance down the hall.

The front door opened and song echoed through the entry-way. *Love and joy come to you, and to you your wassail too...*

Unlikely, Sebastian thought, his pulse spiking as he ducked into the library just in time.

"I apologize for putting you in this situation," Ashford said. "I didn't realize you'd given your word."

"No matter. The entire thing is rather tangled."

The duke nodded. "Once everyone's safely in the parlor, I can send a footman to take you out the back, if you'd like."

It was a reasonable plan, and yet...

"Ashford," Sebastian said. "Might I speak plainly?"

The duke raised an eyebrow, but waved to a cluster of armchairs in front of the tall bookcases lining the room.

"Certainly," he said. "Please, sit."

Sebastian did so, and the duke sat across from him, his expression curious but not condemning.

"I have to confess," Sebastian said, "my next stop was to pay a call on Miss Eliana. And I'm afraid your wife is correct. Under other circumstances, her sister and I may have suited rather well."

Once again, regret twisted through him. If only he hadn't dismissed Miss Eliana Banning so quickly...

"What do you intend to do about it?" The duke steepled his fingers under his chin.

"Tell Eliana how I feel." The admission was difficult to make, yet it was also a relief to unburden himself to someone other than his valet.

"And then leave the country? What if she returns your feelings?"

Sebastian let out a short, bitter laugh. "She does not, I assure you."

"Hmm." The duke gave him a thoughtful look. "Even so, perhaps we ought to save you a visit to Banning House."

"That was my thought as well." Sebastian's heart could be wrung out in the Duke of Ashford's house just as easily as Lord Blake's. "Would you allow me to meet with Miss Eliana here for a few moments, when the singing is over?"

"I believe we might accommodate you." Ashford rose. "I'll have a word with my wife. Until then, make yourself comfortable."

"Thank you."

Chest tight, Sebastian watched the duke leave the room. Had he made a mistake, confiding in Lord Ashford? Perhaps he ought to quietly take his leave now, before it was too late.

No.

He was a prince and a man of honor. And, though it was like a knife to his heart to admit it, a man in love. It might make him the worst fool in creation, but he could not leave London without seeing Eliana Banning one last time.

CHAPTER FOURTEEN

Eliana's toes were growing cold before Lord and Lady Ashford appeared in the doorway, and when they finally did, Selene thought her sister looked a trifle discomfited.

"Come in," Lady Ashford said when the carol ended. "You may all sing more, of course, but the parlor is much warmer than standing about in the cold."

The singers doffed their coats, hats, and gloves, then trooped into the parlor, where the scent of mulled wine greeted them.

"Holly boughs." William nodded at the decorations. "I suppose we should sing 'Deck the Halls.'"

"A splendid idea," Peony said. "But I must take my leave soon."

Eliana glanced at the pitch-challenged Angelica, then back to Peony. "Three more songs, perhaps? Please stay that long."

Peony agreed, and the singers arranged themselves before the gloriously glowing tree and began with "Deck the Halls." After that, they launched into "I Saw Three Ships," and finished with "God Rest Ye Merry Gentlemen."

"That was grand," Selene said, applauding.

The duke joined her, and Eliana saw that Lewis and some of the maids and footmen hovered at the doorway. They added their praise as well, although the singing had not been *that* wonderful. Still, it was an honest and joy-filled celebration of the season, and there was something to be said for that.

"Please, everyone, make free with the refreshments. Lewis, serve up the mulled wine." Selene gestured to the table, then turned to Eliana. "Might I have a quick word with you in the hallway?"

"Of course." Eliana followed her sister into the hall. "Is everything all right?"

"Perfectly fine. It's just that there's something in the library I need you to fetch."

She gave her sister a curious look. "Can't you get it yourself?"

"Consider it in the line of a holiday surprise," Selene said, her expression rather more furtive than Eliana was used to.

"I don't want a puppy," Eliana said.

Her sister laughed. "It's not a puppy. Now go. I'll save you a cup of wine."

Brow furrowed, and a bit apprehensive, Eliana went down the hall and pushed open the library door. For a moment she saw nothing—and then Prince Sebastian stood from where he'd been seated by the bookshelves.

"Oh." She froze, the glass doorknob cold under her hand, uncertain whether to flee or stay. It was rather a shock to have him appear so suddenly, when she'd been thinking of him all afternoon; tall and blue-eyed, his hair finally returned to its normal shade.

"Miss Eliana, I know you weren't expecting to see me here. I beg a moment of your time, and then I'll be going."

The sound of his voice loosened her paralysis, and she stepped into the library, shutting the door behind her.

"Don't go quite yet," she said, then stared at him awkwardly.

Everything she wanted to say to him crowded into her mind at once, so that she was uncharacteristically incapable of saying anything at all.

He came to stand before her, his expression serious, and somehow that jogged the words free.

"Prince Sebastian, I must tell you—" she began.

"Miss Eliana, perhaps you've heard—" he said at the same time.

They both paused, looking at one another, and then he inclined his head.

"Ladies first," he said. "Unless you prefer that I begin."

"No need." Her nerves trembled, and she drew in a steadying breath. "I wanted to tell you that I was wrong to have thought so poorly of you. This afternoon I had a most enlightening talk with my friend Lady Peony."

He winced slightly at the name but said nothing.

"It's clear to me now that I—in fact, most of London— misjudged you, and I'm sorry for it." She swallowed, her pulse speeding. "I understand you're leaving England, and I can't say I blame you."

Stay! she wanted to cry, but forced herself to silence. She would not lay the burden of her affection upon him when he was bent on leaving.

He was silent a long moment, their gazes locked. Eliana was not certain precisely what she saw in his intense blue eyes, but it made her breath catch.

"Miss Eliana," he said at last, "I thank you for your apology, and your honesty. I owe you the same in return. Of course I knew who you were at the Midwinter Masque, though I pretended otherwise. I'd thought, due to your contempt of me, you'd be unlikely to suspect my ruse. And I think a part of me wanted to see who this golden-haired young lady was, whom all the eligible gentlemen hovered around."

"And what did you think of her?" Eliana trembled to hear the answer.

"I should have guessed there was a reason for your popularity, Eliana. You are intelligent and witty, interesting company, loyal, beautiful, and, above all, brave."

She gave a soft laugh. "I'm afraid of many things, I assure you."

"Such as?" He moved closer to her.

"Drowning, as you know. Growing old alone." She summoned her courage, imagining the fire of hope warming her from within. "Seeing the man I might come to love with all my heart leaving me, and England, forever."

He searched her face. "I thought you never wanted to see me again."

"I was wrong."

One more step, and he was standing directly before her. His hands went to her waist, and she set her hands on his shoulders. He looked down at her, lips curving into a slow smile, and she was lost in a storm of emotion—gloriously, desperately. Fearlessly.

She tipped her face up to his, and their lips met, warm and urgent. All the travails and worry of the past few days were swept away by a surge of heat and love, a sense of homecoming so strong that Eliana wanted to weep with joy.

Desire flared, too, and a keen awareness of his warmth and strength, a burning curiosity about how it might feel to press their bodies together, skin to skin...

"Ahem." Someone cleared their throat at the doorway.

Eliana jumped back to see her sister standing there, looking very much like she was trying not to smile.

"I see the two of you have reached an accord," Selene said.

"We have," Sebastian said. "It appears I will not be leaving England after all. At least not immediately." He reached into his pocket and brought out a lacquer box decorated with delicately painted snowflakes. "Eliana, I'd meant this as a parting gift. Now, however, I'd like it to be a promise. Of courtship. And of love. Will you accept it?"

She stared at the box, her mind whirling. Had Sebastian just told her he loved her?

"Wait." Selene stepped forward. "Shouldn't you speak with our father first?"

"As a matter of fact, I have. He gave me permission to court Eliana."

"He did?" Eliana stared at the prince. "I thought he was scolding you."

"Oh, he did that as well." Sebastian's lips twisted wryly. "But in the end, he appeared to think we would be good for one another. A sentiment it seems your sister shares."

"We are a sensible family," Selene said. "Though some of us are unable to see what's right in front of our noses."

"You're a fine one to talk," Eliana said. "Last year, you missed what was plain as day to everyone else."

Selene shook her head. "And this year it was your turn."

Eliana let out a low sigh, and Sebastian caught her hand in his.

"I stand here, still holding this box. It is yours, Eliana, if you'll take it."

His words were serious, and she understood that he was offering more than just a trinket. He was offering his future, and, she dared to believe, his heart.

"Yes," she said, her soul taking flight. "I accept."

He smiled at her then, an expression so genuine on his normally guarded face that she caught her breath. For the sake of that smile, she would do nearly anything.

"I hope your wish came true," he said, handing her the box.

She did not understand until she lifted the lid, to see a beautiful silver pendant glittering inside. A snowflake.

For a moment she was transported in memory to the snowy garden where Sebastian had first kissed her, the snowflakes swirling about them. She had wished then for someone who might love her for who she truly might be. *Loyal. Beautiful. Brave.* His words echoed in her mind.

"Yes," she said, lifting the chain. The snowflake spun and twinkled in the light, but not as brightly as Sebastian's smile. "I believe my wish *did* come true."

They gazed at one another for a long moment, blue and darker blue, like the day sky shading into night. He gently took the neck-lace from Eliana's hand.

"Turn around," he said. "I'll fasten it for you."

He brushed the hair from her neck so tenderly her knees went weak. When she turned back to face him, there was a warmth in his eyes she had never seen before. The Ice Prince had melted away, leaving only Sebastian.

"I love you," she said, her voice almost a whisper.

"And I love you, Eliana Banning." His expression burned with intensity. "I had not expected to, but I do. What's more, I intend to ask you to marry me, if you are willing."

"When, might I ask?" Thank heavens the Midwinter Masque was not an option.

He gave her a half-smile, as if reading her thoughts. "Does Christmas Day suit you, Mademoiselle Red? That will give me time to inform my mother and procure one of the Sayn-Wittgen-stein betrothal rings, along with her blessing."

"Will she give it?" Heavens, marrying Sebastian meant she must become a princess!

For a moment apprehension stabbed through her, but then she lifted her chin. She was brave.

And just as she'd known that Sebastian would not let her fall through the ice, she trusted that he would be there in the future, strong and steady, tying together whatever he must to keep her safe.

"Mother will be pleased I'm marrying an English lady," he said. "It's why she prevailed upon me to come to London in the first place, and now she will think she's won."

"Did she not?"

"No. I have won. Far more than I'd ever hoped." He leaned forward and brushed his lips across hers, heedless of her sister still standing in the doorway.

It was a spark, a reminder, light as snow against her mouth. It was a promise, sealed with a kiss.

"Well, that's settled," Selene said brightly. "Let's go back to the parlor and drink a toast. I'm certain my husband would like to know the outcome of this little meeting."

Smiling at one another, Eliana and Sebastian laced their fingers together and followed Selene down the hall; to the warmth and brightness of the front parlor, to the mulled wine and candles. To the place where snowflakes melted, and the rest of their lives began.

A NOBLEMAN'S NOEL

CHAPTER ONE

Lady Peony Talbot, the only daughter of Lord and Lady Minnerton, hated Christmas.

Indeed, she disliked the entirety of the winter holidays, beginning with the first hint of Yuletide cheer and ending with the celebration of the New Year.

Hate was a very strong word, she knew, and she was not a lady much known for the strength of her opinions. *Meek,* and *kind,* and *sweet*—that was how Society thought of her. *Weak,* the most uncharitable might even say.

She was sick unto death of it.

Which was, perhaps, why she exploded at teatime with the full honesty of her emotions.

"No," she said, setting her teacup down so forcefully that the liquid sloshed over the sides. "I have no interest in attending the Whittington's Winter Ball and attempting to snag Lord Corwin's affections. He is a shallow, greedy womanizer and I don't care if he will be a marquis. I can't stand the fellow."

Her mother gaped at her.

"But, Peony, your prospects—"

"Are shrinking every year." Peony forced the words out past

the lump in her throat. "I understand that, Mother, but your meddling is only making everything worse. Can't you see that?"

"I only want to see you settled. All the eligible gentlemen are being snapped up." Her mouth set in a thin line, Lady Minnerton dabbed ineffectually at the spilled tea spreading on the tablecloth. "You might have had a prince, if you'd an ounce of sense."

Cheeks heating, Peony glared at her mother. "Your interference caused that courtship to end in disaster."

"And then *you* allowed that scheming Eliana Banning to swoop in and—"

"Eliana is my best friend, and I'll not hear another word!" Peony stood and tossed her napkin down on the table, heedless of the servants' wide eyes. "You know as well as I that she believed the lies about Prince Sebastian for an entire year. She deserves every happiness with him. They both do—no thanks to me."

Sudden tears pricking her eyes, Peony whirled and sped for the safety of her rooms, where she might cry in private.

Everything was wrong, and she could not deny her own guilt. Part of her had *known* that trying to trap Prince Sebastian into marriage was a terrible idea, but her mother's voice had been too loud. As had Peony's own fears.

But she was done with such games and maneuvering. She would attend the Winter Ball, but she most assuredly would not be involved in any schemes centered on maneuvering some gentleman into marriage.

"Can you reach that spot, Will?"

William Banning's mother handed him a bag of gilded almonds, then pointed to a place high in the branches of the evergreen tree currently dominating their parlor.

Two year ago, when his older sister had introduced the notion of Christmas tree to the Banning household, he'd thought it a ridiculous idea. But now, helping his mother decorate the fragrant green boughs, he admitted he was becoming a fan of the tradition.

"It's looking so festive," his mother said, echoing his thoughts. "A pity neither of your sisters are here to help this year."

Will made a noncommittal noise, hoping to stave off the next topic.

"You know, marriage seems to suit them both." She wound a gilt ribbon about the lower portions of the tree, then handed it to him with a significant raise of her brows. "I think it's high time you considered the idea."

Drat. Marriage was the last thing he wanted to discuss.

"I'm perfectly well as I am," he said.

"You might think so, but your father and I would like to see you settled, and with an heir, before we get too much older."

"You're scarcely tottering into your dotage." He gave her a fond smile. "There's plenty of time for me."

She sent him a scolding look. "That's what you think—and then, suddenly, it's almost too late."

"There's no one I'm interested in marrying." He tied off the ribbon at the top of the tree, then snagged a leftover bag of almonds to snack on.

"Truly?" His mother cocked her head. "What about Angelica Barrows?"

"Her?" He could not help his puff of laughter at the thought. "She's a notorious gossip, and couldn't carry a tune in a bucket."

Brow creasing, his mother offered up several more names, all of which he found laughable. Finally, when she mentioned Lady Peony Talbot, he could take no more.

"Stop," he said. "You're going to make me choke on these almonds. Lady Peony? I've known her since she was a little girl."

"All the more reason. She is yet unmarried, and she's a sweet, kind young lady."

"She's a silly birdwit. I don't know why Eliana likes her so much."

"Because she's loyal and puts the needs of others above her own."

Others—like her harpy of a mother. He didn't say the words out loud, however.

"I don't think I'd like to have Lady Minnerton as a mother-in-law." He popped the last almond in his mouth. "At any rate, I must be off. The tree looks lovely."

"Some day, Lady Peony will stand up to her mother, and make up her own mind about things." Cleary, his mother was not to be swayed from the topic. "Then perhaps you'll see the light shining from beneath her bushel."

"Perhaps." Though he rather doubted it.

He brushed a kiss across his mother's cheek, then donned his hat and greatcoat, and strode out into the chilly, rain-swept afternoon.

Lady Peony Talbot, a suitable wife? He shook his head. Certainly she had the breeding for it, being an earl's daughter, but she was such a goose.

Pea-brain, he'd used to call her. Oh, but that would enrage her. He recalled her chasing him around and around the willow tree at their country estate—which bordered her family's—brandishing a stick and threatening to whack him until he apologized.

The memory made him grin. Funny, she'd had a bit more spark when she was a girl. Something about growing up into a proper young lady had quite smothered it. Or maybe it was that mother of hers. He'd no doubt Lady Minnerton had been behind the debacle at the Midwinter Masque two years ago, when Lady Peony had all but announced her betrothal to Prince Sebastian.

An announcement which turned out to be unduly premature— if it were even true at all—and had resulted in the gentleman in question withdrawing abruptly from Lady Peony. Will had felt distantly sympathy for the man, who had borne the resulting slights of the *ton* with an icy façade.

Will had been sorry for Peony, too. Since she and his sister

Eliana were bosom beaus, he'd heard her side of the story several times. And while he hadn't taken Peony's innocence at face value, as his sister had, he'd not doubted that Lady Peony's heart had been bruised, if not trampled upon.

Not that the state of her heart was any concern of his.

"Will!" His friend Lucas Atwater hailed him.

Will paused at the top of the steps of their club and waited for Lucas to catch up.

"Dreadful weather." His friend backed into the doorway and shook his umbrella vigorously.

"Isn't it?" Will squinted into the rain. "I thought I'd warm up with a glass of brandy, and hear the news. Join me?"

"Of course."

The two gentlemen divested their wet outer garments into the keeping of the staff, and were soon seated beside a cozy fire, brandy at their elbows.

"Have you heard the latest about Corwin?" Lucas asked.

"I hope he hasn't duped some young lady into becoming his wife at last." Will said. "I pity the girl who ends up in his clutches."

"Word is his father's requiring Corwin to marry and produce an heir by next Christmas, or the inheritance goes to a distant cousin."

"It's not entailed?" Will's brows went up. "No wonder the fellow is getting desperate."

"Well, he hasn't much time to procure a wife and get her with child, that's for certain." Lucas shook his head in mock sympathy.

Will took a swallow of brandy. "His standards are ridiculous, which isn't helping his cause."

"Thus the parental pressure, I'm guessing," Lucas said. "Last I heard, though, Corwin is still insisting he won't settle for less than a duke's daughter."

Dry amusement mingled with the aftertaste of brandy on Will's tongue. "Short of pulling some lady magically out of a hat, I've no idea where Corwin thinks he'll find such a girl."

"Pride and ego before a fall, and all that." Lucas waggled his fair brows. "But tell me, William-boy, are your thoughts tending to matrimony yet?"

"No." Will made a face. "But my mother's are."

"Didn't both your sisters get engaged during the winter holidays? They've started a bit of a tradition, seems to me. Can you blame your mother if she believes it's your turn now?"

"Well, she's wrong." Will finished his brandy and refused to think of Lady Peony Talbot. "Are you going to Whittington's ball tomorrow?"

"Of course." Lucas patted his pocket. "I've a bit of mistletoe that might come in handy."

"Still chasing Miss Basingstoke, are you?"

"Neither of us are weary of the game," Lucas said. "Heaven forbid I ever catch her, of course. Unlike a fish, I'm afraid I won't be able to throw her back."

"You may court danger, if you like." Will rose and beckoned for his coat and hat. "I personally intend to stay far away from even the slightest whiff of matrimony."

CHAPTER TWO

Peony stepped into Lord Whittington's ballroom, her mother at her side, and cast a quick glance at the assembled crowd. She hoped to see her good friend, Eliana, of course—but was less eager to encounter Eliana's husband, Prince Sebastian.

She owed him an apology, and it had taken the better part of the year for her to screw up her courage to do so. This holiday season, she would do her best to make amends for wronging him. But...perhaps not quite yet. Her emotions were still unsettled from arguing with her mother, who simply would *not* drop the subject of Lord Corwin.

"Look." Lady Minnerton jabbed her with a quick elbow. "There's Lord Corwin near the far wall, in the dark blue coat."

"I told you," Peony said between gritted teeth, "I want nothing to do with the fellow."

To her great relief, Eliana chose that moment to appear; and to her even greater relief, Prince Sebastian was not accompanying her.

"Dear Peony, how fine you look this evening." Eliana kissed her cheek in greeting. "What a lovely shade your gown is. It quite sets off your complexion."

ANTHEA LAWSON

"Thank you," Peony smoothed the satin skirts of her teal-colored ball gown.

Though vanity was unbecoming in a lady, she had to admit the frosty blue-green did suit her pale skin and dark hair.

"It is a singular color," Lady Minnerton said. "I've never seen such a fabric, but Peony insisted she must have a gown made from it."

"An excellent choice." Eliana gave Peony the barest wink. "Come, I want to introduce you to someone. If you'll excuse us, Lady Minnerton?"

"Of course." Peony's mother waved her fan at them, already turning away to find her own friends.

"Thank you," Peony said once they were a fair distance away. "She was beginning to drive me mad. But who are you taking me to meet?"

"Sebastian's sister, Princess Margret, will be here tonight. She's barely been out, and I was hoping you might help keep an eye on her."

"In penance?"

"Only a little." Eliana's mouth twitched. "Margret is very sweet, and both Sebastian and I worry about her ability to navigate the currents of Society. Although her dragon of a mother will be here to keep her out of trouble, as well."

Peony couldn't help raise her brows. "You like your mother in law that well, then?"

"Oh, I mean it in the most complimentary way." There was only the lightest touch of irony in Eliana's voice. "Sebastian said they'd be arriving about now. Oh, there they are."

Prince Sebastian's fair hair shone in the light of the gas chandeliers, his tall form unmistakable as he strode though the crowd. For a moment, Peony felt a pang of regret for the chance she had lost.

Then Eliana greeted her husband, and the joy in both their eyes made the last of Peony's jealousy fall to ashes. Eliana and

224

Sebastian were far happier together than she could ever imagine herself being.

"Lady Peony." Prince Sebastian made her a very correct bow. "Allow me to introduce my sister, Princess Margret."

He gestured to the young lady behind him. When she stepped forward, Peony's heart wilted with dismay. The princess's dress was the exact same color as her own.

Such was the punishment for vanity.

"A pleasure to meet you, your highness," Peony said, making her a curtsy. "I must say, I admire your taste in gowns."

Princess Margret burst into laughter, a genuine peal of amusement that helped ease Peony's disappointment.

"Lady Peony, may I say the same! I am full of delight to meet another lady with such an excellent sense of fashion." Margret gave her a conspiratorial grin, and Peony felt her resistance melt away.

The princess was nothing like her brother, who had earned the nickname the Ice Prince for his cold manner. Although Peony had to admit that had partially been her fault. Very well, more than partially, if she were being brutally honest.

"Eliana," she said in a low voice. "Might you lend me your husband for the next dance?"

It was past time she made her apology.

Eliana's look was thoughtful, as if she could read Peony's intentions.

"Of course," she said. "I'll make sure he asks you."

Prince Sebastian introduced his mother, who did not seem as fearsome as a dragon, though she wore a haughty expression. Clearly the woman did not think too highly of London Society. It was easy to see where her son had gotten his icy gaze.

The string orchestra on the dais struck an introductory chord, and Prince Sebastian straightened from where his wife had been whispering in his ear.

"Lady Peony, would you favor me with this dance?" he asked.

Though she'd been expecting it, her throat was suddenly dry with apprehension.

"Certainly." She swallowed and set her hand on his arm.

As he led her to the dance floor, murmurs shivered in her ears and curious gazes pricked her skin. Chin high, she ignored them. If she refused to let her mother dictate her behavior, she would not let the gossip of the *ton* bother her, either.

Though it was difficult. She'd always been an accommodating girl, and it felt strange to turn about and swim against the tide.

Strange, but somehow freeing.

The music started—a lively polka—and Peony took a deep breath.

"Prince Sebastian," she said as they bobbed from side to side, "I owe you an apology."

One of his fair brows twitched slightly upward. "I assure you, there is no need—"

"Oh, but there is," she said in rush. "I treated you abominably, and have regretted it for nearly two years now. Please know that I am so very sorry about what happened."

He said nothing for a moment as they whirled in a turn, and Peony's heart quailed. Was he going to withhold his forgiveness? She couldn't blame him, for she certainly had done nothing to deserve it.

"I'll make amends to you," she said. "I swear it. I'll announce to everyone here that our so-called betrothal was all a ruse on my part."

"There is no need." He gave her a slightly grim look. "I have already suffered, on both our behalves. Your reputation remains intact, Lady Peony. Please do not jeopardize it."

The reminder that he'd borne the brunt of the gossip made her guilt flare.

"I wish there was something I might do."

"Let the past go. Everything has worked out for the best." He looked up, his expression softening.

Peony followed his gaze to see Eliana laughing with her dark-haired sister. Perhaps Prince Sebastian was right, and it was better to let the memories of that awful Midwinter Masque fade from everyone's minds.

"I suppose we're doing well enough in moving forward," she said. "After all, we're dancing together."

"And I am glad of it." A faint smile curved the corner his mouth. "My wife is most desirous that you and I be, if not friends, then no longer seen as enemies. For her sake, I will cross any number of bridges."

"Thank you." It seemed there was nothing more to be said.

Still, she could not help the small current of discontent running through her. Yes, he'd accepted her apology, but it was not enough. She'd hurt him, she realized that now, not only his reputation, but the man himself. But there was nothing else she could think of that would make amends.

The polka ended with a turning flourish, and he bowed over her hand. "Thank you for the dance, Lady Peony. And the apology."

"It was the least I could do, your highness." She curtsied low, relieved that they'd reached an accord. Letting time heal the wounds would have to suffice, she supposed, no matter how unsatisfactory it might feel.

As they returned from the dance floor, Eliana enveloped them with a joyous smile, and the sight of her friend's happiness eased Peony's mood. In truth, she did feel a bit lighter. It was good to know she would no longer have to skitter away like a mouse whenever she and Prince Sebastian were in the same room.

William Banning stood beside his sister, and she saw nothing but approval in his dark green eyes. Despite herself, Peony felt a blush rise in her cheeks. She tried to stuff down her reaction to Will—after all she'd managed to do so for several years now—but the evening had scraped her emotions so raw, she felt everything keenly.

Especially her long-simmering, and equally long-denied, attraction to her best friend's brother.

There was no point in it, of course. Will had always thought her foolish, and Peony refused to enforce that impression by declaring her feelings. When she was younger, she'd convinced herself it was a fleeting infatuation on her part, nothing more, and for a time she'd managed to believe it.

But after the debacle two years ago, she'd found herself thinking of Will a bit too often, looking forward to dancing with him at the various balls where they were both in attendance, standing near him during the Banning's yearly carol-singing event.

He'd been unfailingly kind to her. Alas, kindness could never be confused for romantic affection, and so she'd said nothing. Always careful, Peony had given no indication of her feelings, to anyone. Eliana might—*might*—understand. Or she might not.

Now, Peony's heart did a silly flip flop in her chest as Will held his hand out to her. One lock of his dark brown hair fell across his brow, and she forced herself not to reach out and brush it back into place.

"Care to dance?" he asked, his tone light.

She tried to keep her smile demure as she set her gloved hand in his. "I'd be delighted."

CHAPTER THREE

Will led Peony onto the dance floor, then grinned at her as the orchestra struck up a waltz.

"Do you remember trampling all over my toes, the summer our families took dancing lessons together?" he asked, taking her in the semi-embrace of the dance position.

She fit perfectly in his arms, just as she always had, though he'd never given it much heed until that moment. Of course he and Lady Peony Talbot would dance well together, after suffering through the tortures of the strictest dancing master in the land.

She gave him an innocent look. "I believe it was you who stepped on *my* feet, William Banning. You were always an ungainly lad."

The last was quite untrue, and they both knew it. He laughed at her and spun her into a turn, trying to catch her off guard.

No luck. And why hadn't he ever noticed how bright her hazel eyes were, how sweetly curved her full-lipped mouth?

"You are quite lovely tonight, Lady Peony," he said. "I don't think I've ever seen a dress of that exact shade. It suits you."

A mischievous smile tugged the corners of her mouth. "Haven't you? Princess Margret's is the very same color."

"It is?" He blinked at her. "I don't believe it. Surely hers is a plainer green."

Peony looked up at him, eyes twinkling. "I notice you took the first dance with her. That was kind."

"She seems a sweet girl, if a bit sheltered." His amusement faded. "I see she's dancing now with Lord Corwin. Do caution her against the fellow, when you get a chance."

The mirth faded from Peony's expression, and he was sorry to see it go.

"I don't like him," she confided, leaning a bit closer.

Her nearness made heat flare through him, and he gave himself a shake. Good gad, he could not seriously be attracted to Lady Peony Talbot. Could he?

"You're wise to trust your instincts," he said, hauling his attention back to the conversation at hand. "I don't think his intentions are honorable."

She bit her lip, a habit he remembered from childhood. "I'll tell her."

"Good."

To wipe the troubled look from her face, he spun them into an intricate series of steps, only half-remembered from that excruciating summer.

"Left," Peony murmured, just as he was about to step to the right.

Nimbly, he changed his direction, and they did not end up crashing into the Duke and Duchess of Ashford. Who would not have scolded them too terribly, seeing as how Lady Ashford was his sister, Selene.

She raised a dark brow at them as he and Peony swept past, and he recalled how Peony's older brother had, in fact, left dusty footprints all over Selene's best dancing slippers.

"Do you remember the time your brother and I decided to teach ourselves to joust?" he asked.

"I remember having to read aloud to him and play endless card games after he broke his leg. He was not a happy invalid, and declared it quite unfair that you hadn't broken anything."

"Does your family still go back to your estate every summer?"

"Mother and I do. Your place is rather quiet, though, now that both your sisters are married. I miss their company in the neighborhood."

"But not mine?" He could not help but tease her.

"Oh, everyone in East Winch breathed a sigh of relief when you left, Will."

"Wretch." He grinned at her, to show he didn't mean it.

He'd nearly forgotten how much fun it was to tease Peony and see her expression light up with equal parts irritation and amusement. She was too sober for her own good.

Of course, having Lady Minnerton for a mother didn't help.

The music slowed, and he sent Peony into one last spin. She navigated it gracefully, not a single dark hair out of place, though her cheeks were becomingly flushed.

"That was grand," he said, meaning it quite sincerely.

"Yes. Thank you." Her gaze met his.

Will's pulse sounded loud in his ears as he stared into Peony's eyes. Lady Peony Talbot. Whoever would have thought it?

"Peony." Eliana rushed up to them in a swirl of amber-colored skirts, and the moment was broken. "Have you seen the princess?"

"No." Peony's worried gaze swept the room. "I thought she was dancing."

"She was. With Lord Corwin." Eliana sounded grim. "We must find her. Will, I count on you to assist us."

"Of course." He glanced at Peony. "We'll take the hallway to the left of the ballroom."

Eliana nodded. "Sebastian is outside, searching the gardens. I'll send Selene and Jared down the other hall. Quickly, now."

Trying not to appear as though they were hurrying, Will took Peony's elbow and they made their way through the crush of people on the dance floor. Finally, they gained the ballroom's entrance and they emerged into the hall. Peony took a deep breath.

"I'll check the doors on this side," she said. "You take the ones across."

He gave her a short nod, and she pivoted and went quickly down the hallway. Will began pulling doors open. In short order he discovered an empty parlor, a linen closet, and a dusty library, but there was no sign of Princess Margret.

PEONY SPED DOWN THE HALL, the plush carpet muffling her steps. She'd neglected to take into account the fact that there were no doors on the left hand side for quite some time, as the ballroom took up much of that wing of the house.

At last she reached the first doorway, and flung it open. The smell of old tobacco and leather reached her nose, and in the dim light she identified it as a study. No one was there.

The music room was next, also empty. The third room held an array of potted plants, a scattering of sofas... and someone weeping behind the curtains.

Peony stepped inside and waited a moment for her eyes to adjust. She should have brought a candle. As soon as she could see well enough to navigate the furniture, she moved toward the lump of person hiding behind the drapery. There was barely enough light to see the telltale hem of a ball gown peeking from beneath the curtain; a gown that was the precise color of her own.

"Princess Margret?" Peony asked. "Is that you?"

The sobbing stopped, but the princess did not emerge. Peony went to the curtain and held it open, to see a red-eyed Margret huddled behind it.

"Whatever are you doing here? Are you well?" Peony stepped forward and laid her hand on the princess's shoulder.

"Oh, Lady Peony, I am so glad to see you," Margret said, sniffling. "I am sorry to say it, but Lord Corwin is not a gentleman."

"What did he do to you?" A spurt of anger heated Peony's blood. "Did he hurt you?"

"No—but he kissed me against my will! I slapped him, and then ran away."

"And you were right to do so. Why did you not come back to the ballroom?"

"I look a fright, and Mother would give me such a scold if I appeared like this. I needed a moment to… compose myself."

Peony thought it would take more than just a moment for Princess Margret to restore her composure.

"Come, I'll take you to the ladies' retiring room," she said.

"I do not want anyone to see me like this," Margret said woefully.

"I'll make sure no one is coming."

Peony extracted herself from the curtains. She was halfway across the room when the door flew open.

"There you are," a hard voice said.

A second later, she was wrapped in the strange gentleman's arms, and he was kissing her. It was not a very pleasant kiss. She struggled to get free, but he held her fast.

Fear coursing through her, she bit him. He jerked his head back, and the clock began to chime the hour.

"Curse you," he hissed. "You won't get away this time. And if you bite me again, I'll hit you, mark my words."

She drew in a breath to scream, but he lowered his head to hers, stopping her mouth with his own.

A babble of voices in the hall, then light flared as someone lit the lamp beside the door.

"Oh dear!" a woman's voice cried. "What is this?"

"I'm afraid we've caught them in a compromising position." That was a man's voice, and he sounded rather smug.

The fellow holding Peony let her go and stepped back, a

triumphant smile on his face. She blinked, aghast to see it was Lord Corwin.

His gaze focused on her face, and his expression transformed to shock.

"Where is she?" He leaned forward, his voice a low, angry whisper. "What have you done with the princess?"

Peony only glared at him in reply.

"What's the meaning of this?" Their host, Lord Whittington, shouldered to the front of the gawkers. "Lord Corwin? And, good gad, is that Lady Peony Talbot?"

"It is," she said in a clear voice, her mind racing.

It seemed obvious that Lord Corwin had engineered the whole scene, planning to ensnare Princess Margret. Forced into impropriety, the girl would have no choice but to marry the lord who had compromised her virtue. It was only sheer luck that, in the dimness, Lord Corwin had seen only the hue of Peony's gown and taken her for the princess.

Peony shot a quick glance at the curtains, praying Princess Margret would show a shred of sense and remain hidden.

"I presume you are prepared to do the gentlemanly thing?" their host said, turning his cold gaze on Lord Corwin. "I do not take kindly to scandal beneath my roof."

"Of course." Lord Corwin seemed to have recovered. His arm around Peony remained as hard as iron. "It has always been my intention to marry Lady Peony."

Oh dear heavens! She could not let this mockery stand. And yet, if she denied him, Princess Margret would be in danger. The thought of that innocent soul bound to a cad like Lord Corwin made Peony's skin crawl. At least she had a few skills at her disposal to help her manage the fellow, as well as stalwart friends who would not abandon her. But other than her family, Princess Margret was quite alone in London.

Agreeing to this sham was, Peony realized with a stab of cold truth, the one thing she could do to repay Sebastian. Somehow, she would find a way out of this terrible situation—but for now, her agreement would protect the princess's reputation.

"Lady Peony?" Lord Whittington turned to her. "Is this true?"

"I—"

"It is not!" William Banning thrust his way forward, and Peony's heart rose. "I'm afraid, Lord Corwin, that she cannot marry you."

"Why not?" Lord Corwin's lips twisted in a sneer. "Everyone saw us embracing."

"I did not. And I'll thank you to remove your arm from about my betrothed's waist. You see, just this evening Lady Peony agreed to marry *me*."

Peony stared at him, her mind whirling, and Will returned her gaze, urgency burning in his eyes. He was clearly trying to save her from Lord Corwin—but could he?

So far, Princess Margret had remained behind the curtains, and it would look very bad for Lord Corwin if he tried changing his story—and the purported object of his affections —now.

"She's damaged goods," Lord Corwin said, though he did remove his arm. "Are you certain you want a lightskirt for a wife?"

Peony took a hasty step away from him and searched Will's expression. He was risking his own good name for her.

The determination on his face never faltered as he reached and took her hand.

"Peony," he said. "Whatever happened here, I'm certain you are not at fault. And Lord Corwin, if you touch my fiancée again, I'll call you out—you may be sure of that. Now, if you all would excuse us."

Amid the murmurs and speculative looks, Will guided her to the door, then paused at the threshold.

"May we use your yellow parlor, sir?" he asked Lord Whittington.

"You may." Their host raised his hand. "The rest of you, please return to the ball. There's no need to stand about and gawk. After you, Lord Corwin."

With effort, Peony kept herself from glancing at the curiously lumpy curtains. She would have to trust that Princess Margret continued to show good sense, and would be able to remove herself from the room without mishap once everyone left.

Will bent close to Peony.

"Are you all right?" he asked in a soft voice.

She nodded, her head still spinning with the events of the evening. "We must speak of this."

"Of course."

He led her down the hall and opened a door across from the ballroom—Lord Whittington's yellow parlor, she presumed.

She went to the settee in one corner, while Will coaxed a flame from the amber-shaded lamp on the nearby table. Light bloomed, and Peony stared at her gloved hands, trying to marshal her thoughts.

The cushion dipped as Will settled beside her, but she could not look at him He didn't love her, she knew that as clearly as the stars in the sky.

"Thank you for rescuing me," she said. "I won't hold you to the engagement, of course."

"Of course. But it was the only thing I could think of in the moment. Were you able to find Princess Margret before that cad assaulted you?"

"Yes." She gave him an ironic smile. "She was hiding in the curtains the entire time."

"She was?" Will released a bark of grim laughter. "I'm glad she didn't jump out and make matters worse. Clearly, Lord Corwin was trying to force her into marriage."

"And I stumbled in and ruined his plans."

"Yes." His expression grew darker. "We've both made an enemy of him, today. Be careful, Peony."

"I shall. And I pray Princess Margret treads lightly, as well."

"She ought to, if she's got any sense at all." Will cleared his throat. "I expect we should go find your parents and inform them of our happy news."

Peony's breath pinched in her chest. Her mother would be delighted to hear of the engagement, no matter how it had come about. And when the betrothal was broken, her disappointment would know no bounds. Quickly, Peony stuffed down the treacherous knowledge that her own despair would be even worse.

"I hope this solution isn't entirely unpalatable to you," Will said. "There wasn't time to do anything else."

"Of course not." She mustered up a smile. "Considering the situation, this is the best outcome that could be hoped for. Though I never expected to end up betrothed by the end of the evening."

"Neither did I." He shook his head. "At least we both know it's not real—though I suppose we'll have to keep up the pretense through the holiday season. After the New Year you can cry off, and no harm done."

Except to her heart.

And her reputation. Two broken betrothals would not reflect well upon her. But she would not quail when the time came. She would not force Will to keep a promise he never meant to make. Better she end up a spinster in truth than married to a man who did not want her.

CHAPTER FOUR

Will stared into Peony's bewildered eyes, trying to wrestle his thoughts into coherence. When he'd heard Lord Corwin's false claims about her, he'd acted on rage and instinct. He could not stand by and see his sister's friend coerced into marrying one of the most vile men in the *ton*.

And, he reassured himself, the betrothal was only temporary. They only needed to maintain the sham for a month or so, and then life would go back to normal.

"There they are!" Peony's mother, Lady Minnerton, swept into the room, followed by her husband.

Eliana followed at their heels, along with Will's parents. The expressions on their faces ranged from hope to disbelief

He quickly rose and bowed to Peony's father, his heart sinking to his boots at the displeasure evident on the man's face.

"What's this?" Lord Minnerton asked, his voice like stone. "How dare you presume upon my daughter's affections, you impertinent—"

"Father!" Peony jumped up, an imploring look on her face.

"Now see here." William's father, Lord Blake, stepped forward, his hand palm up. "Let the boy speak for himself."

Will shot his father a look. He felt older than he ever had, and quite removed from boyhood.

He turned to the Earl of Minnerton with a brief bow. "I apologize for the haste with which I declared myself to your daughter. The events of the evening demanded it, however. May I have your blessing?"

"You may n—" The earl broke off with a grimace, and Will suspected his wife had just stomped hard upon his foot.

"Will has secretly been courting me," Peony said, threading her arm through his. "You all know we've been friends since childhood."

Eliana sent Peony a sharp glance, then transferred her gaze to Will. Questions burned in her eyes, and he prayed his sister would hold her tongue.

"I understand that Lord Corwin attempted to secure Lady Peony's hand tonight," Lady Blake said.

"Thus forcing my own." Will gave his mother a strained smile. "Not that I feel forced in any way in my affections for Lady Peony. I was planning to ask her to marry me at Christmas. In keeping with the family tradition."

"Ah yes." Eliana arched an eyebrow. "The family tradition."

"Whatever was Lord Corwin thinking?" Lady Minnerton asked. "I never took him for a scoundrel."

"Perhaps you should have," Peony said, a bitter edge to her voice. "At any rate, that unpleasantness is behind us. I'd rather concentrate on the future."

"Of course." Peony's mother clasped her hands in excitement. "We have a wedding to plan!"

Peony's expression froze, and Will felt a stab of alarm.

"Surely there's no need for haste," he said.

"A springtime wedding," Lady Minnerton continued, paying him no heed. "In the cathedral. Wouldn't that be lovely? Just think of the flowers. Narcissus and iris. Or, better yet, hyacinths."

The earl cleared his throat and glanced at his wife. "Before you go about planning the nuptials, my dear, I believe I have a few items to discuss with Lord Blake and his son."

"But you do give your blessing." It was more a command than a question.

A sour look upon his face, Lord Minnerton gave a grudging nod.

"William and I will call upon you tomorrow afternoon," Lord Blake said. "If that is amenable to everyone?"

"It is," the earl said.

"Yes." Will would be a fool to ignore the warning in his father's eyes. Despite Lord Blake's mild tone, there would be a reckoning ahead.

And not only with his parents. The gleam in Eliana's eye bespoke a mountain of questions. Of anyone, though, she would be the person to confide in. He had little doubt that Peony would tell her the truth, too.

They could use her help with their subterfuge, he had to admit. Having Eliana as a co-conspirator was not necessarily a bad thing. His sister had always been a clever one.

"Are you ready to go home?" Lord Minnerton turned his stern gaze on his wife and daughter. "I think we've had enough excitement for one evening."

"Certainly," Lady Minnerton said. "Peony and I have so much planning to do."

Looking slightly ill, Peony nodded to her father.

"Peony." Will caught her hand and gave it a squeeze, trying to infuse her with strength. "May I call upon you tomorrow morning?"

"Yes," she said, her expression clearing a little as she met his eyes.

They would manage to get through this. Somehow.

As soon as Peony and her family left the room, Eliana rounded on Will.

"What are you doing?" she demanded. "If you're simply toying with Peony's affections, I swear I'll make you sorry."

"Gentlewomen don't swear," their mother said in quiet rebuke. "However, I am inclined to agree. Whatever were you thinking, William?"

"I was thinking to save Peony from being shackled to Lord Corwin for life," he said, suddenly angry with the world. "I'd like a bit of respect for that, please."

"It was well done," his father said, his expression thoughtful. "Eliana, stop staring daggers at your brother. I'm certain his solution makes the best of a bad situation. And we all know that Peony is a sweet girl. You could do worse."

"However did she let a cad like Lord Corwin entrap her?" Eliana asked. "She has more sense than that."

"You'll have to ask her." Will wasn't about to divulge secrets that weren't his to share—especially not in front of his parents.

"Where is the prince?" he asked.

"With his family," Eliana said. "His sister is not feeling well."

Will gave her a pointed glance. "Perhaps you ought to rejoin them."

She'd hear the full story from Princess Margret soon enough, and Eliana would give the girl good advice—namely, not to breathe a word of tonight's events to anyone beyond their immediate families.

"Perhaps I shall." Eliana shot him a look full of menacing promise. "We're not done talking about this."

Will swallowed his irritation. His life had suddenly become complicated beyond reason. All for the sake of Peony Talbot.

"What kind of flowers does she like?" he asked, suddenly desperate not to muck things up even further.

Eliana paused on her way out the door. "Not peonies. Far too many people have thought it clever to give her a namesake bouquet. Beyond that, use your wits, Will. It's not my job to woo Peony Talbot for you."

241

With that, she sailed out of the room, leaving him feeling prickly and defensive. Which was absurd. He'd rescued Peony, after all. Why should *he* be the one made to feel as though he'd done something wrong?

"Don't fret." His mother patted his hand. "You've been acquainted with Lady Peony for years. I've always thought the two of you would suit."

"You have?" He blinked at her in surprise.

"You might have forgotten what a charming, lively girl she was, but I did not."

Charming and lively—hardly how he'd describe the current meek incarnation of Lady Peony. And yet, his mother's words recalled his own thoughts while he and Peony had been dancing.

"What changed her?" he mused, then realized he'd spoken the words aloud.

"I don't like to speculate," Lady Blake said. "But the weight of her family's expectations would crush a hardier soul than hers."

"Nonetheless," his father said. "You have proclaimed your intentions publicly, Will. You must go through with the match, or you'll leave Lady Peony worse off than before."

Stung, Will glanced at his father. "I'd never cry off. I hope you know that. You've raised me to be a proper gentleman."

His mother set her hand on his arm. "Of course we have."

"Then don't doubt me. If anyone ends our engagement, it will be Peony herself. And now, I bid you both goodnight. It's been a long evening."

He bowed to his parents, then spun on his heel. The music from the ballroom drifted down the hallway, but he had no desire whatsoever to remain a moment longer at the Whittington's Winter Ball.

CHAPTER FIVE

Gray winter light filtered through the tall windows in the Earl of Minnerton's parlor. Peony wished the sun would shine—but at least it was not raining. She tried to remind herself to be grateful for such things.

Like the fact that she was betrothed to Will, and not Lord Corwin.

"Excuse me, ladies," the butler said, bowing at the parlor door. "Mr. William Banning is here to see Lady Peony."

"Show him in," Peony's mother said.

As soon as the butler left, she turned to Peony with an encouraging smile. "Don't forget, darling, that although he is merely Mr. Banning at the moment, he will inherit the title of Viscount Blake."

"I'm not overly concerned about such things," Peony said. She was beyond weary of her mother's constant harping on status and suitability.

"Well, you ought to be." Her mother's tone was snappish. "Despite what the rest of the people in this house might think, such things are of great importance."

Peony drew in a breath, resolving not to argue with her

mother over the matter. Lady Minnerton had come from a family on the barest edge of the nobility. Catching an earl for a husband had been the triumph of her life, and she was ruled by the fear that Peony would throw away the status of her birth and marry beneath her.

At least Will was acceptable in her mother's eyes. Barely.

It would be the worst betrayal, when Peony ended up unmarried. Thank goodness she had an older brother to keep the family name alive and well. He had married two years ago, and Peony was hoping that there would be grandchildren soon, so that her mother might be distracted from constantly trying to manage Peony's life.

Will stepped into the parlor, carrying a bouquet of hothouse lilies. They shone like little stars, clear yellow and orange, and the sight of them made her smile.

"Good day, Lady Peony," he said, holding the flowers out to her. "I brought you some lilies."

"Thank you. That was most thoughtful." It was, indeed, a kind gesture.

She was equally grateful they weren't peonies, or the type of lily that overwhelmed the air with their cloying scent. No, these were bright and straightforward—a bit like Will himself.

"Lady Minnerton." Will inclined his head. "I hope you are well this morning."

"Well enough," she said. "I'm still recovering from the shock of last night."

Peony tried not to roll her eyes at her mother's theatrics.

"Indeed." Will bowed over her outstretched hand. "It was an eventful evening."

"Sit." Lady Minnerton indicated the chair beside her. "Peony and I were just discussing the specifics of your wedding."

They had not been, and Peony sent her mother a wordless glare. There was no better way to frighten Will off completely than to raise the spectre of their upcoming nuptials.

Indeed, a hint of panic showed in Will's eyes.

"Sit by me," Peony said, moving over so there would be room for him on the low settee. "And don't worry about the details. Mother and I will take care of such things."

Lady Minnerton's mouth pinched in at the edges. "I hope you've brought a ring, at any rate."

The panic in Will's expression intensified. "I… er. I've commissioned one to be made, you see, and it's not ready yet."

It was an obvious untruth, but Peony's mother smiled at him. "How romantic of you. Peony's favorite gemstone is sapphires, you know. I hope you've taken that into account."

"Actually, I like emeralds better," Peony said. "But Will knows that."

He nodded quickly. "Yes, yes. Emeralds. Peony, would you care to accompany me to the Fitzwilliam's holiday musicale next week?"

"We'd be delighted," Lady Minnerton said. "My husband doesn't care for such things, but I'm sure you're aware that both Peony and I are quite musical."

"Of course." Will's smile was strained. "If you recall, Peony and I sing carols with my sister every holiday season."

"Will has a fine voice, too," Peony said. "In fact, aren't we practicing this Wednesday? I believe there's a new book of songs your sister would like to look over before the caroling party."

"Yes, she mentioned it." He glanced at her, his expression easing. "I'll call for you on Wednesday afternoon."

"That would be lovely."

And thank goodness this was one outing where her mother couldn't foist herself upon them. Not that Peony would be allowed to go about London unchaperoned, even if she were engaged to Will in truth.

"Well, I must be going," he said, rubbing his palms along his thighs. "So many details to attend to."

Yes—such as meeting with her father later that day to discuss things like her dowry. She was sorry Will had to go through that interview for nothing, but it couldn't be helped.

"Good luck," she said softly.

A bit of humor crept into his face. "Thank you, my lady. Perhaps you might give me a token, as the knights of old before they rode into battle."

She met his eyes, certain that they were both recalling how she'd braided him a garland of daisies to wear for that ill-fated jousting match.

"Here." She broke off one of the yellow lilies at the stem and tucked it into the breast pocket of his coat. "Courage, my knight. And don't fall off your horse this time."

He grinned at her, then stood and bowed to Lady Minnerton. "Thank you for the delightful company."

Peony rose, too. "I'd best get these flowers to the maid, before they wilt. I'll accompany you to the door, Will."

He nodded and gestured for her to precede him. As soon as they were outside the parlor and away from her mother's hungry gaze, Peony halted.

"I'm sorry about that," she said. "Mother is sometimes quite dreadful."

"Don't fret." He scooped up her hand and squeezed it. "Do recall that I've been acquainted with your family for most of my life. We'll get through this. Just a few weeks, and then everything can go back to normal."

She suppressed the stab of pain his words brought. "Did you tell Eliana yet that our betrothal is a sham?"

"She suspects. But I thought I'd leave it to you, since you're in full possession of the details. How is Princess Margret? I assume she escaped unseen from that room last night?"

"As far as I can gather, yes, but I'm certain Eliana will inform me how her sister-in-law fares. She's invited me for tea this afternoon."

"Fleeing the battlefield?" His tone was light, but she saw the flash of apprehension in his eyes.

"Don't worry about meeting with my father," Peony said. "Just remember, it's all a sham."

The words stuck in her throat, but he seemed to take heart from them.

"You're right," he said. "And now, I really should be going."

He leaned forward, and for one tremulous second Peony thought he was going to kiss her upon the mouth. She closed her eyes, her body vibrating—but his lips simply brushed her cheek. When she opened her eyes, he let go of her hand and was already turning away.

Curse her foolish heart, which yearned for him to return her affection. Clearly he didn't—and never would. She dipped her face to the bouquet to hide the stinging in her eyes.

By the time Will had collected his hat and overcoat, she was sufficiently composed to bid him a cheerful-seeming goodbye. He gave her a jaunty wave in return as he stepped out the door. The butler drew it closed, and she was left standing in the hall, holding her flowers as though they were a shield.

You saved Princess Margret, she reminded herself. And she must remember that instead of Will meeting with her father that afternoon, it could have been the odious Lord Corwin. Truly, she was beyond grateful that it was not, no matter the foolish state of her emotions.

WHEN PEONY ARRIVED at Prince Sebastian's elegant mansion, she found that not only was Eliana waiting for her, but the prince and his sister as well.

The moment Peony stepped into the rose-decorated tearoom, Princess Margret leaped up and enveloped her in a teary embrace.

"Lady Peony!" she cried. "My savior. How can I ever repay you for making such a sacrifice on my behalf?"

"There is no debt between us," Peony said gently. She shot a look at Eliana and Sebastian, who had also risen upon her arrival. "I presume you know everything about what happened last night?"

"Yes," the prince said. "And we are eternally grateful. You saved my sister from a terrible marriage."

The irony was not lost on Peony, and her lips twisted in a wry smile. "After nearly foisting the same fate upon you, your highness, it was the least I could do."

"Nonsense." Eliana said. "It's a lucky thing Will was there, and leaped to your rescue. Come, sit." She indicated the chair at her right.

The princess, sniffling, resumed her seat at the oval table, and Peony went to sit beside her best friend. The maids brought in the tea service and a silver platter stacked with tiny sandwiches and cakes, and Eliana began pouring out.

"There is one point I am not wholly satisfied on," she said. "Are you and my brother actually planning to wed?"

"Oh, not at all." Peony pasted a smile upon her face. "After the holidays, I will let him go."

"Ah." Eliana handed her a cup of tea. "Well, if both of you think that's for the best, who am I to argue?"

"We wouldn't suit," Peony said. "Besides, I know your brother thinks I'm rather foolish. There is nothing between us except a long-standing acquaintance."

"Not even friendship?" Princess Margret looked disappointed. "Are you certain he has not hidden a secret love for you all these years?"

"I'm quite certain," Peony said crisply. A pity the reverse was not true.

Eliana took a sip of her tea. "You'll be here for rehearsal on Wednesday, will you not?"

"Yes. Will is bringing me."

Eliana's eyebrow went up, just the slightest bit. "You must put up a good show, I suppose. At any rate, we'll have a new alto joining us."

"Oh? Who might that be?" Peony asked, though she had an inkling she knew. Her guess proved correct when Princess Margret leaned forward, a wide smile on her face.

"It is me! I am excited to sing with you, and now that Eliana is my sister-in-law, Mother agreed."

"After the events of last night," Prince Sebastian said, "we were able to persuade our mother that sheltering Margret is not, perhaps, the best course. Had she been out more in Society, she would have known to be more careful of villains like Lord Corwin."

"I have learned my lesson," Margret said. "And Eliana has promised to look after me. I would very much like to become your friend, too, Lady Peony. You are the kindest lady of my acquaintance."

There it was again—*kind*. Not brave, or intelligent, or resourceful. Peony took a bite of cake.

"It is not a flaw," Eliana said, as if reading her thoughts. "Your unselfishness is to be admired, you know. Generally speaking."

"I suppose." Uncomfortable, Peony changed the subject. "What new carols are you thinking of adding this year?"

The conversation moved onto safer ground, though Peony did catch Eliana looking at her thoughtfully from time to time. Of all the secrets they had shared over the years, Peony's attraction to her best friend's brother was not one of them. Nor would it be. She could not stand to be pitied in that regard.

And if she were to be commended for unselfish behavior, well, releasing Will from their false engagement would certainly be one of her crowning achievements—second only to saving the princess from Lord Corwin's machinations.

She supposed she must take some comfort in the fact, no matter how cold.

CHAPTER SIX

As promised, Will arranged for the carriage on Wednesday and went to fetch Peony for the rehearsal. Disembarking in front of Lord Minnerton's he couldn't help a momentary stab of discomfort.

The interview the other day had not been particularly pleasant. The earl had been unyielding, and working out all the particulars of Peony's portion had left Will feeling unsettled—especially as none of the provisions would come to pass.

But there was nothing for it but to move on. Christmas was in ten days, and the New Year at its heels. In a months' time, both he and Peony would be free to pursue their own lives, as usual.

The thought did not cheer him as much as it should have. After all, what was he currently in pursuit of? Happiness, he supposed, though that was a rather nebulous concept. Upon reflection, he was not quite sure where in his life he would find it.

Certainly, he'd never felt more alive than the night of the Winter Ball. It was quite gratifying to be someone's hero.

The butler showed him in, and a few moments later Peony appeared at the top of the stairs. She was dressed in a burgundy gown that emphasized her pale skin, and her dark hair was drawn up in a smooth bun. She smiled when she saw him, an open, generous smile that made him feel as though he'd stepped into a beam of sunshine.

"Ready?" he asked, holding out his arm for her as she descended.

"Yes. My maid will be along shortly as a chaperone." She reached him and tucked her elbow through his.

He dipped his head, pitching his voice for her ears alone. "At least it's not your mother."

"True enough." Her eyes sparkled as she met his gaze.

The butler fetched her hat and pelisse. She donned them, and then she and Will stepped outside, to find that it had begun to snow.

"How lovely!" Peony paused.

One hand on his shoulder, for balance, she tipped her face up to the softly falling flakes and closed her eyes.

Gazing down at her, Will realized with a jolt that Lady Peony Talbot was quite pretty. He didn't know why he hadn't noted it before. Perhaps because he'd been in the habit of thinking of her as his sister's best friend and not a person unto herself.

At least, not until now.

The small flakes vanished when they touched her skin, but remained on her hair for a few seconds longer, a dusting of sugar. She opened her eyes, and found him watching her. An endearing blush swept over her cheeks and he was possessed of the strangest urge to kiss her.

Then the maid hurried out, apologizing, and the moment was gone.

Will shook himself. He shouldn't let this sham betrothal of theirs affect him so. After all, Peony had made it clear she had no interest in actually marrying him. He believed her assurances that she would set him free after the holidays, and he was glad of them.

Wasn't he?

It was a quick carriage ride to the Duke of Ashford's town

house. He kept the mood light by recounting the strange assortment of ornaments his mother had begun collecting to place upon her Christmas tree.

"A carved hedgehog, of all things," he said. "With straw bristles sticking out. I poked myself in the thumb any number of times, getting it into just the right position."

"I wonder if this idea of Christmas trees will go out of fashion soon," Peony said. "Like the mania for filling the drawing room with ferns, or drinking only out of yellow teacups."

"Perhaps—but as long as the Queen and her husband continue to feature a Christmas tree at Buckingham Palace, I imagine it will remain the custom. I hear the notion is even taking hold in America."

"I hope it doesn't go out of fashion," she said. "I think it would be lovely to have a tree in the house—but Mother has forbidden it, on the grounds that the needles are too disorderly when they shed."

"You'll have a house of your own at some point." He smiled at her. "Then you can have all the trees inside you like."

"I suppose I may," she said, but there was a touch of sadness to her voice.

Will wondered what he'd said wrong, but they'd reached his sister's house. He handed Peony out of the carriage. It had stopped snowing, he was sorry to see, leaving only damp sidewalks beneath the gray clouds.

Eliana's butler took their outer garments and ushered them to the front parlor. Along with his sister, a few of the other carolers were gathered near the cozy fire in the hearth.

"Stop!" Eliana called as Will and Peony stepped over the threshold.

"What?" Will halted and glanced about, wondering what his sister was up to.

"Look up," she said, with a sly grin.

He did, and tried not to groan aloud. A sprig of mistletoe, gaily decorated with a bright red ribbon, hung directly above where he and Peony stood.

"You're engaged now," Eliana said. "It's perfectly acceptable to kiss your betrothed."

And rather odd if he did not; curse his meddling sister. What game was she playing?

"Of course." Will kept his voice cheerful as he turned Peony to face him. "Shall we, my darling?"

She gave him a strained smile, a flutter of something in her eyes he could not name. Fear? Embarrassment?

He'd have words with Eliana after this. How dare she put her best friend in such an awkward position?

Keeping his hands on Peony's shoulders, he bent forward and touched his mouth to hers.

The moment their lips met, fire leaped in his belly. His fingers tightened and he could not help drawing her closer. His pulse beat through him, loud and insistent. Her mouth were soft, and sweet as honey.

She slipped her arms around him, her warm curves pressing close. She let out a faint sound of pleasure, barely audible, and desire closed its jaws on him; a hungry wolf he hadn't even known was at his heels. And now he was being devoured.

It was supposed to be a short, chaste kiss, but he could no more let go of Peony Talbot than he could stop his own heart from beating. Just another moment of tasting her mouth, of feeling her against him, of hearing the wolves howl under a perfect, starlit sky.

"Ahem." His sister cleared her throat, laughter plain in her voice. "I believe you've made your point."

Will forced himself to raise his head. Peony opened her eyes and stared up at him, her expression dazed. Slowly, she pulled out of his embrace. As though her were letting go of something precious, he released her shoulders.

Damnation.

He was falling in love with Peony Talbot, and had no notion of what to do about it.

DIZZILY, Peony let go of Will and stepped back. What had just happened? She'd expected a peck on the cheek, or perhaps a quick brush of his lips over hers. Instead, he'd kissed her as though... well, as though he loved her. As though they were truly engaged to be married.

Regret for everything she could never have twisted inside her, dimming the glorious memory of Will's mouth fused with hers. He was a marvelous actor, that much was plain.

"After that display," Eliana said, "certainly no one can doubt your intentions, Will."

He shot his sister a wary glance. "I suppose not."

One hand at Peony's back, he guided her into the room. All her senses flared at his touch, and she was glad to move away from him in order to greet Princess Margret. She concentrated on catching her breath and taming the heat she could feel burning in her cheeks.

The princess shot her a conspiratorial look.

"Goodness," Margret said in a low voice, "if I didn't know any better, I'd think that William Banning truly had feelings for you."

"Well, he doesn't." Peony kept her voice light, despite the turmoil of her emotions. "Have you had a chance to go over the music yet?"

"Yes. I am rather nervous, though. The rest of you have been singing together for years."

"Don't worry." Peony gave her an encouraging smile. "'It Came Upon the Midnight Clear' is new to everyone. You'll do splendidly."

The rest of the caroling group arrived in a noisy bustle, and soon Peony was able to distract herself in the music. Mostly.

Once or twice she looked up from the page, to see Will watching her, his green eyes troubled. He was not worried that she was going to make him go through with the betrothal, was he? As soon as the rehearsal was over, she'd reassure him on that point.

It was dusk by the time the singers were satisfied, and Eliana had the servants light the candles on her Christmas tree. It looked lovely, sparkling in the window as Will escorted Peony back to his carriage. Her maid followed quietly behind.

Other trees shone in the windows of Mayfair, and Peony was careful to keep the conversation to safe topics on the trip home. When they reached their destination, she turned to her maid.

"Give me just a moment," she said. "I must have a word with my fiancé."

"Of course, miss." The maid sent her a coy look, implying she suspected Peony and Will would be exchanging more kisses than words. "I won't say a thing."

As soon as they were alone in the carriage, Peony turned to Will. It was difficult to make out his expression in the dim light.

"Don't worry," she said. "I promised you I won't hold you to this engagement."

He did not respond for a long moment, and her pulse beat in her throat.

"Do you dislike the idea of our betrothal so much?" he finally asked, his voice tight.

"Of course I do. You've never had any intention of marrying me, Will. Don't pretend otherwise."

"You don't think I'm husband material?"

She let out a short, unhappy laugh. "I'm sure you'll make some girl a very fine husband."

"But not you?"

"Are you behaving like this because of our kiss?" She could not let herself believe he had any feelings toward her, or her heart would surely be dashed to pieces. "It's all just a sham, Will—don't you remember?"

"I don't think *this* is pretense."

He leaned forward, his arm going about her waist, and captured her mouth with his. Despite her intention to protest, her mouth opened in a little sigh instead and—oh heavens—his tongue dipped in and tasted her. Delicious warmth ignited through her, and she melted into him. Her hands slid up his shoulders, and her senses swam with his smell, his touch. It was what she'd always wanted.

And what she couldn't have. Gasping, she pulled back.

"Are you toying with me?" Her voice trembled.

"Can you deny this attraction between us?"

"No. But—oh, please try and understand, Will. It's only because we're pretending to be engaged. I believe our emotions are confused."

She meant his, of course. Hers were as true as ever.

"You really think so?" His face hovered over hers, his warm breath tickling her cheek.

It was all she could do not to pull his head down to hers, and kiss him until they were both bright candles, aflame against the night.

"Yes, I do think so." She made her tone firm. "It's a passing fancy, nothing more. Nothing to base a marriage on."

He sighed, and leaned back. "It sounds as though you're determined to jilt me."

"It's for the best." Somehow, though, it was becoming harder to convince herself of the fact.

No. She would not force Will to marry her. He was in the grip of a physical infatuation, that was all. Once it wore off, he would see reason.

"No more kisses," she added. It only made things worse.

"No? You are too cruel, Peony. Just one more…"

Before she could argue, he'd caught her in his embrace, and

she could not bear to push him away. She was lost in a wave of emotion; desire and sorrow tangling together, bound up in the sound of his name. *Will.*

"What's this?" His thumb brushed her cheek. "Are you crying, Peony? Good gad, I'm sorry. I didn't mean to overset you."

"It's not because of our kisses. I mean, it is, but..." Oh, she could never explain. "I need to go in."

He let her go. Wordlessly, he opened the carriage door, then jumped down and handed her out. When they reached her front stoop, he paused.

"I never meant to offend," he said. "Please forgive me."

"There's nothing to forgive."

He stared at her a moment, his expression troubled. "I feel like a cad."

"You're not, Will. You could never be."

Mouth set, he bowed over her hand. "If you say so. Do you still want me to call for you on Saturday, for the caroling? Or would you prefer to arrive at Eliana's on your own?"

She hesitated. It would be so much easier on her emotions if she broke things off with Will now—but it was still too soon after Lord Corwin's despicable actions. The *ton* would fasten upon it, and it would be obvious that their betrothal had been a ruse from the start. She would suffer through the rest of the holidays, for the sake of both their reputations.

"You may fetch me," she said. Then, before she could say anything else and betray her true emotions, she lifted the latch.

"I'm glad." He bowed, his green eyes still shadowed with worry. "Good night, Peony."

"Good night."

She closed the door, heartsick that the growing ease between them had been shattered. The next two weeks would prove difficult beyond words, but she would get through them without breaking in two. She must.

CHAPTER SEVEN

Will did not sleep well that night, nor the next. His dreams left him exhausted—he chased a silver fish, but every time he was about to catch it, it slipped out of his grasp. Or he was crossing an icy cliff, each step sure to give way and plummet him to his doom.

When he awoke, one thought remained clear in his mind. Lady Peony Talbot did not want to marry him.

It should not matter so very much—indeed, he should be glad of the fact. Yet the edge of misery dogged his steps. Finally, he tired of trying to unsort the tangle of his thoughts. There was one person who could help, though no doubt she would laugh at him first.

On Friday morning, he presented himself at Eliana's house. The butler showed him into the parlor, where the tall Christmas tree perfumed the air with the scent of spruce. Hands laced at his back, Will paced back and forth before the cold hearth.

"William?" It was not his sister, but Prince Sebastian who strode to the room. "Is everything well with your family? Eliana will be down in a moment."

"Yes, everything's fine." Will halted. "Well, mostly fine."

Sebastian gave him a curious look. "Then what is the problem?"

"Peony won't marry me."

The prince's brows rose precipitously. "Have you asked her?"

"Yes! I mean, well, no. Not exactly."

"Then how do you know she will not wed you?"

Will blew out a frustrated breath. "Because she keeps assuring me she'll break off our engagement as soon as the holidays are over."

"Hmm." Prince Sebastian folded his arms. "Perhaps she does not want you to feel trapped. Do you?"

"I don't know." Will ran a hand through his hair, and turned to stare out the window. "I don't know how I feel—about anything."

"Excellent," his sister said, stepping into the parlor. "That's a very good sign."

"What do you mean?" Will pivoted to face her. "That I'm losing my mind? You shouldn't look so cheerful about it."

"Of course not, goose." She shook her head. "I think you're finally falling in love with Peony Talbot."

"What? Why *finally*?"

"Don't you remember? When we were young, you were always the knight and she was your lady. You even had a pretend wedding once, in the pasture. I believe the sheep were your bridal party, and Selene was the minister."

"I'd forgotten about that." The tips of his ears went warm with embarrassment.

"I haven't—and I suspect Peony hasn't either. I think she's loved you for years, Will."

"Oh, I don't think so."

Eliana cocked her head. "She's hidden it well, I give you that."

"She's never said say anything to you? Then how can you know?"

"Precisely because she never mentions you."

Will threw up his hands. "There you have it. She doesn't care for me."

"You're wrong." Eliana advanced on him, her expression intent. "If she didn't care for you, one way or the other, she wouldn't be so very careful to ensure your name never came up in our conversations. Over the last two years, I've noticed it more and more. Every time I mention you, she changes the subject."

"That's hardly convincing evidence." Despite his doubts, his felt something in his chest ease. Perhaps the treacherous cliff was more stable than he thought, and he'd make it across safely.

"I think your sister has the right of it," Prince Sebastian said. "For certain, Lady Peony never loved me."

"And lucky we are, because of it." Eliana went and threaded her arm through her husband's. "Really, though, Will. I think there's something between the two of you. Something that could truly blossom."

He shook his head. "I can't believe it. She seems determined to jilt me as soon as reasonably possible."

"Of course she does. She thinks you don't care for her, and she must protect her heart. Tell me, how did it feel when you kissed?"

His ears heated again. "That's none of your business—and it was unkind of you to set such a trap for us."

She gave him a smug smile. "It worked, didn't it? And I have to say, you both seemed quite—involved—with the result."

Will crossed his arms. "Very well. Maybe she does have feelings for me. What am I supposed to do about it?"

"What my so-wise husband has suggested." Eliana gave the prince a warm smile, then looked back at Will. "You must ask Peony to marry you. In truth, this time."

Will's heart gave a lurch. "What if she turns me down? She seems to think that, if anything, I'm in the grip of a passing infatuation."

"Then you must convince her otherwise." Eliana arched her brow. "I'm certain you're up to the task."

He was not so sure. But, as he left his sister's house, Will's heart felt lighter than it had in ages. Perhaps happiness did lie within his grasp, after all. He just had to have the courage to reach out and catch it.

PEONY CLOSED the book she'd been trying to read, and stared at the flames in the parlor hearth. She truly disliked this season of the year—more so with every passing day. Thank goodness her obligations to Eliana's family were almost at an end.

Today was the annual carol singing, and after that, Peony thought she might catch a terrible cold and take to her rooms until the New Year arrived. She'd almost begged off the singing, but her sense of responsibility was too strong. Her voice was needed to keep the sopranos on pitch, and she knew that Princess Margret would be deeply disappointed if Peony did not put in an appearance.

So, although Peony's heart was not in it, she would go, and sing about joy and merriment, and try to smile. And try not to look at Will too often, or too long. And most certainly stop daydreaming about his kisses—as she had caught herself doing all too often.

"Mr. William Banning is here," the butler said from the parlor door.

Peony jumped up and patted at her hair. He was early, by nearly an hour, and she wasn't even close to ready.

"Show him in," she said.

She would say hello, then bid him wait for her in while she prepared herself to go out. Why ever had he come now, instead of an in hour?

Will strode into the room, smelling of fresh rain. Drops sparkled in his hair, and he was holding something behind his back.

"Good afternoon, Peony," he said. "I'm terribly early, I know, but there's a reason for it. I brought you a present."

She eyed him warily. "A present?"

"Yes." His smile was crooked. "I hope you like it."

He pulled his hand out from behind him, and she blinked to see he was holding a small evergreen in a red clay pot. The tree was less than a foot high, draped with a bit of crimson ribbon and decorated with tiny silver and gold balls.

"Happy Christmas," he said, handing it to her. "I know your mother won't approve, but I thought you might like a tree of your own."

Her heart tumbled in her chest. It was thoughtful of him. More than thoughtful, that he had listened closely enough to her to know exactly what she would like.

She pushed down the ever-present, foolish hope that he might eventually return her affections. It was just a gift—and he was expected to make such gestures during the course of their false engagement.

"How clever," she said, holding the tiny Christmas tree up for inspection. "Wherever did you find such tiny ornaments?"

"They're beads," he said. "Do you know how difficult it was to string them up? I lost at least a dozen under the chairs and sofa."

"You made this?" She inhaled the crisp scent of pine and couldn't help smiling.

Who would have imagined Will would do such a thing? And for her?

Though, thinking back, she recalled he'd always had an artistic streak, fashioning clever figures from bits of clay and wood, or dabbling about in paints and charcoals.

"There's a present, too," he said, nodding to the small, wrapped box beneath the lowest boughs.

Her breath caught, and she scolded herself. It was just a token, surely. Nothing more.

"Shall I open it now, or wait until Christmas Eve?"

"Now," he said, sounding both nervous and excited.

Forcing her hands to remain steady, she set the tree on the mantle and removed the present. The box was light, the paper easy to slip off. She opened the lid, and the room tilted for a moment as she glimpsed the shining emerald ring tucked inside.

"What...?" Her throat dry with hope, with wonder, she picked it up between her thumb and forefinger. The emerald, surrounded by tiny diamonds, winked at her with a clear green light.

"Peony." Will reached and clasped her free hand. "I'd like to do this properly."

Still holding her hand, he went to one knee on the floor before her. She gaped at him.

"Will, get up. You can't do this. You don't really—"

"I do, actually." He gave her a crooked smile. "I love you, Lady Peony Talbot. It's not a momentary fancy or infatuation. I want to marry you. A true betrothal this time."

She could not breathe. Surely he was making a terrible mistake.

His smile faded. "Will you have me? Or... was I wrong in hoping you cared for me?"

"Oh, Will!" Her legs couldn't hold her any more, and she sank to her knees beside him. "Are you sure?"

His gaze met hers, and the certainty in his eyes quite undid her.

"I am," he said. "It took me far too long to recall it, but you've always been my lady fair. I'll ask you again, and this time I expect a true answer. Peony Talbot, will you be my wife?"

"Yes." She did not hesitate as her long-held dream materialized before her eyes. "Yes, William Banning, I will marry you."

"And not in a pasture this time, I promise," he said, laughing. "Might I borrow your ring for a moment?"

She handed it to him, only to have him slip it onto the fourth finger of her left hand. It fit perfectly.

Then he drew her into his arms and kissed her—tenderly,

feirociously, until she thought her heart, indeed her entire body, would catch fire from joy.

"Heavens! Peony, what are you and William doing, sitting on the floor?" Lady Minnerton's scandalized voice pulled them apart. "Well, I never."

Peony smiled at Will, then slowly rose and faced her mother. "We are celebrating our betrothal."

"That's a most improper way of doing so." Lady Minnerton's mouth pinched into a disapproving line.

"It's what we choose," Peony said. "What's more, we're getting married in January, and it will be a small wedding with just our families, in the chapel at our country estate. With yellow lilies." Her voice grew stronger with each word. "Also, Eliana will be attending the holiday musicale next week as our chaperone. Though you are welcome to go in your own carriage. And make Father come—it will do you both good."

She could hear Will's muffled laughter as he got to his feet. He put his arm around her waist, and nodded at her mother.

"Good day, Lady Minnerton. I trust you are well."

She blinked at him, then at Peony. "I scarcely know *how* I feel, when my own daughter behaves in such a singular fashion. Cavorting about on the floor. Peony, whatever has gotten into you?"

A backbone, she was tempted to say. But there was no need to be cruel—not when she'd only be living beneath her parents' roof for another few weeks. She pulled in a breath, feeling as though all the windows of her soul had opened at once, flooding her with light and air.

"Forgive me, Mother. Would you like to come to the party this afternoon, after we finish our caroling rounds? Lady Ashford is hosting, and she's known for her mulled wine."

"Perhaps." Lady Minnerton sounded a bit mollified.

Her mood improved even more when Peony showed her the engagement ring sparkling on her finger.

"Will arrived early, to give it to me," she said. "And my tree—which I'm taking up to my bedroom."

"Foolishness," her mother said, but didn't argue when Peony lifted the potted Christmas tree off the mantle.

"I'll make a star for the top," Will said. "I meant to, but I ran out of time."

Peony gave him a smile. "We've plenty of time now."

"Yes," he said, the look in his eyes full of warmth. "We do. All the time in the world."

CHAPTER EIGHT

"*Noel, noel*," the carolers sang. From her place between Will and Princess Margret, Peony lifted her voice, letting her words ring up to the heavens.

They stood in a half circle outside the front stairs of the last house on their caroling tour—the town home of the Duke and Duchess of Ashford. Dusk was falling, and the huge tree in the bow window glowed. The smell of cloves and cinnamon wafted from the open door, where the duke and duchess stood listening, their hands linked.

Peony's fingers were laced with Will's, not that anyone could see. Every now and then he would give her hand a squeeze, and she would press his in return. Truly, she did not know how she could possibly contain so much happiness.

It was a good thing that she could open her mouth and sing it out—but no matter how much joy she brought forth, more welled up from deep inside.

"Come in," the Duchess of Ashford said when they had finished. "I've mulled wine waiting."

The singers trooped up the steps, laughing. Princess Margret looped her arm through Eliana's, and they went to meet Prince

Sebastian, who had arrived in time to hear them sing. Peony recalled that Eliana and her prince had gotten engaged at this very party, last year. And Selene, the Duchess of Ashford, the year before.

And now Will.

"I think I like your family tradition," Peony said to him as they mounted the stairs. "It makes the holidays even more festive."

"I do, too." He grinned at her. "I can hardly wait to turn our house into a forest of Christmas trees next year."

She gained the top stair, then turned and put her gloved hands on his shoulders, stopping him on the step below.

"Now we are the perfect height," she said.

"For what?' He gave her an innocent look.

Laughing, she leaned forward and kissed him, letting her mouth relearn the taste of him, her arms feel his sweet, solid warmth as their heartbeats matched in perfect rhythm. There was nothing else she needed in the world than this moment. This man —and the future they would build together.

"We're about to close the door," the duchess called. "Are the two of you going to stand outside in the cold all night?"

Slowly, Peony broke the kiss. Hands clasped, she and Will went into the spice-scented warmth. Candles shone brightly from the tree and blazed on the mantel, with the fire crackling below. Someone was still humming the refrain of their last carol, and boughs of holly did, indeed, deck the halls.

Lady Peony looked up into her betrothed's eyes and quite suddenly realized that Christmas was, in fact, her very *favorite* time of year.

And she had no doubt it always would be.

ABOUT THE AUTHOR

~*USA Today* bestselling author and two-time RITA nominee~
Anthea's books have received starred reviews in Library Journal
and Publisher's Weekly, and she was named "one of the new stars
of historical romance" by Booklist.

Anthea lives with her husband and daughter in sunny Southern
California. In addition to writing historical romance, she plays the
Irish fiddle and pens bestselling, award-winning YA Urban
Fantasy as Anthea Sharp.

Contact her at anthea at anthealawson dot com, and join her
mailing list, tinyletter.com/AntheaLawson, for a FREE STORY,
plus all the news about upcoming releases and reader perks!

Find all Anthea's books at your favorite retailer, or visit her
website at anthealawson.com

www.anthealawson.com

www.ingramcontent.com/pod-product-compliance
Lightning Source LLC
Chambersburg PA
CBHW031611240626
47153CB00002B/719